CW00687529

The Rules Of June

G H SHAW

The Rules Of June

G H SHAW

Chapter One

Therapy Session 0172

S o, you find apples sexy?' It was a question, obviously, and one only a therapist could pose with such, well, inhumane distance.

'I don't think I said that, exactly.' The air in June's head thickened. It did this when she was here. Often, she wondered if it came simply from opening her inner thoughts to this other person, or whether it was more simply a result stemming from of the atmosphere of this room. Then there was the smell that emanated from the furniture that looked to have always, like forever, been here. Furniture that appeared to have been cut and pasted from the dulled pages of a 60s conversational magazine—w*hatever that was.* And the light...

'June?'

'Barking,' she said, sitting up on the divan and gripping it with both hands, and with her eyes looking hard at the door.

'Barking?'

1

Turning those eyes on him and smiling at his face, a face void of expression, she said, 'Yes.' Allowing, or at least not preventing, or maybe knowing full well—well of course she did—the sex that showed in her smile. 'Yes Dr Michaels.' She dropped a hand to her open inner thigh, knowing her expression pretended that she had done so absently, and knowing that Dr Michaels would accept no such premise. He might be a Doctor of Psychiatry, but he was no fool. 'Barking.'

Taking his glasses off, and slowly placing them on the table before him, he leant forward on his forearms and raised his shoulders. Fiddling with those glasses, and looking at them, he said, 'Is this about your recent visit with your mother?'

Clapping, June stood, flattening out her skirt with her smile directed at her shoes. June stepped to the chair opposite the good doctor and dropped herself into it. 'Of course,' she said. Picking up a pen, she began to doodle. 'If you like.'

The Doctor's breath could be heard coming in through his nostrils. 'You know full well June that *this*,' wagging a finger between them with slow enthusiasm, 'only works if we both take part.'

June watched him intently. This was after all a game. She was certain that they both knew this and that the other knew it, and yet they kept doing it. He stood from his chair and turned to make coffee. She watched him take two cups. In the seven years that she had been coming to see him, he had always made two, and he had never asked her after that first time how she took it or whether she wanted one. He merely made two and she drank it or not.

'I know why you're doing this,' she said, though she would acknowledge to herself that it had sounded bratty. It was bratty. Here she was living a life that entitled her, afforded her, the luxury of seeing a therapist, regularly, even though she was convinced that she really had no need of one. It was... well that was not somewhere she was willing to delve into in this moment.

With his back still to her, preparing the coffee, he said, 'But why are *you*?' He went statue.

Watching him, this man whom she had known for so long in this capacity, somehow, she felt beholden? Responsible? Something. She noticed the slight rise in the fabric of his pants. Only a slight rise as the muscles of his butt tensed as he halted mid-coffee-prep. Crossing her legs, she felt the small heat rise up into her face. *What the fuck is this?* Her thoughts ran independent. *Thoughts*, coached as they had been for so long. She said, 'Is this guilt?' Watching his head dip forward just a little before he continued his task. She set back to her doodling. Only looking up at him from time to time. Well really it was every couple of seconds, but needs must and all that.

The thickened air within her skull changed direction until the appropriate sounds and peripheral movements indicated that the Doctor had completed the coffees. She let her nostrils seek that smell. 'You do make good coffee,' she said. Her smile this time was one she didn't require an internal definition of, but of course she couldn't hide from the knowing of how this statement might imply... *or was it my tone?* Doctor Michaels sipped his coffee, and June felt that she could hear his response to his first sip, even though no audible sound came from him. It never did.

'I think it's inappropriate how you look at me,' she said, looking into her cup between sips. Hearing only the lightest of chuckles coming from her therapist. Knowing that he wouldn't entertain any such attacks. Deciding not to waste

3

any more time on such obvious acts of avoidance, she said, 'I called her a cunt.' Placing her cup back down on the table, she let her flat fingers smooth over the surface as though she were flattening a tablecloth.

'Mint?' he said, holding up a small bowl of chocolate mints.

'Mmm.' Perky, she sat up and took one of the packets from the bowl. 'Where do you get these from anyway?' Smiling again as she thought, *So much not to say with this guy.* 'No really,' she said, almost laughing as she unwrapped the small square of chocolate mint before biting into it, taking a corner, 'I have looked absolutely everywhere.' She snorted just then. She snorted a laugh that made her begin to cry.

Trying to stop it, but not wanting to enough, or simply unwilling to, June felt the child of her fill the flesh of her arms and shoulders. And she could smell the hair of her own head... when she was nine. The mint and chocolate in her mouth was flooding with the sourness of so much bitterness as it spilled up from the eyes and lips of her own desperate emotional self. She squeezed her eyes so tightly together, she knew in a useless, utterly, attempt to hide what was obviously happening. Knowing that with her mouth wide open as it was, she... 'Looks like I'm eating shit!' It was very nearly a scream—more of a wail really. And she didn't mind the soft chuckle that came from the Doctor this time. She heard it all; the endearment in his sounds, the honest care, a kind of love... 'Uh-har-har-har!' she actually said this. June herself was even a little more than quizzical over the fact that she actually sounded as though she had spoken this. And she bawled like a... 'Baby bitch!' she said this too.

Taking the tissue that he handed her, June tried to wipe up the drops of chocolate that lay on the desktop in front of her, and on seeing another flap of white and lifting her eyes

4

to the second tissue being offered, June saw the wet in Dr Michael's eyes and lost her shit all over again.

A time passed. A whirlwind really, but a relatively small one, or so she judged. Nothing was broken, or so she assumed.

'Thank you,' she said, allowing herself a fractured fragment of real eye contact with him as she dabbed at the corners of her eyes like some girl in a movie she had seen sometime.

'Oh, that's okay,' he said, lifting the bowl of chocolate mints. 'Would you like another?' he asked, smiling.

'Oh no you fucking don't!' Her own laughter was so honest that it washed her mouth out and cleared a little pain from the muscles in her cheeks.

With her eyes dry, but still sticky, and her nose clear, June let some air out and turned her head to those large windows to her right, looking out at that golden eggshell sky. 'Do you think it will ever end?'

'Do you really want it to?'

June turned her face, but only halfway back to him with her finger-knuckle now between her teeth. A gave a quick suck on that knuckle, almost a kiss. June turned back to that sky. 'Not ever.'

Stepping from the bathroom door out into the reception area, June felt her squinted smile appear as her eyes met Sarah's. Her eyes were tracing over the middle-aged receptionist's dress, and the luggage it held within, before reconnecting with the grey eyes above. Eyes through which June knew, *knew*, what evaluation had just been carried out... *perpetrated* upon her person. Grey eyes that accepted this cursory judgement, saw its conclusion, and responded with an affirmative, *Fuck you*.

Lifting her hand high in the air for a high-five that only *Elasti-Girl* could ever hope to connect with over the fifteen feet that separated them, June said, 'Right on Sister!' And she turned left and walked on down the hall. Not at all missing Sarah's definitive head shaking as she did.

The doors to the elevator opened. June's hands were on both hips, appearing as though she had been waiting for ages. When her eyes met those of the older woman in a buttoned-down faun coloured jacket, she pretended the shock of recognition. 'Rebecca?' June said, dropping her hands to her sides. Seeing the doubt, superimposed by discomfort, literally grip this stranger as she exited the lift, June placed herself too close, far too close to the Doctor's next appointment. So much so that the woman was forced to sidestep and shuffle.

'Sorry I don't know you,' said the woman before hurriedly making her way, away from June.

With her hand holding the elevator door, staring after the woman until her last look back, June stepped onto the lift. She pushed the button and pulled her pack of cigarettes from her bag. Drawing on that smoke and leaning against the rear elevator wall, she blew the smoke out so that it hazed her reflection in the golden panel.

The reflection she liked. Everyone liked it, liked her. She was pretty. Everyone knew this. It was how she made her living. Every woman she met fawned about how slim she was. Whilst all the while she could smell the acid that pooled in their mouths as they spoke their flattering words.

When the doors opened on the fifteenth floor, three people stood waiting. Two women and one man. Their expressions varied for obvious reasons, and naturally only the man entered the lift. June ignored the mumbled words from the others. She sucked some more and let the smoke fall from her mouth as the doors closed, and she smelt the three squirts too much of cologne on this man in the blue suit, but June knew that this was already too much attention from her. After all, he was her bitch the moment he stepped into the elevator.

'How am I supposed to ignore it?' she said, but only softly to herself.

'Excuse me?' Super helpful and yet?

Turning part way to him, opening her eyelids again, June clearly wasn't going to say a word. She turned to him fully, blowing smoke. Watching him, reading his *stupid*—no really, it's not even being unkind—*expression,* June stepped closer to this man as he straightened, backing up somewhat as he did. With her eyes looking him over, standing very close to him, seeing his confusion, his excitement swamped by the subsequent self-doubt, she said, 'What are you," blowing smoke, 'thirty-eight?'

'Ah,' a chuckle, 'thirty-six,' he said. His eyes shifted.

Drawing deeply on her cigarette, hearing the bell of the lift chime, knowing it had to be the ground floor, June said, 'You wear too much cologne.' And she pushed the cigarette between his lips, turned, and left the elevator.

Ten feet from the elevator she heard the cough followed by those staff voicing their objections... and she strode into the foyer.

It was the little things.

Or so June thought as she stepped through the still opening doors of her therapist's building and out into the warm air of Tuesday afternoon.

Chapter Two

The Tennis Lesson

You don't even like tennis,' he said as he looked up at her.

'What's that got to do with it?' June watched as he lowered the grin on his face back down and returned to sucking the sweat from the skin of her arse just below her yoni. The stubble on his cheek and chin was scratching against her softest skin. The knuckles of his left hand pressed into the flesh of her high upper left thigh. The sensation was almost soft in comparison to the cut of her white undies into her skin as he held them tightly dragged to one side. 'I can feel the air on my pussy,' she said so softly that she knew he could not even hear if he was listening. But she could feel it—*the air.*

Laying back on that table in the back room of the tennis club, June could feel the skin of her back pull against the linoleum tabletop as she was handled by Mark. The sensation, she imagined, was like that a carcass might experience *if a carcass could feel*. 'Oh, I'm riddled,' she laughed into the back of her lifted hand as Mark licked roughly at her, and she felt her own fluids being facially wiped about her.

She was just beginning to enjoy herself when he stopped, lifted his face from her and said, 'But you keep coming in every Wednesday?' And he shoved two fingers deep into her and turned them like an idiot feeling for the warmth of a pie. 'Aw,' she said, pushing herself against his hand with the skin of her arse squeaking on that caramel linoleum, and she shook her head at herself as she knew she had pulled one side of her lower lip in between her teeth. She wanted to laugh at him, but she knew if she did that, he might stop hand fucking her. So, June lifted her blouse enough for him to see her hardened right nipple. Knowing that a man with such an IQ—a man—could not pass up such a distraction. But as he kept hand-fucking her—which she knew he would—pushing a third finger in and causing the nerves to shoot and tingle through and up into her eyes, June felt the fabric of his tennis shirt, wet with sweat, as he sealed up onto her enough to get his greedy mouth to her breast... and right then she resigned herself to the truth that what she was engaging in was nothing short of bestiality.

A part of her wanted to hold his head as he slid up onto her. Words, possibly from an online psych lecture, began to sound throughout her head. She laughed as she felt her eyes go soft at the feel of his tough and accompanied stubble. Her hand, regretting her enjoyment, tangled in the thick, dark, sweaty hair at the back of his head. June allowed herself to pull on it as she pushed his face harder into her chest. She knew she was making noise now. Could hear it at one separation as it bounced around that large room, and yet,

June still heard herself considering the appalling truth of the average IQ of the population in which she lived. Knowing that even as Mark here pushed off of her with his strong hand and fumbled to free his substantially meaty girth from his too tight tennis shorts, that he, her *tennis coach,* definitively resided somewhere much south of that average. And June thought, *What is it about you morons that I find so...?*

WHACK! Came the brutal sound from a window behind her. June made to squeal at the socking noise even as her mind made to make sense of it. The heat that was rising into her face, she knew, was the embarrassment she could not argue with. An embarrassment that in some way she sought. Of being caught in such an act.

And then her body was yanked like that carcass again before she had time to steady herself.

Mark's hand pressed into the flesh of her hip and arse. 'Bird!' he almost yelled as he pushed his cock into her.

'Ugh.' A small sickness in her belly was quickly overridden by the pleasure of such an impolite punch. Her mind was slipping on the windowsill of her analytical capability to comprehend *what the fuck* was happening. Her teeth were showing as this man Mark, less than a decade older than her or there abouts, pulled a little too hard, separating the cheeks of her arse enough to cause a pinch of pain. 'Bird!' she said, laughing as she lifted her shoulders forward and slapped him hard across the face.

As she lowered herself back again, watching the shock on his stupid face, the slow motion began. June even saw the spray of sweat that she had slapped from his ridiculously even features, and she continued to laugh as he did only what he could do—manhandle her.

11

Her hip bones banged a little bit on the tabletop as he flipped her, and she laughed. June could feel his anger as it bled with his lust for her. She had been fucking him most Wednesdays for nearly half a year. He was no *Rubik's Cube*. 'Ow,' she said, pointlessly she knew, when her knees stung as they were drawn up along the linoleum. Her nipples were then licked by that same table covering before the weight of his hand pressed them into it, ringing bells she loved to have rung. And as Mark's hands fumbled their grip on her lifted arse on that tabletop in the rec-room of this stale tennis club, with her head lolling to one side, June saw the bird responsible for that earlier *whack* lying dead, or almost so, on the windowsill just across from her. Her body jolted like a corpse as her tennis coach heaved his thick cock into her... even as the pleasure of it resounded throughout her, causing her to lose some breath, and June felt the sting in her eyes as they fixed on that bird... and she drifted.

The palms of her hands were pressed against the hard, now sweat slippery surface of that table, and with her tongue licking at it through her open lips, June felt the air around her shudder as a tune from a bygone era drifted lightly to her ears. The grunts of the man fucking her carelessly, boomed flatly behind her. The rhythm of her skin was squeaking against the tabletop with each heavy thrust that opened her over his cock. Her body was shaking with the growing orgasm that was rounding the bend, and still her own tongue was licking that linoleum unbidden. And she heard the gentle melody of that tune. She could only imagine that it played through the old speakers mounted high near the ceiling of this tennis club back-room. Speakers, she imagined, that had long since been disconnected from whatever kind of system...

'Awww... uh-uh-uh,' she began to pant as thoughts of herself running with a pack, of the heat of the chase, and the hard ground pounding beneath her feet ran through her pleasure-fractured mind. Even the drums in her ears picked up the tempo, and she screamed, 'FORGIVE ME!' And her nails clawed at the old caramel linoleum as the afternoon light creased in her watering eyes. And her body shook. Her mouth stretched open so very wide, and right then, June felt her eyes were drawn to the tickle of the line of saliva that spilled from her open, extended mouth. She watched it run to pool on the brown table between her clawed hands... before her hair flung forward with the final heavy thrust of the moron behind her... so very deep within her. The burst of his spunk was so very hot as it forced its way into her, and yet even as its heat plumed within her core, June felt her tears run at the hateful enjoyment, the devilish pleasure, she loved more now than she could find any reason with which to agree. But without doubt, it was a pleasure she craved even as her body was wracked with its electrical tendrils.

The air went quiet as her body thrummed with the intensity of the wave that had crashed through her. Her breathing still piqued as this man's cock began to shrink even as his hands squeezed her still risen arse until it ached the muscles there. She felt a drip of his sweat land on her lower back as his sopping penis slid from her, and he drew his finger slowly out of her arsehole, the final departure from her body. June stayed there on that table then with her most private parts exposed and open and her eyes closing as the cum from this man she had allowed to fuck her began to run from her body and splash onto that hard linoleum. The air of the room cooled then, making her more aware of her exposure. The extent of which was not more possible, and the harsh lights of that back-room offered only a chill as June knew she wanted more...

Her heart ached at this, just for a moment, for the truth of it... *her need*. A need she felt might never be properly sated.

Quickly, she dropped to her side and moved from the table before the other thoughts that she knew barked at the small doors of her inner mind could break through and make her *pay attention*. Those barking thoughts that hated her more than she could believe they could have a reason to. But there they were, and June was no fool. *Not any longer*. She would not entertain them.

Squatting to the floor to retrieve her clothes, out of habit rather than bending, she laughed, ignoring Mark's confused look as he pulled on his shorts. Ignoring everything about him. Ignoring even the fluids began to dry on her smooth skin. She pulled on her underwear and easily dressed in her tennis outfit. Adjusting her bra, June knew she would not shower before she left. For as much as she had no interest in this man who smiled dumbly before her, she wanted to feel the stink of him on her as she walked from this building and on down the street of this city.

'See you next Wednesday?' Mark smiled in a knowing way, that was not nearly as close to the truth as he imagined, and he cracked open the top of a bottle of water and drank like he'd just won the match.

'Maybe not.' June slung her bag and walked from the room. The sounds of Mark's laughter were echoing down the institution green linoleum hall as she swung her legs one in front of the other. Her reflection did not show the whirlwind that froze within her. She smiled, still walking, as she drew a cigarette from the pack in her bag, and lighting it,

14

June breathed out and smiled the smile she had become known for.

She tried to ignore the usual glances as she strode through the sporting facility's foyer, blowing smoke into the open air, but her eyes snagged on one or two of those looks before she made the door with her smile showing that she knew they wouldn't confront her *inappropriate behaviour.* They never did. No one ever did.

Chapter Three

The Interruption

What are you reading?'
Audibly exhaling, not wanting to, but still dropping the second-hand paperback book to her lap, and with her eyes unwilling to adjust to this *person's* face who stood before her, June said, 'Well, I'm not reading it anymore, am I?' Still seeing not more than a middle-aged man in jeans, she found her head shaking just a little, and her mouth opened again in response as she watched this intruder turn and take a seat beside her. There wasn't much room in her these days, nor had there been in many years, for the kind of patience and courtesy that might allow one to avoid any outward displays of annoyance, and consternation, at such an obvious and unwelcome intrusion upon one's liberty.

Her chin had come back down to its usual position. 'I can smell you,' she said, referencing his proximity to her, and not caring, nor mistaking, the obvious connection that would most likely be taken; that his smell must be offensive. Which it was not. And so, June nodded in the affirmative at her own statement.

The softness of his chuckle was so light as he crossed his legs and leant back into the park bench. Resting his elbows on the top of the back rest, he said, 'It's just wonderful here this time of year. Don't you think?'

'Well, it was.' June made it clear that she was looking at, and mentally measuring, the distance of his left elbow to her shoulder and that her decision on the outcome of this measurement had already been concretely decided at the outset.

His laughter was so open, round and deep, and its timber so relaxed that it was clear that he was deeply self-assured. An assurance, June surmised, that came with no relationship to any popularly agreed upon reality.

And the air settled around them as they sat on that park bench somewhere near the middle of those grounds. Others passed by. Birds found their way to their seemingly designated spots and tasks. An older gentleman stooped to pick up the shit that had been squeezed from the arsehole of his wife's twenty-centimetre-tall dog.

But neither June nor her uninvited park bench guest appeared willing to give up their position.

She opened her book on her lap and began to read.

'Ahhh,' he said.

June read the line on the page... a third time.

And he began to whistle, but not a tune. He just whistled.

It was ten o'clock in the morning.

Still keeping the book open and holding her eyes as though she could still read it, June said, 'I take it you're not employed?' Tapping the place on her wrist where one might wear a watch. Hating the sound of her own voice with this statement that in no way affirmed her real views on this matter. Still, she felt her statement was fair under the circumstances.

Again, with his laugh. 'Do you mind if I smoke?' he said, taking a cigarette seemingly by magic from his jacket pocket. 'Yes.' But of course, she didn't.

When he lit it, the cigarette smoke curled and drifted... 'Oh give me one.' June held out her right hand, wanting to shudder at his chuckle as it came through a corner of his mouth as his lips clamped over his smoke.

Placing it between her lips and leaning in for him to light it, June could see the shine in his eyes through her peripheries. It was a light of intelligence, but it bore no indication of the possessor's intent. When her cigarette was lit, she drew back on it. Her whole body drew back as she pulled on the smoke. She turned so that she was facing him with one knee crossed between them. 'So, what's your deal?' she said, drawing again on her cigarette. With one arm resting atop the back of the bench, June held her eyes directed and squarely on this man. Lifting her face in the space before his answer, seeing the line of his jaw, the angle of his cheekbones and the cord of muscle in his neck as he faced forward not looking at her but out over the park, June reminded herself not to be too curious.

Taking his left arm from the top of the bench, leaning forward as he shook his head, he crossed his legs, and he revealed an open-mouthed smile. A smile that conveyed that he knew of, had observed, and maybe—*well certainly,* June thought as she took another hurried drag—the power this smile could have.

'Crazy,' she said, fixed, watching as his eyebrows moved in a question he obviously knew the answer to. Her eyes moved over him then. Unfortunately finding in this evaluation that there was nothing, not a thing, that she could pinpoint to be disparaging about. And she was stunned. Not enough to prevent her eyes from scanning a second, though be it swifter, time. 'Oh, you're quite good at this.' There was no reason not to say it. Or so June imagined. After all, it was a trade she understood very well herself. One that she believed she had mastered to a degree that had left her, almost, bored with it. She sucked on the cigarette and felt an eagerness to engage this man who had swanned into her personal space with such a perfectly unassuming lack of grace. She felt she had no option but to acknowledge that he had excited in her a kind of zeal that she had all but forgotten. 'Show me,' she said, and actually, really, began clapping.

But the man did not move. His face was frozen for several moments. His stare fixed on a place much further away than she could see. June's attention was captured. Her mouth began to open as she watched the moisture well in his left eye. She even felt a boot on her chest as this tear spilled. Watching as it fell, following it as time slowed, until it landed in this man's open palm. The hand that closed over it, the fist, now turned over slowly, gracefully. A twist and it opened again, showing her a single Frangipani flower resting in his palm.

Again, she clapped, not caring for the dangers that may lurk here. She smiled, not caring that she responded like a child.

20

She sat straighter now as she watched this man's hand close over this flower that she remembered from her childhood... and the park bench that sat beneath the tree in the garden of her dear grandparent's house. She watched now as wisps of what appeared to be smoke rose from between his thick fingers just a moment before he opened his hand to show that the flower had disappeared. And again, that boot on her chest, now pressing deeper at the knowing of her loss of these dear people... who had loved her so as a child.

As his hand lifted, June's eyes followed it to the level of his eyes. To eyes that bore into her with a kindness, and a knowing that now lighted the earlier shine she had observed. And she felt her heart pulled from her chest before his head leant to his left, and he began to transform. With the movements of the slowest dancer—so slight as to betray that any real movement was occurring at all—June watched this man's appearance shift.

Her eyes swam as he morphed as a master of bearing, a Yogi of the art of posture. June sat stunned as he straightened somehow. She watched as his shoulders became stronger, wider, straighter. She watched as the strength in his chest asserted itself. She watched as, from where just a moment before he had looked like a man living the physical result of years of inactivity, now, he presented an increasingly athletic visage; a man some ten years younger than the one who had sat beside her only minutes before. And then turning, he presented the sophisticated bearing of an aristocrat from a century ago.

'Stunning,' she whispered, watching as her sounds carried to this man before her. Seeing as they landed, that a new smile grew. This smile swimming over his face, articulating and lifting the forms of his now so very clearly handsome

21

features until the muscles that lay under that skin shifted to display such perfectly formed cheek bones. Cheek bones that held such deeply penetrating hazel eyes like two hands cupping, and offering them, just to her.

June found herself reaching out to him. Unable, in that moment, to see the humour of her current state. With her eyes wide, she chirped as this magician stood from that park bench and rose onto his toes with the smooth strength of a practiced ballerino, and she found herself mirroring the tilt of his head as his arms lifted like those of a crane. His whole body becoming fluid before her. He moved without self-consciousness. He was confident in a way she had not ever seen. He danced before her with a quality that drew her within her own imagination, and she would, in that moment, swear that unicorns were absolutely real. His feet touched the ground with such lightness and surety that June herself began to weep.

Her hands lifted to cover her heart, sitting on that park bench, and her tears ran in tiny streams down her face. Tears that sprouted from a well she had forgotten as this man she had never met before... danced for her in the middle of the park.

It wasn't until he slowed the arc of his superbly graceful movements that June became aware that he had been singing *to her* as he danced. She became aware of the steady crescendo of his deeply narrated melody. With his hands held one atop the other before him, she saw that he sang to her from the face of a mime, and the first tiny sob bubbled up and out through her now quivering lips.

And he was there then, before her. So quickly had he moved, that he was there in the time it had taken for a tear's blur to clear from her unwiped eyes. Somehow her heart tore just then. As this man, this stranger for whom she had not pretended her initial disdain, now stood before her speaking words to her in a language she did not know; showing her their meaning as he pressed a folded tissue under each of her eyes.

June gripped those hands then, so very tightly, and heard him say, 'Magari.' And she believed that only he and herself, in that moment, could know the true meaning of that word and the intention that carried it.

And she was lost just then, June. She had fallen into the belly of her own well. She had been torn fully open and shown the cliff upon which she stood. Shown the very ground that she *had* believed was firm.

With her eyes so very tightly shut, as her mouth whispered the howl of pains she had so long ignored, June felt his lips touch her forehead with such very deep care. Hearing from between those lips, one word that rumbled with more gravel than its volume should command, one word, 'Rocambolesco.'

And she could not open her eyes...

She knew that he was leaving.

She felt his hands fall from the sides of her head like a gentle breeze, and the smell she knew now to be cedar... swept away with them.

She did not want to open her eyes.

For the longest time she sat there with her lips still trembling, her jaw aching... and her chest dissolving.

'Are you ok my dear?' The smell of lavender.

The light hurt as she opened her eyes, and a great lung full of air poured into her as though she had been holding her breath. The lady standing beside her was far into her years. Those years all showing a depth of understanding at what

June would have only moments ago believed no-one could possibly know.

June wanted to tell this kind lady that she was fine, and to explain... 'What?' verbally asking this question of how she would ever be able to...

Her eyes caught on the concrete path before her.

She stood from the bench then and rushed to those words written in large curling letters, in red chalk, before where she had sat.

She looked back to the elderly lady standing beside the bench. Seeing her own state reflected in this woman's expression, she read the words out loud, 'Non tutte le ciambelle riescono col buco!' She read this as though she or the caring stranger would understand.

But still, even as she pulled her phone from her pocket and attempted to google their meaning, June stumbled back two steps... and dropped onto her butt like a child. She dropped to her arse onto the grass, and she began to cry.

'It's okay my dear.' The elderly lady was by her now, shushing gently. 'It's going to be alright.'

Chapter Four

The Shoot

The clock ticked, and the room was hot.
Hot enough to make the tan and orange coloured décor look like candy.

June refused to wipe the sweat from her brow but deigned to drag a sleeve across her upper lip and peel each leg off the vinyl chair without straightening her skirt. She wore no make-up to smudge or blur. She never did when she was booked. It only resulted in longer times in the chair, and there was nothing quite as uncomfortable—emotionally—as another person wiping off your make-up. It touched on a level of degradation for June that made the all-but-dead butterflies in her belly give a last kick and remind her of that uncle who always licked his lips over Christmas dinner.

As she lowered each leg, she just knew her nostrils listed and spread, and it wasn't only due to the retching feel of her wet leg-backs making contact with their discomfort's cause. Since the age of fourteen, June had been encumbered by a nearly desperate fear of smelling her own vagina. And such a preventably unfortunate situation as sitting on a chair in an environment such as she did currently, only exacerbated thus mentioned fear. She could almost hear her skin squeak when the elastic of her undies curled as she shifted about in her futile attempt to relieve herself from her tacky situ.

'Ms Bone et?'

Standing to her feet so fast that her lower back gave a single jolt of pain, ignoring a run of sweat tickling the back of her right leg, and pushing down on her skirt—sniffing for her own potentially whiffy underbelly as she did—June snatched up her bag, remembering to look bored as she passed the assistant who had called out an attempt at her surname, and she said, 'It's Bonnet, you mental dwarf.' Passing through the door, she continued, 'Like the fucking hat.'

Gerard, which was obviously not his given name, turned in exaggerated camp while looking over his needless glasses at her as she entered the large white cornerless room. 'June-bug,' he said, returning his attention to the piece of photographic equipment he fiddled in his small hands.

Eye rolling couldn't speak to this guy, and June wanted to get this done as quickly as she could, so she took the coffee from the make-up girl. A girl she had sat before more than a few times but couldn't care enough to record her name. And she sat, knowing, at least, that the make-up girl was a professional and wouldn't piss about. Gerard, on the other hand, was a total bag of shit and had never—as far as her memory of her own time in the industry could recollect—been known as anything other. Well, *that*, and an amazing photographer. June knew this, of course, but where she failed was in the how. It's built into us, that anyone who is

27

given even a middling measure of talent must be of above average intelligence and character. *And yet?*

As the girl worked on her face, June felt the whine before she heard it.

'Juney, I know you won't mind, but I've booked another girl for the shoot with you today, and she's kinda new to the scene, so I know you'll help us out in there hey?'

She never spoke to him.

'Good, good,' he trailed his smirk as he turned.

June herself had been seventeen the first time he had *photographed* her.

It was the way of the industry.

But only minutes after he walked away, June felt the air around her freeze, and her fingers tightening over the edge of the armrests of her chair as Patrice—she did remember her name—supplied her mask. June could feel the bone of her teeth as a desperation swam like a snake in her upper gut. The chill of her sweat was lifting the small hairs at the backs of her arms. She sat straight in her chair, ignoring Patrice's attempts, and her head cocked like an animal hearing those far off calls, the signal of something stirring the innate instincts strung through a thousand years of need.

She stood from the chair as the atmosphere thickened. The room about her filled with the water of her heightened senses. June walked from the chair and past the equipment that stood like black metal branches in this otherwise forest of white.

And still the air grew colder.

The curtains that divided the space fluttered as she glid past them, pushing them smoothly away as she followed the call that drew her.

28

Sound had all but ceased. The music that played ahead of her nothing but sticks and stones as she rounded the last partition... and June felt the whole room of glass within her... collapse.

The next few moments can only be told through the patching of those slides of her fractured memory that remained after the event. After what took place. These pieces, only those that could be filtered through the cacophony of emotional debris that flooded her system amidst her internal chemical-fireworks.

It could have been the glare that sent her running for him. The harshness of the washed-out photographic melange that overlay and threaded with the real catalyst, that triggered her action. The small sounds—so small—issuing from the young model in the room she entered, that burbled forth one hundred images from the dungeon of her own recollect. Imagery so buried in the soil of her need to *maintain* that it was as though the chill required to lift their corners in that hidden grime could only be allowed... through the need of another.

She screamed. She knew that much. *Wailed*, is what Patrice heard before she came running. Though *her* statement of events would be absent on any record. The sound poured and shook that viscous atmosphere, hardening it instantly before shattering it as her heart's call twisted its pitch and flung into her mind a very real image of her mother's breast... leaking milk... as her infant's mouth released from feeding.

It could have been the photographer's hand; the colour of it against the skin of the teenaged girl's most tender place. This, at least, was the frame that had frozen in her memory. As far as June had allowed herself to piece it. The single frame that her mind had overlain with a shooter's crosshairs. The image her eyes glassed on as she moved like a *Fury* through that room. And yet even the sound of her bare feet slapping on that hard white floor—a desperate staccato that kept the time of her attack—rang so loud in her memory.

She did not hear the photographer's shriek. If at all he made such a sound. His face most assuredly pretended this. Why would it not? For June was a professional of long standing. Known for her ease to work with. Known for holding her shit. And what this, *now never to be named again*, photographer witnessed in that moment would most certainly haunt him, and most deservedly so, during the hours when he felt most small from there on in. And, as surely, it undid one's former impression of June Bonnet—even her own.

June would be left believing that her most inhuman actions to this point would, no doubt, be remembered as her most human. But of course, even June knew that nothing is ever that simple.

She would never be able to forget the feel of his bones breaking as they did. So tight within her own grasp were those two fingers of his as she applied such viscous force upon them that her own nerves felt those fibres crack and tear even as her own throat leaked the bitter fluid of the rage she let loose.

She could not remember any of the young model's responses, in that moment. Other than that she froze. Her eyes, wide and brown as a story book nymph.

Violence—the smell of it like the blood and fluids she had recalled from her sister's birth in the backroom of their family home.

Her knuckles stung as she took the young woman's hand, spitting on the fallen, beaten photographer as she stepped over him... leading the now willing model from the room.

Through the foyer.

To the elevator.

The doors of the lift closed, and the usual pace of time zipped back together. Time as it had been, resumed. June's breathing staggered, and she believed she might feint. Her lack of breakfast, a pleasant reminder. Her skull filled with the helium of a post adrenaline dump. June wanted to cry but could not. And as she pulled a cigarette from her bag like a neurotic from the age of the Mary Tiler Moore Show, June felt the heat of the younger model's arms as they flung about her neck. She felt the time slow, just a dot, as the heat and smell of this girl filled the, still, animal nostrils that had only just sunken beneath the surface. And her breath was lost to her.

She saw her own mouth open in the warped reflection of the brass panelled wall of that elevator. She watched it open a little wider as Rebecca's tears pressed against her cheek, and the firmness of her left nipple pressed into the outswell of her own breast.

The light of that lift, yellow and bright, highlighted an amber light in June's eye then. The one she could still see over the plaited, parted, straw coloured hair of this young woman she had saved from the repulsive actions of that man in the white room. And June was rooted by the shard of light in that elevator wall reflection... and the truth it told. In fact, she could've sworn she saw her own image laugh. Laugh, as she slowly dropped to her knees before that young woman. Feeling the delicious sensation of her small dress's fabric slide up. Slide up and allow her to press her face—the bones of her right eye and her upper cheek to the side of her nose—firmly into the hot cotton fabric that covered Rebecca's vagina... and she breathed in all she could take.

31

June's mouth pressed into the skin of her most high inner thigh, and her tongue felt the slight buried stubble as it slid under the outer edge of the girl's white cotton undies. And she hit the stop button by the elevator door.

She was aware. Of course she was. Though still, as her mouth filled with the flesh and taste of the young woman before her, and as the floor pressed hard against her knees, June pretended to wonder at terms like *Conflict of Interest*, among others. Nothing that could stop her from pushing her fingers deeply into this *Innocent* whom she had just rescued. Nothing that could stop her from pressing hard against her own now hot undies and heave against the fingers of that same hand.

'I know who you are,' Rebecca breathed.

June felt a sting in her left eye as she mouthed this girl. Looking up at her as she tore at the T-shirt fabric covering those small white breasts, and squeezing so very hard with her palms at those pink nipples as they made air. And June moaned. She moaned, even as she couldn't be sure if her stinging eye was being caused by a tear, her smudged make-up or the sweat or quim fluids of this young woman she only now began to anally finger.

Somewhere near the sixth floor of a building's address she couldn't care to remember, June heard the pitch of the young girl's voice shiver as she called again...

'I know who you are!'

Chapter Five

Therapy Session 0173

What, no mint?' she said, adjusting her skirt beneath her with the knuckles of her hands sliding across and against the heavily woven fabric.

She rolled her eyes, and she sat there without any apparent indication as to whether she could expect a positive outcome from this visit. But she wasn't going to bet on it. It was the best she could do, given the situation.

Dr Michaels, giving the pen he held a final twist, placed it on the table before him, knowing that June would note its position. A position in which he would never usually place it. He sat up straight before his desk. 'No June.' Folding his hands beneath his bearded chin and allowing a flat smile, he said, 'Not yet.' And he meant it.

She began picking at the imagined lint on her skirt. Her eyes, a second level *whatever*.

A few minutes passed.

'Well?' said June.

Taking the sheet of paper before him, Dr Michaels began to read from it, 'It says here, that after you seriously physically assaulted,' again that flat smile, a bearded line really, 'a *Mr...*'. 'Don't say his fucking name!' June's eyes, she knew because she could feel it, stared as a loon whilst her index finger stood adamantly tall at the end of her extended hand as she thrust it toward the doctor.

Bearded line maintained; Dr Michaels continued. 'After you seriously assaulted *The Photographer*,' looking to check that his choice of words satisfied June, he went on, 'that the Fire Brigade...' his smile stretched to show some humour, and incredulity, as asserted by the incline in the Doctor's pitch, '...having forced open the elevator doors to said *Photographer's* building...' his thumb now rubbed at a corner of his brow, 'that they came upon you...' blinking, 'fisting a young woman whilst yelling at her to...' holding up a finger of his own, 'and I quote, *Say my fucking name.*' Clearing his throat before taking a mint and placing it into his mouth and shaking his head at June's request without looking at her, Dr Michaels continued, 'And...' clearing his throat, 'excuse me... and that you bodily prevented them access into the elevator...' Looking a little defeated, with a large exhale he said, 'And again I quote... *Until the bitch cums.*' Dropping the sheet of paper onto the impressive desk like a freaking microphone, he said, 'And you say, *Well?*'

June sat up, looking into her lap, about to say something.

'No!' Dr Michaels said. 'You have a charge of *Intentional Grievous Bodily Harm*,' raising one finger and holding it there for a moment before he continued. '*Assaults* on three firemen and one on an ambulance officer. And it says here...' tapping a second sheet of paper, 'that one of these assaults included an attempt made by you to push several fingers into the mouth of one of these officers.' Again, tapping the sheet of paper, he said, 'Yes. It actually says that it was... *the same hand* you had repeatedly inserted into the young woman's vagina. Oh, and yes... her anus.' Taking a deep breath, leaning back in his chair and crossing his legs, he said, 'Oh there's more.' He turned in his chair to look out the window. 'I just don't want to say the words.'

'You sound a bit judgemental.'

'No!' he said. 'No, not I Ms Bonnet. Not me, but the entirety of society at large that judges this kind of activity as not quite of the kind...' waving his arms, 'that at the very least...' leaning toward her, 'is *not* to be carried out in public.' Quickly picking up the sheets of paper before him and tapping at them, he said, 'It's actually one of the charges here! *Public Indecency!*'

'Well, I don't see why you're so mad.'

His eyes went wide. He fought to get the words out, 'Because, they are asking me for a recommendation.' His eyes looking out from under his heavy brow, were kinda shaking a bit.

'And you don't know what to say.'

He laughed then. For the first time, and this wasn't the only first of her visit thus far, Dr Michaels laughed openly, and like a man who had found that the *hens* had gotten into the *fox's coop*.

June took the opportunity to light a cigarette.

'Have fucking mint!' Dr Michaels literally threw a small handful of them at her before standing, pulling up his belted pants, clearing his throat repeatedly, and making his way to the very large windows that opened onto a really very

36

impressive view of the city. And he stood there catching his breath.

June ashed into her hand until she was sure he wasn't looking. She then calmly stood and took a thing from his desk that looked like it could hold a few butts before sitting again and crossing her legs.

When it appeared that he was indeed going to take his time, June chose to offer, 'It was only four fingers.'

Wheeling, he said, 'What?' His eyes darting to the object in her hand that she was using as an ashtray.

'I wasn't fisting her.' Her eyes lidded. 'I was hand-fucking her... with four fingers. Three mostly.' Taking a drag, and looking at him with Agent 99 eyes, she said, 'She couldn't take the thumb.'

The doctor sat on the window's ledge and briefly held his brow in one hand before lifting it and pointing at the desktop. 'It says that the young woman... *eighteen years old*! Which by the way...' But he couldn't continue down that avenue, and so he moved on down his original path, after a bit of a stutter. 'It says that she was, *screaming like she was being murdered*. Their words, not mine.'

'She was screaming,' her eyes wobbled a little bit, 'because no one had ever made her cum properly!' Sucking the cigarette and beginning to nod, she said, 'That's the real crime here.' And of course, she knew how that sounded... once she'd said it.

'I'm sorry,' Dr Michaels said, 'but you really are leaving me with no choice in this matter.'

'Oh no you fucking don't!' June was pissed. 'If you and your so-called fucking therapy was worth a pinch of shit then maybe...' shaking with her rage, she went on, 'maybe after a hundred and fifty *PAID* visits, a person might find that the progress they have made... might in fact not leave them psychologically fracturing whilst in the course of their chosen profession... and totally losing their shit!'

Dr Michaels smiled then, for real. The theatrics of the previous minutes dropped from him like a veil, and as he moved toward her, he was nodding. He said, 'Good.'

June strode to his desk, shoved her hand into the glass bowl of mints, withdrew a handful and began to feverishly unwrap more than a few. Keeping her eyes on Dr Michaels as he moved to the coffee station where he began to pour two mugs, slowly, with her eyes locked to him, dragging the pile of mints with her, she eased herself into the chair at the desk opposite his... and proceeded to shove snatched handfuls of unwrapped mints into her mouth.

Stepping to the desk, not looking directly at her, the Doctor placed his mug down before him and hers before her. 'This might help wash that down.' His smile, genuine and at ease.

She lifted the mug and began slurping. The chocolate and coffee were ill-contained. She tried to speak, but it took a few moments before her mouth was clear enough. Then she said, 'The burn!' Referring more to the mint than the coffee, of course.

Taking the proffered tissue from the Doctor and pretending as though this were just another chat, June said, 'So what the fuck was that all about?' Sipping at the coffee now, like a *lady*. A lady with choc-mint dribbling from more than just the corners of her mouth... but still.

'I'm sure you know you have a very good lawyer June.' Sipping from his own mug and placing it down, he said, 'Mr Jericho called me straight after you contacted him from the police station. And he assures me that we will be able to avoid all charges. If certain conditions can be met.'

June let the tumblers tumble. It took only a moment. 'And?'

'And I believe that if you are willing to participate,' he said, hardly a look with the pause, 'that we can make such arrangements.'

'Well?'

'During your outburst,' he said, indicating the position she had held just minutes before, 'you described yourself as *someone who had psychologically fractured and lost their shit.*'

'Yeah.'

'Which shows that you understand that your actions were not those of a person following a rational course of action. Not those of a person with a healthy state of mind.'

'Un-huh.'

'Which demonstrates that you are able to discern the difference, and yet, accept that those *said actions* were, at least, socially unacceptable.'

'No shit.'

'I also have information about the actions of the photographer in question... and how some of those actions may have been directed toward you, in the past. As well as a number of others.'

This time, June did not speak.

Dr Michaels nodded short. 'The cleanest way through all of this mess, June, is for you to voluntarily sign yourself in to a facility of my recommendation... for a short period of time.' He looked to her for her reaction, and then continued, 'If you agree to this and stay at this facility and participate in the program for a period of no less than thirty days,' again looking to June, 'then Mr Jericho assures me that with these conditions met... then all charges will be dismissed, and no further action will be taken against you.'

Taking another wrapped mint from the table, and turning it between her fingers before placing it back on the table unwrapped, June said, 'Where is it?'

His shoulders relaxed. 'The retreat is called *Bridges*.' Taking a brochure from a drawer beside him, he placed it on the table with his hand over it. Looking to her, sincerely, he said, 'June, this is a place I have worked with for many years... and we have had many successes.' He took his hand from the brochure. Watching, as June lifted it and began to look at it. 'It's about an hour from here. It's tucked away at the end of a bay on a very large *private* section of land. You would have complete privacy. The beach there is also private.' Waiting, he then said, 'You won't be disturbed.'

'Har,' she said, 'disturbed.' They both laughed at that. More out of a kind of relief than anything else.

Turning the brochure over with a question showing on her face, she said, 'It doesn't say what kind of rehab they do.'

'It's not a rehab facility.'

Her eyes told the story. Especially the left one.

'I'm going to ask that you trust me here June Bonnet.' The way he said it.

June felt it fall from her shoulders then, the façade, like a thick antique fur she had once tried on in the home of a wealthy designer. It fell, slid from her shoulders, and here in this office she had visited so many times, over so many years, June felt a crisp air surround her. An air she hadn't felt since she was twelve years old. And she knew, at least in part, that the time for trying was almost at an end. That this bullshit way she lived... 'The fucking struggle of it all.' Her voice was so small as the air fell out of her, and her lip shook like she was about to cry.

40

She took the pen that Dr Michaels offered her in her right hand as her left took the form she was to sign, and sitting up with a small swallow, June signed her agreement to both the deal and the contract for her stay at *Bridges Retreat*.

June watched as the Doctor silently took the paperwork after she'd laid down the pen. Watched as he lifted his phone immediately after and called through to her lawyer. His words blurring as he conveyed the information that would save her skin... and she felt *defeated*. She felt... like she had lost the war.

The sound of the phone being placed down in its cradle, so light. She felt numb.

'I'm proud of you June.'

And she coulda swore she heard the Doctor's voice shake a little.

Looking up at him with her hands folded in her lap... June began to cry without sound.

With her eyes running, focused on Dr Michaels, she felt her arms go up as he rounded the desk. And as his arms surrounded her, hers surrounded him… and so quietly, he held her... and June Bonnet fell apart.

Chapter Six

The Introduction

Its call drew her out of the car.

Stepping out onto the sandy soil, dragging her bag after her, she closed the door of the car without another word to the driver.

'Where are you?' Her face angled high into the trees as the car pulled away behind her.

Again, the bird called. Shrugging the bag up further onto her shoulder, June began to walk down the path and past the sign that pointed to her destination. Every step in the new runners she wore, the lightness of their bounce, contributing to her now childlike state. June looked for the Pied Currawong. The bird she had first become aware of as a child while holidaying with her parents.

'Look Daddy it's a crow.' She had been *maybe nine? Maybe younger*, now she came to think about it. 'No, it's not.' Even now as she walked along the narrow path leading through the large trees that overhung it, some eucalyptus, June remembered her confusion at noticing that this large black bird was not a crow. 'It's got white on it.' The indignation of a child felt on her face even now as the memory painted its reality upon her.

She had looked to her father. The choke of this memory was so strong as June remembered the love she had for him... when she was maybe nine. A love that never dimmed or shook or altered as she grew, as she became more aware. Had he been looking for the bird? But no. Her young eyes had seen that he looked directly at it. Still. His face so steady and calm. The joy he always seemed to carry, just under the thick warm skin of his face, was there as he looked at this confident bird. Her Daddy, always looking as though he saw something there that others did not.

'That's right baby-girl.' His voice had always seemed impossibly deep, and yet, like that of a child himself. His arm slowly gathering her small form to him. His smell covering her like a blanket. Her eyes following his hand as it rose and pointed to that grand black bird. 'You see the white feathers under his tail?' Knowing that she had.

'But it's not a magpie Daddy,' she had said, squinching her mouth to one side, looking for the answer she knew she did not know.

And she jolted in her child's form as the bird opened its beak, turning its face toward her and her father, only a few metres away. Little June had watched as the birdsong played out through its open beak. Her own mouth had opened unconsciously, mimicking. Her young mind awed by how this was possible. Her heart lifted and carried. Her young mind attaching words to her feeling; words like *Robinson Crusoe*, *The Island of Dr Moreau*. Stories her father had read to her. He, whose arm held her a little tighter and whose smile she now saw through the corner of her eye as she watched this beautiful music come from this beautiful bird. That smile that caused her own to open. This smile that made her known.

'You know they can live for over twenty years in the wild?' The voice loud, slapping away the past, bringing with it the cooler morning air of the here and now.

June heard her own shoes grate on the gravel underfoot. She felt her eyes stunned. Flashes of memories lost and then regained. 'Who the fuck are you?' The accusation defensive.

The ginger headed man with his hands deep in the pockets of his cargo shorts stood smiling like he had enjoyed giving her a fright. He nodded with a pinch of his nose like he was winking but wasn't. 'Gotcha,' he said, pointing his finger at her like this was funny. 'Yeah. Well, welcome I guess.' Thrusting his hand out before he made the large step toward where June stood on the path to Bridges Retreat.

Not having developed the necessity for the kinds of expressions required to make others at home in her company, June looked around her, seeing no place that she had yet arrived at. She made no attempt to take his hand.

'Sure, well I can see you're busy...' he said, smiling again and then not and then again. 'Um, arriving huh? Yeah, yep, okay so I'll...' Hooking a thumb, the ginger man began to step around her on the path. 'Oh!' Raising his hands at her reaction. 'Sorry.' Slowly taking a step backwards. 'Hey, you know...' pointing up to a large tree behind her and to her right, 'they can live for over twenty years in the wild.'

He appeared not to notice her expression, or else he was simply used to it.

Turning to the tree he had pointed at, June looked up high into its branches. 'Ooh,' she said, pointing entirely for her own benefit as the Currawong began its song once again.

Then from behind her now, maybe ten metres down the path, she heard the ginger man call, 'That's more than most of us could make it.'

But June forgot what he had said the instant she heard it, along with the fowl expression she was hatching. 'There you are,' she breathed the words as she walked closer to that large old tree and that beautiful... June froze... even as more of it hit her. Cool on her skin. Not wet at first. At least not to her senses. Her mouth still open wide. The taste of it beginning to spiral. And of course, she began to spit. With her hands still frozen in a *surprise,* she gagged as her mind caught up, and she felt her tears begin. Real ones, as she frantically spat and gagged and swallowed and finally began to retch... as she saw the painting on the wall. Well, not paint, and not the wall.

She wanted to scream at that bird. That bird who had once brought her so much happiness. 'Orhhh! Urpt!' And on she went for a little bit. And then a bit more.

'It's more the texture if I'm right?'

As she spun—a small fart, a leap and a turn really—June caught a tiny reflection of herself in Ginger-man's sunglasses. She saw the splashes of white down her mouth, eye, and parts of her hair and hands...

Nodding like he had got it in one, he said, 'Ooh and WOW that one really...' Holding his hands to his red hair and blowing out air like he'd taken a long run. 'But I'm right, aren't I? It's the texture more than the taste.' A finger, pointing right at her again.

June hurled, bent double.

'Some's coming out of your nose,' he said.

Panic gripped her chest hard then as fear spoke its steady heated words down the back of her neck. The heat of knowing that she could get no air in and no air out. Her hands flapping in small paddling movements as she fish-mouthed towards Ginger.

'Oh shit, alright, okay um right, righty-oh, fuck it eh, fuck me!' Jason Mackie, not a large man, with ginger hair, in front of June, began to flap his hands exactly like her. Until one of her hands—not accidentally—swopped him and felled him like an infant.

And the sweet air, in a tiny stream like it was coming through a straw, entered June's lungs. And then a little more... and she could feel the muscles within her throat begin to relax more and more. She paced in circles with her hands on her hips like a runner who had just finished a race, breathing hard through pursed lips.

Then she began to smile. Covered in the shit of the Pied Currawong, covered in her own regurgitations and a few tears, June began to really smile. Still pacing a few rounds before dropping a hand to the flattened ginger-man.

'Monkey-grip!' he called as he linked hands with her and allowed himself to be hauled to his feet. 'You gave me quite a fright there,' he puffed. 'And the...' leaning in, 'accidental...' He threw a wink as he mimicked her swing that had dropped him. 'Oh here...' Swinging a small bag from his back, Jason pulled a bottle of water from it and handed it to June. 'Just in time I guess.'

June pulled the lid off the bottle as she took it from his hand. First, she splashed some over her face before taking a large mouthful and swishing and tilting her head right back and gargling before spitting it out onto the ground between them.

'Oh, a spitter! Am I right?' Pointing again briefly before performing a mock boxer's dance and throwing a little rabbit punch toward June's shoulder but stopping well short of full extension. 'Ahhh,' he said as June stood before him flat eyed and performed a second gargle whilst keeping her eyes on him. Extending his hand, 'Me name's Jason Mackie, but everyone calls me Blue!' He smiled too loudly. 'Well not really.' Looking to the ground as she took his hand, shaking it loosely twice before letting it go. 'They generally call me Jase or Jason or Big Mackie!' he said, leaning back with this last one.

After washing more of the bird shit off her face and using the last of the water on her hands, June said, 'June.'

'Yes of course. Well then, June, should I escort you back to *The Lodge*?' He smiled, throwing a thumb down the path.

'If you have to,' she said. But the truth was that she was beginning to enjoy this strange little man.

'Ooh!' Excited, Jason dropped to a squat and rummaged in his bag. Extracting what he sort and handing it to her with the happiness of a puppy, he said, 'An umbrella!' His wide eyes signalling his great idea. He pointed skyward. 'You know? In case of more,' using his fingers for inverted commas, and nearly losing his balance, 'bird-strike!'

June's smile was small but sincere as she popped the small button clasp on the wrap of the umbrella. She looked at him kindly before pressing the button to open the umbrella, and she lay it over her shoulder before giving it a little twirl.

With his hands on his hips and his mouth hanging open, he said, 'Gee. You're really good at that.' Tilting his head and snatching up his bag, he made to link arms with her, but on seeing that this was not going to be accepted, he swung a crooked arm in a march, calling, 'Hi-Ho!' And he led the way down the increasingly sandy track.

Her room was small, but the windows were large.

June opened the French doors that stood just a few steps from the bed that would be hers for the next thirty days and felt herself let go. The salt air rushed in and swum about her as though it had been waiting all day for her to get home.

Stepping out onto the small veranda, she felt her hair lift with the breeze, and she leant into it. She felt herself tilting her head just a little bit as she rested her hands on the faded paint of the railing that stood between her and the sand of the beach.

She breathed.

And for a time, that's all she did.

She did not think.

She chose not to give words to the feelings she felt.

She did not give her attention to the reasons of why she was here.

She just stood on the small veranda of this little shack on this beach and breathed.

After a time, June heard a sound like the first pebbles falling from the top of a cliff… as they rattled to the base.

But even this… she chose not to entertain.

She had not gone Zen. No. But for some moments, she was not swallowed by a single question, doubt or concern. Nor was she captured by a burgeoning sense to self-judge or flagellate.

'I've simply run out of rope,' she said to the wind.

The brightness of the sun then dropped like a large hand had turned down the dimmer switch. Looking up into the clear blue sky, knowing that there must be a cloud up there somewhere, June felt a small chill as that wind ran over her bare shoulders. Her mind went still. The ocean, far out before her, grew somehow darker. The crests a little whiter. She felt the heat of her fear then, and she wanted to run. But the only place she knew she could, was out onto that beach. There was nowhere else for her to go.

But that fear.

June closed her eyes tightly.

Shaking her head just a little as she gripped that weathered railing so very hard.

Forgetting to breathe, June opened her eyes. Leaning forward, she peeked up under the small tin roof, not wanting to see... what might have dimmed the sun.

Chapter Seven

The Awakening

O h, you like it don't you.'
That voice smooth, feminine and accented. 'Yeeees,
you like it very much.' The words just cutting
through the lifting fog and drawing June to the surface.

'Hey!' June lifted her head from the pillow, watching her
own hands slapping at the white bed covers, and staring
wide to clear the sleep from her eyes. Her heart was
hammering in her race to comprehend the picture she was
met with. The sea breeze, warm and fresh, blowing in
through the open doors of her cottage, and a woman
standing at the end of her bed, folding a towel, silhouetted
by the morning sun. Her wide smile, the only part visible as
June's eyes fought hard to adjust.

'Who the fuck?' Sitting herself up, hands pressed into the
bed, June scrabbled the bedclothes up around her as she

began to slap together pieces of where she was, and who, and how, and what was happening?

Laughter, free, maybe too free, spilled from this currently towel-folding lady's face. June was able to discern more of her features as she turned, with the morning sun so bright behind her. June watched her taking a few paces to where she placed the folded towel on a sideboard.

'I was watching you sleeeeeep.' So much *sexy* in her voice.

'Just who the…?' June's eyes scanned the room, and she saw by the detail of rearrangement in the room around her that this woman must have been here for some time already. This piece of information connecting those fuzzy dots that swum in her mind, and now knowing where she was, she said, 'You're a housekeeper.'

'What because I'm from the Philippines you just assume I'm the freaking cleaning lady?'

'I need coffee.'

'I don't make coffee Dr Jones.' Laughing hard as she lifted a spray bottle and a cloth. 'I clean.' Wagging a finger, luridly swirling her hips, raising her arms overhead and lifting her hair some in the process, she said, 'I don't do extras.' Bucking her hips forward three times. Leaning down, placing one hand on the bed, minxy, she purred, 'But in your case I could make an exception.' Her laughter seeming to propel her back up off the bed.

Still struggling with the inappropriateness of the *Dr Jones* comment as she seesawed with her fight or flight response, June said, 'Aren't you supposed to knock?'

'Oh, I knock baby.' Her laughter bubbled out from her. 'I knock long time.' She sprayed a surface and wiped in one action. 'It not my fault you...' Her head flipped back as she made snoring sounds. Snapping out of it while somehow masking the steps that had brought her now directly beside the bed. Leaning in close to June, she whispered, 'You were dreaming.' And then she mimicked sexy dream time.

'Oh, I really don't see how this is appropriate. Really.' Hearing her mother's tone speaking in her words before the pillow beside her was lifted and thrown into her face.

'Oh, you need to lighten up.'

'Really?'

'My name is Sally,' she said, turning and dropping the cleaning gear into a square bucket on a chair, 'and you are sexy-dream-girl so what?' Turning and walking to June, taking an arm, clearly without permission, she began to haul June out of bed.

'Awrp! No.' There was really no way for her to go with this kind of treatment, and yet, there was simply no way not to. She couldn't be sure, as she was bodily dragged down the bed by what was truly an impossible grip, how to right the situation. She felt the end of the bed, under the rumple of sheets and duvet, disappearing under her belly, and she said, 'ARFPT!' More than once as she crashed off it and to the floor.

With her head completely covered, and limbs—someone else's—in the mix, June began to laugh.

At the sound of Sally's laughter, June lost the last of her composure. Within moments, they were rolling around in the tangle of bedclothes. The sunlight cut through in peeks and splashes. Sally's long dark hair bunched in her face before June realised that in her lost state, she had breathed some in. Which only made her laugh harder.

In time, they lay there side by side in the mass of linen. Both blowing hair out of their faces. 'Urgh.' June lifted her hand, pulling with it a length of Sally's hair from between her own lips. The length of it having been swallowed, now coated in her own saliva. And looking into each other's eyes, like two girls, they laughed like children.

Defeated by the situation, June felt her whole body let go. She felt herself relax. Her hands stretching back over her head, really stretching. The sunlight, the sea air, the old white paint of the cottage's interior...

June let out the air.

'Awp!'

Sally had curled into her and had begun to tickle her.

June, unable not to react, felt the muscles of her face form the kind of laugh she had lost. The laugh, she now understood, she had lost too long ago. And she screamed the unbound delight of a child, of a person who could bear no reason greater, a person caught unawares, a person without...

'How did you do that?' June's question was sincere as she looked in amazement to where Sally stood beside her own still prostrate form. 'But you were just?' Pointing at the floor by her side.

'It's an Asian thing.' Blowing more hair out of her face, and holding both hands out to her sides, Sally said, 'Be like water baby.' Laughing it off. 'Hey, breakfast here is served between seven and nine.' Showing fingers with each number before pointing to the clock on the wall. 'And it's written on the wall Doll.' She cocked her hand like a gun and fired one off.

It was a quarter past eight.

June looked this way and that, to get her bearings from the tangle on the floor.

'You want me to help you get cleaned up?' Sally was licking at the back of a wrist before giving a demonstration of cat bathing. 'No really I can do that,' she said, belly laughing. 'No really,' she said, letting the laughter trail away. Looking back to that clock, absently, June said, 'You're crazy.' When her face drifted back. 'Argh.' Sally's face was right there in front of hers. Her eyes blank, and her voice flat, Sally said, 'You're never to say that word here.' Her lips too wet. The pooling saliva beginning to spill. 'It's a rule Dr Jones.'

June walked, carrying the key that had been attached to the note she had found upon first entering the facility yesterday. It had been stuck on a door of the administration block. A note that had only *June Bonnet* written on it in large handwriting beside *Cottage 17*. And so, June walked, appreciating the well-tended gardens as she looked for the dining area.

Aside from Sally, she had still not met with another staff member. Like Sally, she presumed, they did not dress in uniforms. Her mind drawing a conclusion to probabilities of some kind of *Method*. Whatever the reason, this suited June just fine. The thought of being processed and controlled with a whole list of rules had been the one consideration that had almost prevented her from showing up. That and the fact that Dr Michaels had called and informed her that he had arranged a car to bring her here. To which she had mumbled something about *liberty*.

'There she is!' The voice instantly recognisable. 'Up for some grub I see,' Jason said, and laughed at whatever joke this constituted. And before June could decide on where he had come from, he was right beside her saying, 'May I escort you to your table?' He giggled like a child.

The sunshine, maybe it was this. Maybe it was the magical style of landscaped gardens. Maybe the birds that flew around them so free. Whatever it was, June felt disarmed. And happily, this time she took Jason's proffered arm and allowed herself to be led along the garden path.

It was the clinking and the ticking of plates, cutlery and glasses, that sounded their imminent arrival. Maybe for the first honest time since she was a child, June's mouth fell open as they rounded a corner, and she felt Jason's hand tighten on her forearm. She saw what appeared to be a large glasshouse filled with tables and chairs and fine tablecloths and glassware... and people. More than she had expected.

Her eyes drank it in, the hanging plants, the small fountain off to her left, the voices of these diners, the... everything froze.

Everyone, at every table, stopped like a record that had been fingered mid-roll.

'Come on,' said Jason. His voice the only sound other than the lightly splashing water of the fountain. His eyes a little excited, he walked her through the faces of the other guests, and in a moment they all returned to their former activity as though nothing had happened.

She had never felt like this. Not ever. Like Alice.

In a dream, she sat in the seat that had been drawn for her. Feeling like her dress was too tatty for such a place, June sat and rested her hands lightly on the tabletop.

'I chose this table so that we could ease in you in a little bit.' Jason smiled as he took the seat opposite her. A table set for five. His eyebrows rose in time with his shoulders. 'Cool huh?' Raising his hand and clicking his fingers before dropping both to his lap, he said, 'Just kidding.'

Time, like glue, like melted sugar, swam.

The sounds of glassware in use and the voices of the other diners surrounding her humming a full two octaves, June sunk into this atmospheric beanbag and felt her own mouth open just a quarter inch. The back of her seat holding her like an egg. Her eyes creasing in their corners from the lightness of it. Of her surrounds.

Too many things. Too many faces and colours, though they were mature colours. Colours of a real painting. They fell together so seamlessly, so perfectly, even with all their movement, that for the first time, June believed, no, she knew, that she was herself now a part of this beautiful composition. She knew in fact, in that moment as her head turned to see Jason with his smile still fixed as he arranged his knife and bread plate just so... that she was now an active collaborator, that she was one of the many who held the conductor's baton, the artist's brush, or maybe the coach's whistle.

The smell of hot toast.

The sound of Jason's hands rubbing together in anticipation of this most simple of foods. The shuffle of the food's bearer as he arrived at their table. A song of laughter spiralling to her right. June's mouth lifted to the angle of her eyes. The smell of the toasted bread threaded, she knew, with a very thin taint of the metallic tray on which it was carried.

Is it silver, she thought in a dream.

And then the butter. *The butter.*

Like a fist slowly pushing up within her from the bottom of her gut, her hunger spread its fingers at her throat, stirring the taste buds fast. She leant into the table. Her hand absently taking her butter knife. Her eyes latched to the butter as it was still lowered to the table. Her peripheries picking up the jam to her right. Jason's smiling face out of focus behind. His eagerness clearly hinged on her enjoyment. And her stomach growled like a waking troll. Her mouth felt the sounds of mewls as her body leant into the table with her hands lifting and her mind taking her into *the zone.*

She watched herself butter and jam her first piece of toast even as Jason lifted and lay her first cup of hot milky tea before her. The small crunches of that bread, like a still crisp brown paper doughnut bag between her fingers, sounded in such a way as to cause her eyelids to drift and her lips and teeth to part. June could almost see her taste buds leaping like leaches on a tropical trail as her head moved from side to side... like a baby seeking out its mother's nipple.

'Hmmm,' June heard herself say.

'It's good right?' she heard Jason reply... in slow motion.

Chapter Eight

A Wreck

The note on her bed simply read, 'Take a long walk. We'll talk soon.' No name at the bottom.

She stood there with her hands on her hips, looking down at the small square of paper. Its top edge torn. She couldn't feel anything. Internally, nothing. Her eyelids lifted a little. She turned to the still opened French doors. The breeze was warm, so light and easy against her skin. June forced her eyes about her surrounds, digging until she found it. A reason. She felt that knot in her lower chest, that fist, begin to pulse.

'How easy is this?' Her fist bopping in agreement. A sourness in her mouth now as she stepped about the room looking at all the evidence of how entitled she was. Her laughter beginning and only that. 'Poor Juney.' But there was little steam to it.

Snatching a towel, June walked out the doors, pretending not to notice how good the sand felt beneath her bare feet. She lowered her sunglasses, kicked her chin up a notch, and strode down the sandy path towards the Pacific Ocean... like a model.

Cresting a dune brought her face to face with the water's edge and pulled that fisted knot into a deeper recess. Involuntarily, she sucked the salt air into her flaring nostrils until she could taste it. Her eyelids drooping under her shades as she let it out. And she let it out, just so she could draw more in.

With the sand beneath her still not hot enough to burn her feet, lifting a corner of her skirt for no apparent reason, June walked on down until her soles felt the damp of that brown sugar sand. Smiling, she slapped her feet on it until more water rose to the surface. Holding the towel out to shoulder height, she lifted her hands to the sky, knowing in that moment that she had forgotten to bring her cigarettes.

With a nostril raised, June turned to gauge the distance back to the cottage and saw someone hurrying along the same path she had taken. The person lifting something in one hand while waving wide with their other.

Lifting a hand to shade her brow, she tried to recognise who it was. Another small feeling in her lower gut springing at the idea of it being Jason. A feeling she quite assuredly was not going to investigate, not wanting to know its cause. She began to walk toward the ungainly waving... 'Woman?'

The woman arrived, stopping just a few feet away from her, puffing hard at the effort she had just made. Her wavy hair sticking to her forehead in parts under a brimmed hat. With her hands on her knees, raising one unmistakeably keen eye to June, she said, 'Aw, thank fuck you stopped! Har! Hoo!' Laughing, panting, as she caught her breath.

Reaching for the water bottle she didn't have and looking at this woman—not in great shape—guessing somewhere in her middle fifties, June felt herself like her. 'You're a sweaty mess,' she said, smiling as she made to help the lady at least stand straight.

'No,' she said, such a big honest smile, 'I got it. Woo!' Reaching into the bag she carried, withdrawing a bottle of water, wet with the condensation of its obvious chill, she snapped the lid open like a metaphorical sailor. She offered a cheers to June before lifting it to her upturned mouth. Dropping it back down before raising a finger and repeating the same. When she had done this—her face a scrunched bag of consternation—she turned back down the path she had just run and said, 'What? That's got to be fifty or sixty metres I just ran!' Hooking a thumb as her laughter flew from the centre of her roundish middle. 'Oh, forgive my bad manners.' She thrust a hand toward June. 'I'm Sharon,' she said, smiling as though that explained it.

Unable to keep her own smile from being painted, June reached for Sharon's hand and began to say her own name but was halted by this lady's waving hand as she snuck another gulp.

'Nah, I got yours my dear... Urrrp!' Burping like it was a beer she held in her hand. The whole charade was completely off balance with her outward appearance, more housewife than hooker. She continued, 'That's why I'm here.' Nodding her head in big nods.

'I see,' June said, crossing her arms and taking an unconscious step back. Of course, she did not see.

'Come on.' Stepping forward and taking June's arm, turning her and pushing her back down the path toward the beach. 'I'll explain as we walk.

But she didn't.

They just walked to the water's edge. June so overtaken by this woman that there was simply no time to piece together any concrete thoughts. And so, June kinda gave up on the trying.

The water was perfect. With her arm still gripped by this strange, yet somehow lovely, woman standing beside her, ankle deep in the ocean, June smiled as she caught the knowing; that the water's temperature felt the same as her own.

'Just look at it!' Sharon called out to the open space. Her hand pushing out before her, she called, 'Fucking Majestic.' A free hand, though there appeared to be none, produced a pack of cigarettes which she handily opened. And with a quick, short, up-down jig, she caused several to pop up above the others in the pack. She stood that way, still not looking at June, with her eyes fixed as though on an object far distant out to sea.

Smiling—knowing this would be her default around this woman—June took a cigarette, and she leant forward as Sharon casually lit it without a hand covering the small flame. June's eyes rattled at this little, but impressive, trick. And she felt herself pulled away as she drew on the smoke.

June looked out over the water, past the small waves that broke a few short metres from where she stood. On her third exhale, Sharon had draped an arm around her. Her strong arm giving a few short pulls into her soft form before she released.

A sound like a sob broke from June's lips as she made for her next draw. Only a sound though. She drew on the cigarette and noted that the sea breeze shortened its lifespan, and she pretended not to notice the tiny tear that was soon driven away and into her hair.

'Salt air,' Sharon said, thumping June on the arm. 'Come on! There's something I want to show you.'

This woman, taking her hand the way she did and dragging her off down the beach, gave her no pause. *Like a favourite aunt?*

June was empty now. Somehow empty. And as she heard herself chuckle at this woman dragging her along the wet sand, she considered in an offhand way that maybe this was the feeling a shell had when its host either outgrew it or died.

'Not far!' Sharon called back through the growing wind.

Flicking her cigarette out into the water beside her, June began to trot to keep up.

The sand beneath her feet was now dry, powdery, soft. Beginning to like holding this woman's hand, June felt herself come to a stop.

Placing her hands on her hips before pointing at the large, rusted structure that lay before them, Sharon said, 'See?'

June stepped forward. The air around her was swimming, playing about her. As she took her second step and then her third in the deep soft sand, she heard the tinkling chimes of the laughter of her child's memory. Her neck already beginning to ache as she craned. Her eyes climbing the formidable structure now just twenty feet or so before her. The deep red lines of the weather cut rust on the ship's external hull like ladders for her eyes to step from. She wanted to turn back to Sharon, to say something to her. But she couldn't. Not only gripped by the visual impressiveness of this mighty thing, so out of place where it lay partly buried in the sand so far from the water, June was drawn by it.

And her feet kept moving her to it.

'Be careful...' she heard Sharon calling. The rest of her words trailing from June's ears. She could guess at the reason for the warning.

But still she moved closer. She needed to touch it. Her heart beating its little fists at the walls of her ribcage. 'Hello,' she heard herself say as her right hand, palm spread, pressed against the many layers of deep rust that constituted the outer walls of this wreck.

Her mouth opened as the long rending sound from deep within this ship's hulk reached her, seeming to speak to her of this contact. And she heard herself say, 'It's okay baby.' Placing her left hand beside her right, unafraid of cutting herself.

'It's so soft!' she called back to Sharon, hearing the child-like joy in her voice, the awe.

'... it's dangerous!'

Spoken so only she could hear it, June said, 'Then why did you bring me here?' Smiling open-mouthed as her hands ran over the surface, feeling it, moving along it, about it.

June was inside the massive, rusted hull of the shipwreck before she was aware of it. It wasn't until a hard line of light struck her face that June woke to her position, her situation.

She stood on broken boards, somehow preserved, partially buried by sand and rusted debris, within those walls. Her eyes caught by a corner to her left still in shadow—*maybe always so*—where paint still remained on the steel walls. She moved to it. Her feet finding their way without conscious aid. The sound of something else—something alive—

skittering away around a near but unseen corner in what June knew must be a maze of rust and memories.

The beam of sunlight running its warm hands over her head, hair, and shoulders as she passed into the instantly cooler shade. Her eyes running over this relatively intact corner in a so far otherwise completely degraded structure. And her hands reached out. She couldn't help herself. Her heart felt wisps of wrongdoing, of inappropriateness, but still June couldn't restrain herself. It was as though, through her touch, she could feel something so much deeper than only the rust and now creamy enamel paint that were the remnants of this huge vessel.

Her hands still running, trailing and tracing, June squatted before the steel desk that had no doubt been bolted into place many, many, years ago. 'The smell of...?' June tried to find some way to describe it. As her hands ran over the drawers, she was thrown by how they could be so intact when all about her had fallen to such total decay.

'The smell of man,' she said it. Hearing the echo as she smiled at her lack of a need to find or even decide upon a clearer explanation of her own words. She tried a drawer, and it came.

The sound of its opening, so large in this place. The rending echo that followed, like a call from another time. 'I suppose it is,' she said, knowing that she was pushing the bounds of something here. *At the very least,* she thought, *common sense.* June looked above and over her right shoulder at what had to be many, many tonnes of rusted steel that could—she could see this now—actually fall. And so, knowing that the entire structure could possibly collapse upon her, June proceeded.

67

That smell again, she thought, *but sharper*, pulling the drawer open as far as it would go, *something like an alcohol?*

'Whoop!' Two small eyes stared back out of the deepest shadows within that three-quarter opened drawer. June found herself both too afraid and too responsible to run away. And so still squatting, she began to flap her hands at her skirt covered thighs as she watched those eyes moving in inhuman ways. A tacking sound, *clack-clack-clack!* Sounding louder than she knew it must be. Her fright lifting the tiny hairs about her body, making her aware that she sweat between her breasts. June tried to laugh, but said, 'Erghhh!' As the clattering clacking became skittering, and she felt her butt-hole contract maybe two times, maybe three. And her hands were flapping under her drawn-down mouth... 'Oh... really?' She wanted to pee out of relief. 'Hey little guy,' she cooed, getting all Disney as a crab, and not a big one, dragged its blue and orange shell along and over the edge of the opened drawer. June's cow-eyeing stretched as the crab fell out of the drawer and clacked to the rusted mess of a floor in front of her. Seeing it fall like that, like it must have broken something, June said, 'Oh, are you okay?' Timidly reaching out to help it before it righted itself in a single flip and began snapping its little, but still somewhat dangerous, claws at her, moving swiftly in her direction. 'Urgh!' she said, her heart pancaking. June's hand thrust out and her fingers catching the underbelly of the wee beast, effectively flinging it so fast and high that she heard the squeal issuing from her own mouth before her hands could cover it. Her eyes followed the crab as it lifted up, over and through a large rusted out section of the wall to her right. June stood there, feeling bad the whole short journey.

Catching herself, head dipped and tilted, still listening for the sound of the crab's undoubtedly harsh contact on landing— no doubt taking longer than it possibly could have—June's eyes caught on something glinting in the recesses of that same opened drawer.

Only her hand moved. The fears of a child now swimming within her, reminding her of the darkness and the unknown creatures that may, *no must*, inhabit such unknowns, still June's hand moved to that partially shining thing.

Her hand snatched before she had known it would—clearly bitten by the same bug that had creased her inner workings—and she withdrew it. Staring at it before her mind would attach the word for what she knew she held the instant her fingers locked onto it. A key. Not rusty. Not decayed. A still shiny, key.

That's when the shadow alerted her, before the sounds could reach her alarm, before her sense's panic button could be pressed. But just like her hand, June's whole body was on the move before her analytical mind could find the pictures or words to support her gut's reaction.

She was running so quick, with her feet picking safe enough places to light upon, just enough to carry and yet propel her slim form fast enough, to avoid the devastating weight and brutish sharpness of the large sections of falling rusted steel that beat and thumped and rained down around her.

Even her own thumping heartbeat couldn't sound in her recognition amidst the sheer awesome calamity that she ran through as her will—seemingly acting independently and previous to any conscious thought—forced her to *MOVE!*

The tremors still wracked her even as she fell to the very soft sand. The immense collapse still occurring right behind her, so close that June fully expected that still she must not have run far enough; that still she *must* be bitten by that screaming, decayed, tortured steel.

And she could feel herself screaming as her hands covered her ears, and her face pushed itself into that sand. Her feet desperately scrabbling for purchase as her lizard brain still protested for *further distance* from this great and violent threat. The noise, the thunder of it, quickly dropped, and those sounds withdrew. Still, they were sounding, but now they are leaving her immediate space, pulling back like a curtained line. Her body was shaking, feeling sharp debris the size of grasshoppers still falling upon her prostrate body... and then quickly, to mostly dust.

June now heard herself cry. And unable to look back upon what she had undoubtedly caused—a very near personal, *and let's be honest,* mortal disaster of her own absolute creation—June bawled like a newborn baby... as she lay there covered in the dust and debris... in the hard light of day.

The first words she heard, unable to discern how long she had been laying there like she was, were, 'Oh really.' Sharon, tut-tutting as she both lifted, dusted, and carefully wiped at the shit that covered June. 'You've made a right mess of your hair,' she said, fluffing at her before her face dipped, and her wet eyes looked straight into those of this girl who had just very nearly died, and she said, 'What do you say we make our way back?' Her eyes, smiling now. 'They'll be about to serve morning tea!'

Her heart in a masher, June allowed herself to be held and led under this older woman's heavy arm. And feeling her tears still running like her eyes had been pierced, June closed her fist ever so tightly around the key she had withdrawn from that drawer; the key that had lain in the heart of that ship... that wreck.

As they walked back down the beach, Sharon spoke of many things... all of them food related... more than half, about jam.

Chapter Nine

The Dip

O h look, they float.'
Looking across from where she sat at the little table
while threatening her buttered scone with a knife
loaded with red jam, June stared at Sharon standing in the
pool. She watched her looking down at what she first took
to be her breasts as they bobbed lazily in the clear turquoise
water.

Pointing down to one of the half scones that floated in front
of her then looking up to June, Sharon said, 'It floats.' The
squint in her eyes at the angle of the sun making it unclear if
a smile accompanied the hopeful childlike enthusiasm of this
observance.

'You want some jam?' Holding up her knife.

Tapping at the scone in the water, she said, 'Nah, yeah, nah.'
Her big tits appearing like knees. 'I'll let it soak for a bit.'
Sharon disappeared under the surface. The scone drawn
under with her.

'I think she...' Jason said, holding up his hand and imitating
several quick hand-draws of a smoke, 'you know?' Looking
at the woman in the pool as she surfaced, Jason picked up a
scone and casually lifted the knife from June's hand and

spread the jam from it, on it. Sitting back in his chair for only the time it took to take a bite before he quickly leant forward, he said, 'We all think we know that she...' His eyes still on Sharon with his left-hand lassoing in the air as he took another large bite of the jammed scone, sans butter.

'Well,' she said, not at all sure that she was following his meaning as she took another knife, cut and buttered another scone, keeping her eyes on Jason while loading her knife with the jam, 'she sure knows her jam.'

'Mmm hmm.' His own mouth loaded, leaning back at a crazy angle, he could only point his hand at Sharon in the water, in recognition of June's statement. Which he did a few times.

The air crackled then. Or so it seemed to June. With the jam covered scone so close to her mouth that the scent of it tickled her nostrils, June looked at the early afternoon light through her amber shades. 'The colours,' she said. But she heard no response. She was not requiring one. She was speaking with herself, watching the burnt yellows and buttery oranges spreading with the mustard wash of that light. 'Just now...' Her eyes turned to Jason. 'What the fuck are you doing?' she said, observing this man wearing shorts, a light blue shirt opened to the waist, sitting up at the table they shared with both hands on its top, holding and fingering a scone.

'Aw no,' he said, the back of his right hand going to his mouth, covering his smile. 'I see.' Still covering his mouth, and then pointing at the whole scone impaled on his left middle finger. 'Oh my god.' And he let himself laugh now. And then slowly he withdrew his finger from the scone, looking at June blankly. He lifted the butter covered finger and put it wholly in his mouth... sucking on it before speaking around it, 'No jam.'

June reached for a cigarette with one hand and her coffee with the other as her eyes sought a lighter somewhere on the table. A wave, a small one, began to rise within her. It was a small heat. With her hand taking the lighter, she felt her thoughts dropping down their tentacles to that heat of emotion. Thoughts she had chosen not to entertain. Questions, confusions about this place. And she began to vocalise. 'What is this place?' she said to her hands. 'Who are these people?' June raised her eyes and saw that Sharon had stilled in the water. Turning, she saw that Jason had frozen too, with his finger half buried, again, in the scone. Knowing that the heat had risen to her face. Knowing that the animal of her emotion, now linked with her thoughts, was in real danger of taking her over, June felt the rope, the ribbon, slip through her fingers. 'Who the fuck are you guys?' June had gotten loud and was hating the expression she could feel on her face. 'And where the fuck are the doctors?' Seeing her hands shaking as she made to light the cigarette she held between her fingers. Taking a draw, and then another before she exhaled. Feeling that emotion beginning to take hold of her mouth. The sour taste beginning to pool around her tongue. The tremble in her lips. 'I mean for fuck's sake!' Her head leaning forward, unable to ignore the statues, who just a moment ago had been Sharon and Jason. 'I've been here for a fucking week and nothing but these...' she said, snatching a crumpled piece of paper from the tabletop before her as she blew out a heap of smoke, 'fucking notes!' She drew heavily on her smoke, throwing the balled square of paper back down onto the table.

CLANG-ALANG-CLANG-ALANG-CLANG-ALANG!

A beating hammer where her heart should be, June said, 'ARK!' Her wide eyes shooting to her right, to the source of that sound. 'Really?' At the top of the stairs leading down to the pool area stood a wee man in a dinner suit, holding a triangle up in one hand and its metal wand in the other. 'It's almost as big as he is.' June knew she was speaking to no-one in particular. Her anger was still spewing, and her words were not coming as she watched a procession of other *patients* making their way past the man still holding the large metal triangle up as though he was about to have another go at it. 'Oh, this is too much!' She made to stand... and felt a hand on her forearm before she had noticed that Jason had moved at all.

He didn't say anything, Jason. But June could feel a warmth. *An authority?* She couldn't be sure in that moment, of anything. She wanted to cry and scream. And if it wasn't for much effort, she was sure she would not be able to prevent herself from stamping her feet under the table. But something *in his touch.* Something *in the way* Sharon had moved toward her in the pool. *Was it a calm?*

'Ohhhh,' called the posse of strangers, a few she recognised, many she did not. All of them in bath robes. All of them walking in a measure. Their faces bland. Their expressions flat. All sounding as one, 'Ohhhh.'

'Oh alright,' June said, 'I'm outta here.' Annoyance flaring her gums as the pressure of Jason's hand increased. 'Let me the fuck go!' As the last word issued, June felt the air pull out of her space. Her eyes lifting. Now a line of people was standing along that poolside, expressionless, facing her as one.

'June,' Sharon's voice sounding from her left. The single word sounding with a depth of recognition that June believed she did not deserve.

She felt the terror then. June felt it boil. She felt the sound of her scream rising from the lowest parts within her belly. She felt it tearing its way through the bones of her chest like a banshee loosed from its cage. She felt her mouth beginning to open...

CLANG-ALANG-CLANG-ALANG-CLANG-ALANG!

The triangle rang.

June's tongue stuck in her throat. The echo of that, *fucking sound*, calling to a place she had to know, stilling her. Feeling big slurps of air pulling in through her nostrils. Her mind silently screaming that she didn't know what was happening. 'What is going on?' she said, so softly. *Nothing* finding a place here.

'Yip! Yip!' the woman at the front of that crazy line of bath-robed folk poolside called, hollered even. Her face turning to the sky. Her hands first clasping the collar of her fluffy pink bath robe... then casting it straight down to the ground. This woman's expression: the practiced wide smile of a cheerleader as her robe was flung to the tile at her feet. Leaving her naked body lit by the full sun. The flesh of her pale, and not without signs of life. Her body full and stark.

June's eyes fixed on this woman. The boil of her terror somehow churned as the spoon of this unfathomable happening struck her dumb and slowed her waters. And yet still her hand holding the cigarette found her mouth, and she puffed as the naked woman lifted her arms straight above her like a synchronised swimmer, with a smile to suit. A dark thatch of pubic hair opening as her outside leg lifted, and she plunged into that pool.

'What the fuck?' June spoke around the cigarette clenched between her teeth. She was no stranger to... but her sentiment was clear.

A man, tall and greying at the sides of his regal head, standing half a step behind the fallen pink robe, turned. He too holding the collar of his brown bath robe. His eyes sparkling like a loon. He lifted his chin and cried, 'YOW-YOW!' Somehow sounding like a wolf as he too stripped himself bare. His long cock swinging above his shaven balls as his long legs bent until he squat like a frog and called, 'YEW!' And with his hands pressed together above his head, he sprung like one, with impossible agility for a man his age, and dove into the pool.

June simply stood now with one hand crossed over her hips. The elbow of her other arm sitting atop that hand holding the cigarette. June stood, chewing a fingernail. And in truth, as one after another of these crazy people stripped bare and leapt hollering into that pool on this fine sunny day, June felt herself cough a laugh through her curled smile as a few sweet tears, she never knew she had, leaked down her cheeks.

She was wiping at those tears as Sharon took her left hand. She hadn't seen her getting out of the pool.

'Don't worry dear,' Sharon elbowed her lightly, 'you were distracted.' And she gave a good-natured chuckle as she threw a pointed hand at the pool now teaming with naked folk. 'Whoop! There he goes!' Clasping her wet self onto June's arm as she pointed stair-ward.

Trying to get her lips over the butt of her smoke, June's eyes hooked right, squinting at the very loud, *CLANG-G-G,* as the wee man's giant triangle clambered to and down the concrete stairs.

'GO JERRY!' Sharon's voice was deafening at such close proximity. She let go of June, stuck the middle fingers of each hand between her lips and tore the fabric of sound with a trucker's whistle.

June was laughing, bent with it. The back of her left hand lifted to cover her face as it stretched beyond her *public expression level* at Sharon's outburst. Then as she turned, her arm dropped, and her mouth formed a wide stretched *O* as the former *dinner triangle banging Jerry* got the rest of his dinner suit off, then at a full run—a cock the size of a hammer slapping at his thighs—he leapt fully into the middle of a clapping mass of nude swimmers in this, only moments earlier, idyllic swimming pool.

June felt herself shaking. There was no room for the questions. Her emotions had split. And even this she couldn't find the answers to. The *why's* were many. With herself now laughing like a loon, she felt the ribbon of her sanity slipping between the very real fingers she grasped before her. The sound of music now filled the air around her. She saw it. Her eyes leaping to the speakers on their posts at either end of this recreation area. She saw them shaking, or seeming too. The music, a kind of jazz, filled what was now an arena of swimming nakedness. The craze of it all. The break from anything connected to any kind of normalcy she could grasp at. The snare drum, with its rhythm cycling, drawing her mind and her gut further afield from any bearings. June felt she might fall. She felt the strong steady hold of Sharon's hands on her left arm and shoulder. She saw Jason risen from his chair. The accosted scone out of site. This man, who had born a certain comedy with every interaction, now serious. And in a circumstance, such as this. 'How?' her voice so small. Wanting to disappear as he approached her, rather than face whatever he had to say. *Stern,* he looked stern. 'How?' Her question, more than could be answered with a turn of phrase.

A foot from her now, and standing so still, with his hands pressed together as though he were about to deliver her with a wisdom drawn from a time spent on high, a sermon even, he said, 'Well?' And stood looking straight into her crying eyes.

June's mouth moved as she sought for something to say. Her eyes, those of a dear caught in the face of an inescapable danger. Her mouth moved... without any sound.

Jason said, 'Don't you think it's time for some...' A long pause followed, stretched. Thoughtful, with his eyes cast to one side before returning to hers, he said, 'I mean to say...' Another pause, and finally a shrug. 'Wouldn't you say it was time for some... ginger-nuts?'

June could feel her head shaking at these words. Memories from her own childhood flash-carded. Memories of visits with ladies, all elderly, some kind. The tension of a child hoping to be found *of good behaviour,* never leaving her. Of politely accepting the proffered brown biscuit; the kind that no child really sought. The texture hard, the *taste*...

But June had no time to entertain her deeply drawn memories a moment longer. Before her, on that mostly dry concrete and already shirtless, Jason had dropped his shorts. She was frozen in place. Her chest torn in so many differing directions. Another cough of laughter causing her face to turn red. *Embarrassed.* A sick turn in her lower belly. With a fear of a kind that brought forth the smell of citrus. The silence of this *Sharon* standing to her side... June swore she could smell her own vagina. And again, her mouth—faced by Jason's implacable expression as he stood completely naked before her—moved without sound. Her eyes, no matter her want, unable to stray from the light that played on the ginger hair of his lower belly, and on the ginger hair that thatched above a cock. She couldn't remove her eyes. She couldn't close her mouth. Swearing, in her near silent mind, that she could see that there was blood moving into his organ. Her eyes informing her that it was thicker than she had believed it would be. And this, informing her that she had thought of her *friend's* cock.

Wanting to be somewhere else. Wanting to press her hand against herself. June felt her nipples tighten and her teeth want to grit. But her mouth would not close. And sweat, she could feel it, sprang from the very top of her brow by the line of her hair.

With a voice deeper than she could have credited, as his arms rose and his cock a little with them, clapping his hands together above his head, Jason called, 'WOE-WOE-WOE!' His arms dropped, his hands fisted, and his elbows lifted in an *Exit Stage Left*, or right in this case. And as time in June's reality slowed, ever so much, she watched this man Jason flop his head to one side and then the other... as he ran for that pool. Calling loudly, even deeper in the slowed frames, as he did, 'It's time for some...' His foot slapping so hard as he kicked off from the pool's edge that, momentarily, June's eyes snapped shut. As they opened in slow motion, she saw him high in the air out over that glinting turquoise water... and the quickly parting nude bathers. Their shocked and yet expectant faces beaming up at him as he held a hand under each leg... somersaulting. June's hands came together, unbidden, before her. Her neck stretched to its full limit as though she were attempting to give Jason some extra lift. And she watched his body turn. And she watched his dark

81

arsehole appear in full view. She watched his partially engorged cock coming up and under as his whole body spun. And she felt herself cry out something she could not hear as she heard him yell, 'GINGER NUTS!' Which in that very moment, with her air pushing out of her in sobs regardless of her agreement, filled the focus of her vision. June stood, held in the viscous grip of slowed time, with her mouth still drawing open wider still…. staring at Jason's red hair covered balls as his body spun *ever so slowly* in the air.

From between his parted legs, in just a flash, a moment before time slipped back to the *normal track speed*, June saw his face—Jason's. His expression, replicated in her memory, June had only ever seen… on the face of Eckhart Tolle.

Wondering for the very first time if what she was experiencing was the same—in her former opinion and still maybe so—*delusional* rapture that she had only seen on documentaries of cult followers and their devotees, still June found herself tearing at her own clothing. She did so, watching the raised and clapping hands of the many people in the pool before her. Their feverish eyes all fixed on her as she got her shirt clear. This act feeding an excitement she knew had to be more than a little concerning. And yet she couldn't stop the grunting sounds… that came from her own lips as she disrobed.

'You show them,' said Sharon.

But June couldn't process this in the moment, and yet she knew she was glad that she could not. Her hands needing to get her skirt clear and under her feet. Her undies, half pulled down in the process. Her tits swinging over the slip of sweat that had gathered under them. Her mouth aching for reasons she felt had to have something to do with long buried pain. June wanted to pee, to shit, and wipe her nose all at once. Her air coming in quick pants. So far beyond any sense of decorum. So far outside her sense of balance. June screamed, 'YARP!' Half folding as her tears pushed out of her. Her face now a burning mess. She could feel her own snot on her upper lip, and even then, glad that it was probably the clear kind. She laughed like a fool. She made sounds she could not discern. She let her now red eyes go to the sky above her and then to where her hands met under the self-conscious bend in her neck. The sounds of the clapping, louder now, joined by the many emotionally strained voices whooping their encouragement and heartfelt congratulations.

And she stood before them naked, and again she screamed, 'YARP!'

And she ran. She might never know why. But June ran for that pool. Completely naked before these people. Her tits swinging free. Her vision all but hidden under her crying eyes as she felt her right foot slap against that pool's edge. And she felt her body lift into the arc of a somersault she had never before performed.

Again, for June, time slipped.

She could see fragments of the world around her, through her flying hair.

She could feel her own hands gripping the backs of her knees.

She could feel the full spread of her arse.

She could even feel the parting of her labia... as she heard her own voice scream, 'Lamb's tongue!' Before she entered the water... with a hard slap on her right side.

Chapter Ten

A Sign

There was light on the horizon, a little, *a glow.*
The sun hadn't cracked this part of the world just yet.
But it was about to.
June's eyes, like balls floating in a jig, found their level as she
turned her head. From right to left she turned her head.
From the trees—*somehow pubic in this light*—at the far south
end of the beach, she turned her head. June's chin held the
sway. Her eyes held to the water, so flat, impossibly flat,
smooth, silken. The rises in it, *bumps,* undulating, unfixed,
and yet permanent in the way they reappeared elsewhere,
drawing her eyes to ever differing parts of its whole.
The smell, she thought. The sand under her feet damp, a little
cool. She said, 'Like... teenaged sweat.' She breathed through
her nose. Her eyelids still. Her hands hanging weightless by
her sides. June could feel her hips, her knees, and the sand.

Three quarters of the line to the north end of the great curve, *the carve,* of that beach, the Sun's yolk spilt. The light, *its light,* opening, spilling, but quick. Its result on the world here, quick. The colours around her different. So fast was the change that she was unable to recall those former colours. That's how fast that light had sprung. And her mouth fell open just a bit. And she could taste that sweat. And her eyes felt the salt now. The salt that had been in the air the whole time. Somehow now it had become apparent in the moment the top arch of that big ball of yellow crested that far away horizon.

A splash brought her down. And she felt, *so fast,* like a child knowing the promise of fun. She felt that *fun* was giving her a chance to play. Her lips stretched. She could feel it. And she heard a high laugh coming out of her as she watched her feet spread *fast* like a family pet... when their loved one grabs the ball.

The next splash was bigger. *Closer?* June fixed on that direction. Seeing ripples to her right again. Now a ring, *rings,* spreading from where the creature—*it had to be*—had submerged. June felt the water, *cool,* on her toes, on her feet, to her ankles, somehow embracing kindly.

SPLASH, and June felt the bones from her cheeks to her collars. She felt every part of them. Her eyes opening wide enough to tilt her head back. The *mannish* sound coming from her chest *more felt than heard* as the enormous creature, mostly black and so large, crashed back down into the still ocean. And June knew she was hopping up and down because she could feel it. She knew she was laughing because of the tears the breeze touched on her face. She knew her heart was full... because it seemed to shine the

86

water before her... as her hope stretched and pulled from the bottom of her basket... until it started dragging out the need. To her knees in the water. A lapse and then to her short's bottoms. The denim there wet to the metal zip... and past.

With her palms on the top of that smooth salt water, June was in it to her ribs. Her eyes, her heart, seeking that animal she knew couldn't be so close to the shore. A small alarm sounding a cautionary murmur, a whisper of logistics, and a memory of ocean topography.

'Trench,' the word carried away and gone.

The *groan*! The best word her mind could find in the split between the normal run of time and the gel of time she was pulled into as the beast... 'Jonah!' she said. Her mind correcting her immediately, but she stepped forward, not at all caring. Her hands still pressed to the water's line as the Humpback—*it had to be*—broke through that line... and entered the same air as June.

There was nothing for it really but to gawk. *The sound of it*! The power of this impossible creature bursting through, out, up and up and up and shaking, shuddering the very air around her. And she screamed. The best kind. Her chest was shaking with it. Her mouth and eyes and heart—sorry but it's true—all wide open and roaring with real, very-very real... *Delight*!

She was giggling, even as the monster was turning in the air. Its tail *and probably midriff,* by June's calculations, were still in the water. She began to grab at the top of the water, bracing or attempting to. Her knees were bending, her nipple line submerged, and her glee was sparkling—had to be. June's hands were opening and closing on that water even as the spray of the whale began to paint her, even as she was in the belly of her nervous system's freeze on time. It stopped and

June heard a chain rattle somewhere far down within her. The top of her head was wet now from the impossible situation in which she had found herself. *Unbelievable even to tell a child.* June felt the top of her head heat with a fear so deep, so green, so beguiling... that she felt her teeth freeze. And she stood like that, frozen in that moment, gripped by her deepest fear, unknown as it was, tits deep in the Pacific Ocean. So near, that with a leap she could maybe touch it— one of Earth's grandest creatures.

With her face moving so slowly upwards, her eyes locked on the large, clear, *so very deep*, eye of that whale. It too, seeming to know that *it* had been caught in an inexplicable moment, in an impossibility made possible by the somehow. June saw it. Her reflection, captured, swallowed whole, drawn within the forever mind of this mighty animal... And June saw it know... her need.

A *crack* of time! June felt it snap. And she saw the green flash of light in that hair of a moment. *CLAP!* The enormous burst of energy. *The whale's?* She had no way to know. She had no way out. Sure she must shit her shorts in that water, again, June screamed a proper scream. Not the kind one sees in the movies. Not even the kind brought about by a kind of tragic loss, of news we all beg not to hear. But the kind one knows... that tears a soul in two.

The sound then, June's—no matter its honesty—halted. It ceased as the impact of that beast's re-entry pushed her under like two massive hands folding her into dough. And she was without bearings, without a handhold, without a place to press her feet. Taking in water, all June could see was the torn ribbons of light and the enormous darkness. The enormous dark weight of—she had to believe, in those fractured moments—the whale. A creature she knew capable of...

The second impact was slow, and from below it came like a groan. She was pushed, it appeared, by an immovable thing, up and through the salty water. Her speed increasing until she heard her mind offer, *VELOCITY.*

She was still unable to conceive of what was taking place, of course, as it was happening. Her hands were pushing down on the thing that was lifting her, thrusting her upwards, even as the water thinned in the rush... and she popped through it.

The air! The air! June's mind screamed.

The water line beneath her, a sting on her hip, and with the darkness of that huge animal beneath her, now June could see just how huge it really was. And yet still, with such a perspective, unsure of how high she could be... coughing out the sea water as she sucked, *slurped,* in that air past her burning throat... even June, though she knew it true, couldn't piece the truth of it down. And as she flew, cast high and shore-bound by this whale, she knew she was laughing... until she hit the sand.

The wind and too the water she had taken in was knocked out of her. The sand was a mercy, though the impact was still a brute. June tried to push herself up in time to see the creature again, though all she could see were the rings, large as they were, rippling out from its last position.

She sprawled, laying back on that sand with the last small coughs issuing, and with a little more water coming with them. June felt her tears leaking. Warm little lines of water running from her eyes. A joy mixed with a sadness. A pity and a defeat.

She thought, as the light of the new day warmed her wet skin, *No-one will believe me*. And she thought this earnestly.

And as her head lolled to her left side, June said... softly, as her heart broke the news... 'There's no-one to tell.'

So, as her self-pity bled into that sand with which some she was painted, June threw her arms out wide, and then her legs, and then drew them in and out... making a sand-angel... as her eyes looked up into that seeming *forever blue*.

Half covered in the sand, getting to her feet with her mouth hooking at the pointlessness of brushing it off, June simply dusted her hands... and made her way up the beach.

Walking, seeing no one around, not surprised, not disappointed either, she felt that newly familiar childlike sense of freedom urging *adventure*.

Picking up a stick as she came across it, she turned to the ocean. Setting her jaw, June turned again and began to write in the sand. Feeling the end of the stick biting into and carving through the wet sand, her mouth opened into a smile she had never known. She stopped at the final letter and thrust the point of the stick into the sand, feeling nothing as it dropped flat.

Her arms hanging by her sides, standing before the three-foot-high letters, she read them out aloud, 'Jonah, was here.'

She stood there dusting her hands once again and gave a chuckle at herself for even doing such a thing. June left her mark, temporary as it was, and continued her way up the beach with no thoughts, only air and light and the unfamiliar sense of opportunity—*come what may.*

She was almost past it before she stopped. Confused at what state of mind she could find herself in that she could ignore it, she now turned to the wreck and marched towards it. Her arms swinging, her steps big like a kid, June moved without any thoughts. And though she knew this, she did not know how. She did not know that a thing such as this, *this freedom from the mind's constancy of words*, was a reality to experience. But she liked it. And she knew that it suited her, *that it always had.*

The shade under the coconut trees that bordered the large clearing around the front of the wrecked ship looked as though it held the truth of secrets nobody remembered had been kept. Those shadows looked like they held live things—*Watchers.*

And then *it* was there.

June's head tilted to one side as she looked at its large rectangular face. *Rusted.* She could smell it. The face of it so pitted and scarred, she knew, by the exposure to such a place. Some of its white paint, *much of it*, still remained. There was black around the lettering. But it was the red that stood out. 'WARNING!' she mimicked *Will Robinson's Robot.* Scrunching her nose as she realised it was *not* the word the robot was famous for. *Still*, she thought, then said, 'It's what he meant.' Dusting her hands, again.

Pointing up at that sign, with most of the words on it now lost to time, she said, 'I coulda done with that little piece of advice on Tuesday.' Like it could hear her. Slapping her hand against its face as she made her way past... she grabbed her hand... seeing the line of blood beginning to seep through.

Looking back at the sign now three steps behind her as she continued toward the massive, rusted structure of the shipwreck before her, June made to say, *You cut me!* as she sucked at her hand.

But she didn't say it.

Chapter Eleven

The Inner Child

S ome things, are a matter of the heart.
Others, well, they're matters that the heart is not
entirely qualified to tangle with.

June knew, as she strode up to that large, landed vessel in which she had very nearly met her end only a few days earlier, that her heart was playing at least a part in what was spurring her onward. She knew that the sand under her feet was soft. She knew, and some element of her was in no doubt, that her destination was inside of this wrecked ship.

'Heart, fart,' she said, looking at the new wind that rustled the leaves, the fronds, high above and to the left of where she walked.

Her hand rested against the torn edge of that ship's hull. She watched as some of the edges of the many leaves of red-brown metal crumbled, collapsing to flakes and dust under the light weight she applied. Her face cast upward as she made a mental note and questioned if she was going to progress any further. And she almost asked herself whether this was a very good idea. But her feet were already inside.

The coolness of the shade, alerting her to this fact. Absently, she dusted the rust off her palms and set about moving deeper within this groaning beast. A thought very nearly stuck as she made to think on these things. Nearly.

Already ten or so feet within, June got an inkling of how far she had made it in *the last time*. She could see, sense and hear the sheer volume of this place. And she knew that *last time*, she had only just scratched the exploratory surface of what she saw so much more clearly now, was a labyrinth.

Continuing on deeper, weaving her way around and through the many walls and juts, June's mind ran with the information that could help her comprehend the possible layout of a craft like this one. Though she knew this was an impossible ask. She knew that she had no experience at all with any kind of waterborne vessels, other than to ride a ferry or two. She had asked Jason and Sharon, after her web searches came up with too much information on ships in general and zero on this particular craft. This last point, clearly *not possible*. And she had made this point clear when broaching the topic with Jason and Sharon.

'I know right?' was all Jason had said before sipping his tea and looking to Sharon. Something unspoken, travelling between them.

'Mmm,' was all Sharon had said.

Not one to be shy about voicing her *God given pinions*, June had said, 'Well how the fuck can this be a riddle?' And that, apparently, was the last word. It didn't stop her from giving the other two a hard look, through very squinty eyes.

But it was real. *And cold*. This fact surprised her. With both palms pressing up against one particularly large wall, with several of the floors directly above broken through, June leant her face against the surface. Her eyelids closing, remembering the few times she had hugged trees. *But this thing?* Well. 'You're beautiful,' she said. And feeling it this way did something to her. Something she could not place, fit or allot to anything she had experienced before. 'Oh, if only,' saying this without any rational understanding of why. A few short reels of footage quickly spinning through her mind's eye of people, even women, who had fallen in love with and carried on relationships with inanimate objects.

Standing back from that wall and rubbing at it, smiling, talking to it like it were a person, she said, 'Bit of a stretch.' Feeling a flush of embarrassment. But at least, even that sounded lame to June.

A small shadow passed over her. Her eyes quickly shooting skyward, catching the silhouette of wings and tail feathers. Her heartbeat caught before the gallop. With her eyes still high, June kissed her fingertips and pressed them against the rusted wall she was just talking to, and then she moved on, in deeper.

There was no way to tell how long... June made to lift her phone out of her pocket. Seeing it was not there, her mind raced the few steps to ascertain where it must have fallen out. But there really was no way to tell. *Figure that.* But she was too *Alice* right now. Too, well, there's only Alice really isn't there? So, too Alice to make too much of this fact. She was in an unsafe area with no-one aware of her whereabouts... and no way to make a call for help. 'Yup,' she said as she took her first steps into the ever-greater gloom. She knew she was entering the deeper recesses. She knew that she was leaving the outside world behind with each further step.

But June was past the point of reason. Of this she was aware. And it felt great.

The rooms, this far in, were far less decayed by rust. June could see more of the damage wrought by the impact as she stepped through, dodging the larger holes in the floor. The impact, she imagined, that had brought this grand craft to land. The walls in there were buckled in places, torn, folded and crushed. She took two steps to her left and saw a long, long, long, hall. The kind one pictures being in a ship. Doors stood at every twenty or thirty feet. The stretched oval ones. And with no monsters in sight, giddy, June stepped through that outer door and into the hall.

The moment her foot landed on the other side of that doorway; she saw it.

Far off, at least three doorways down, as she turned her head to look, as she brought her right foot over, June saw a flash of white... a drift.

The movement that followed was frantic. Propelled by a scream, down in the belly of her heart, June made to run. Not away and back out the door through which she had just passed, but forward down that long hall.

With her head desperate in its response to her mechanism's need to get, gather and hold its bearings, June felt she was looking through a steady-cam as her feet beat across the uneven and unknowable floor.

And yet still she ran.

She was at and through the next door in moments. With no idea of what was contained, if anything at all was contained in that first room, or anything other than the scraps her wobbled vision could offer her, June passed through into the next room. The toes of her right foot making contact with something hard. The pain, enough to feel like she had been cut.

'Wait!' She knew she was yelling. That flash of white, larger. The shape of it, what had brought the command, the plea, from her lips. And she fought to get her feet working under her again. 'Hey!' Tasting the blood circulating, rushing through her body. June gritted her teeth. An instinct greater than any she had shared time with, surged in her to her bones. It was tearing at her need, and this need was forcing in air, more air. Her elbows were thrusting in an effort to claw her way faster on down that long hall. Only pinpoints of light breaking through the mighty hull and the floors above, in no rational order. This making it impossible for her to judge the distances she must to avoid all of the debris. At what could have been the fifth doorway, *or portal,* June stopped. With her head aching from the effort, breathing hard, her face a mask, she looked down that hall... and saw *her.*

'What?' She was too alive to ignore the bitter plea in her own voice, too astute to pretend that no whine was present in that awful sound that had escaped her lips. Too confused not to scream, 'WHO ARE YOU?' To the child who stood—herself breathing hard—two doorways, two whole rooms ahead and deeper into the belly of this long-ago stranded vessel.

The light in there, broken and washed with the disturbed dust, showing that this girl was clearly standing there. The dust in that light, moving around, altered, by the physical form of this child in the white dress. This fact, yet still proof that this girl was no ghost. June fought to make out her features. The long blond hair, parted in the middle, covering half of the girl's face. But it was the eyes? *Or the mouth?* Or the hint of ear... showing through the long straight hair where it hung?

Softly, though yet it echoed, 'It can't be.'

But the girl darted before June could fit her mind around it. She had picked up the sides of her little white dress and turned her little tanned shoulders and run.

'Stop! URGH!' June lifted her own knees, and spitting on the floor to her right, she flung herself through the doorway. And throwing all caution, trusting that if this child—no more than eleven by the look she had gotten—if she could make it through, then there was every likelihood that June herself could too. But her third step caused her to absolutely disregard this reasoning as she found herself at a full run along a metal beam, exposed where the sheets of steel meant to cover it were no longer present. And beneath it, more than two floors deeper, open and exposed steel beams and structural remnants stitched a scene of an industrial Pick-up-sticks. This only showing her greater, the folly of her choice this day. But once across and back onto more solid footing, June felt the surge of relief, or adrenaline, or both. And not for the first time in her life, June considered the possibility of her immortality.

Naturally, even as her eyes showed her that she had made some ground on this running child, June fell.

And not easy or well.

The pain of the first impact was followed briefly by vertigo. 'Shit!' The word knocked off short... by the second impact. Her full weight landing heavily on a steel girder. The end of which shook, screeched and snapped before June could grasp the pain and begin to suck more air into her winded lungs.

'STOP!'

June heard the small girl's cry, even as she fell.

Turning, her body dropping, June looked up through the space she had fallen... to that voice.

Whether through a magic of time or the body's miraculous mechanisms, the air through which she fell grew thicker. And June saw the face of the child. Her blond hair hanging around her open mouth... with her two small hands encircling it as she cried, 'STOP!'

And she did.

She stopped harder than she had ever stopped before.

The immediate absence of pain ran her skull with the heat of fear. Her belly, though she could not feel it externally, coursed with a sickening pulse. She tried to speak. Afraid, confused, and scared of what she had done, June tried to tell herself *to keep* her *eyes open*. But her voice wouldn't follow orders. Not a squeak. Not a peep. And June knew she couldn't get any air. She knew she was in trouble.

Pushing down on her hands only caused the debris in which she lay to shift, screech and tumble.

June tried to scream from the pain. Her left side felt like it had been caught, speared by some great beast. Which of course, it had. Her whole weight held by what her left hand was discovering, and finding to be true, was a rusted rod of angled steel... that now stood several feet out through a jagged rip in her lower left belly.

I've been shot boy! A movie reel running in her drifting mind. *They got me!* As June, still unable to draw any air... rubbed raw with a pain that was only beginning to show its full rage... went dark.

100

Chapter Twelve

The Womb

The light shook, the trees shimmered, and the smell of it spoke of war zones in which she had never been.

Never had she known such separation. Never had June understood that such distance could be afforded. Unfriendly, unrepentant in its divorce, the loss of her consciousness so complete.

Carried, run in fact, by the rough hands of care that bore her, June had never known or remembered air so sweet. It was this, not the searing jagged horror of the pain, that was the centre of her focus. And although that pain be heavy, it was but the sweetness of the air that cherried this moment.

Their voices, *these rescuers*, foreign in their tone and frenzied with their need. And their need was for her. She had no doubt of this. Had no trouble accepting this fact. But still their handling of her was rough.

It was the sparks that had brought her back. The sparks thrown out from the saw that had drawn her back. They had been fireworks at first. Though the memory of their connection to whatever dream she had floated had now shrunk to a flat circle in her memory, and one that she may never be able to sight again. It was the sparks. Like tiny balls of fire. The burn of the few that touched her, those that flew past the heavy mat barrier these rescuers used, nothing more than angry insect bites. Yes, it was those little burning lights that first drew her back.

The sincerity of their voices, supposed to calm no doubt, pulled at the stitching of the need to be cared for, and releasing those emotions of unrequited love that had so stained her time as a child of nine. She had cried as they patted her, as they spoke those intense words of calm to reassure her. She had cried like a child. Even then, she knew this. She knew it was not the pain that was threatening to pull her under, but their unquestioning desire to simply help her survive.

It came in flashes after that. Her consciousness not nearly solid enough to keep her present as they cut through the steel that pierced and held her to the structure of that ship. As they got a stretcher under her and began to navigate out of that crazy mass of tortured, twisted ruin, June saw her eyes open from within, and she saw the rescuer's faces, mostly hidden by the headlamps attached to their helmets.

'You're a woman,' June said, seeing the smile of one of her rescuers. The smile of this rescue worker holding the corner of the stretcher by her left foot, confirming her statement. And darkness blanked the world out once again.

103

How bright a day can be. Blinding. June's back arched. Her own hands were swatting hard at her chest, swatting at the imaginary defibrillator paddles.

'Easy! Easy! Hold her!'

But she was out again. The pain, sinking her in a pool of burnt orange.

She heard drums. She heard them.

Opening her eyes. Viewing the world from the horizontal. The air shuddering, and those trees, their fronds rippling like the whole world was shaking. She was going to vomit. Her shoulder then hot with it. Desperate, that she would never breath again.

'Fuck it!' A man, ordering the others to, 'Get her down.'

The cold water splashing her as another hand cupped the back of her head and lifted her face forward. The hard plastic of the bottle, banging her teeth. And June smiled at this. She might never know why.

'Try and rinse your mouth darlin,' the woman said again, wiping her face with each splash of water. 'She's good! Let's get her loaded!'

The chop of the wind was so violent.

As she was lifted, June could smell that she had peed herself. And then she could smell *Fruit Loops*. As they moved toward the rescue helicopter through the heavy, so heavy, down push of the air and sand too, June could smell the cereal. Her eyelids closing and opening with each bounce of the stretcher. June saw herself sitting in front of the large, faux wood veneered, box television on the purple carpet of their childhood home in the outer suburbs. She saw herself watching that seemingly never-ending TV series as she sat eating the dry cereal from an orange *Tupperware* container. Watching the on-screen characters in uniform, of *Hawk-eye*, and *Trapper*... and of *Klinger*—in a pink dress. She heard her memory say, '*Hey Hot-Lips!*' And then June remembered that she had never known the years of the Korean war.

Thinking that she may have shit herself as the helicopter lifted up from that beach, June heard, 'She's shit herself.' And found a music in the vibrations of that accelerating craft.

She felt her hand being taken by one similar. 'You're going to be okay,' the voice strong, the breath sweet.

And before she lost consciousness again, and this time for many hours, June heard herself calling as loudly as she could, to be heard over the rotors, 'Thanks Hot-Lips!'

'June?'

'June?' A tapping on her hand.

'June?' Louder.

'What?' Her eyes wouldn't open.

'JUNE!'

'Fuck off!' Her mouth was so dry, but her eyes opened this time.

'Oh good.' The voice familiar. 'No don't.'

'OW!' Her hands shook and lifted from where they had tried to push down against the starchy fabric.

'You've been through a lot June,' he said.

'Jason?' Taking the water from his hand. Seeing so much white. Too much light. Wanting to speak but hearing only the pathetic sounds of pain crawling over her very dry lips and tongue. She drank the cold water through shaking lips. And she knew she was in trouble. She had never once felt like this. The closest she could remember, *was that time in*

Italy, when she had been on a week-long party with some of the other girls, and she had woken on a hot day, sticking to the bed sheets.

'Take your time June,' his voice somehow calmer, more grounded, than she had recalled. 'Don't rush it,' he said with an authority, a care and a voice of experience.

So, she listened. June wanted to cry. She didn't know she already was.

'Here.' Jason Mackie handed her a box of tissues even as he lifted one and dabbed at her eyes. 'You gave us all an awful fright there June Bug.' And June could hear a shake in his voice as he said this. She could hear the honesty of his distress.

But she couldn't speak now. The waves of very real pain scraped her relentlessly, and yet she was unable to prevent herself from struggling to a seated position in the hospital bed.

'Here.' Jason leant forward, taking her hand and placing it on a small button attached to a white cord. 'You just press this when it gets too heavy.' And he lightly pressed her thumb down on that button.

'Aw.' Almost immediately, she felt it like a cool breeze. The hardest edge of the pain lifting like a chiffon throw. This juice, letting her breathe, letting her muscles droop. 'Thank God. Thank God.' And she meant it.

For ten minutes they sat just like that as June allowed the medication to filter through and do its work. They sat there in that room, and June began to gain some clarity.

Finally, she couldn't take his bright-eyed smile any longer and found one to meet his. They just looked at one another. Their eyes doing some to and fro. His seeming to say something, like he was hinting at something. Then he wobbled his head with his eyebrows lifted.

'Should I be getting something here?' June spoke through a smile she couldn't be sure wasn't more drug than joy.

Jason circled his eyes and dropped them and then repeated, looking down at his chest.

June watched him as he repeated this, time and again. Her smile, loose and open, not sure at all what he was doing until he pointed at a name tag pinned to his white jacket.

Squinting, June tried to lean closer.

'Oh no, don't do that silly.' Jason was up on his feet and holding her shoulders and then easing her back down on the heap of pillows, he said, 'Easy Ese.'

'Awpfff!' she said. Then croaking, 'I think that's the masculine.'

'What? Oh, thank you very much.'

Breathing out, feeling herself wanting to drift back into sleep.

'No,' she said. 'Ese. It's for boys. Esa is... for girls... I think.'

And as she said these words, feeling the truth that she was in fact drifting back into sleep, June saw his name tag, close as it now was. She read, 'Dr Jason Mackie.' And then she said, 'What the fuck?'

'Do you think that one can fly?' Dr Mackie spoke around a mouthful of pasta while looking out the window of June's hospital room.

'Uh-uh,' she said, forking something *food like* into her own mouth from the tray hovering across her bed. 'Too fat,' smiling so big as she said this that she lifted the back of one hand to her mouth to prevent any food from spilling out.

'Oh, that's not nice,' he said, with his own smile showing too much sauce. 'True… But not nice.' Jabbing his fork at the window, he called, 'Ou Look! She's doing it!' And he did it. Dr Mackie leant on the windowsill and called out, 'Go fatty! You can do it!' A pained expression on his face as June lost control of her mouthful. Looking across to her and then back out through the window. 'Well, she's giving it a good go.' Now he himself unable to hold on. His laughter honest, childlike. 'Go! Aw nearly! It's flying about *this* high off the ground.' Indicating several inches with his hands. One of which still bearing a fork. Digging back into the pasta on the bench before him, getting another mouthful and speaking as he did, 'She's more hopping really.' And then he kinda let the food fall out of his mouth, back into the bowl. Taking a napkin and placing it over his mouth, looking at June, and on seeing her reaction he began laughing, pointing and snorting, bent nearly double.

'Ahhh,' he said, after they'd got themselves together. Putting his fork down for the last time. Wiping his hands and looking at June as she sat in her bed. 'How about you then Miss June?' Giving some time before continuing. 'You reckon you're gonna fly this coop?'

Placing her hands on her blanket covered lap, she said, 'Then what?'

'Well,' Jason sat on her bed, 'we'd love to have you back for a few more weeks. When you're up to it.' His eyes saying that she understood enough that he didn't need to patronise her. 'We have the facilities there to take care of you once they're done with you here. Probably only be a few days. *CHRIST* you were lucky! Oops didn't mean to scare you. Har-har. But you! By God, how you stuck yourself through.' Giving her a fully enacted and over-animated version of events as he spoke. 'And missed every vital organ!' Throwing his hands up in the air as he said, 'You didn't even slice a single sausage!' Then pretending to pull his intestines out through an imaginary hole in his own gut.

June laughed without sound. The full measure of the realities of what had occurred and the truth of how close she had come to serious long-term complications from her actions, even death, she knew, would ripple through for some time to come. But right now, June loved this man, this doctor. A man she had come to know and had believed to be just another patient. Those ripples, too, had not been fully stilled or answered. But the care she felt just then, as he... Jason... Dr Mackie... performed for her, she knew, to relieve her of her feelings of shame and discomfort. The actions he took to show her that this *place*—the one she had come to inside of herself— was a *place* that was so far out of her realm of experience, a *place* she had no idea how to navigate... to show her that this *place*... was not a *place*... that was unknown to all.

Sitting on her bedside again, this time taking her hand in his, now speaking to her calmly. 'I know it all looks crazy from where you're standing,' he said, taking a breath. A peek into her eyes, that showed a small flash. This peek demonstrating that he did in fact know. That showed that maybe he had some real experience in this whole business. 'But I believe that if you'll allow me Miss Bonnet. *Love that name.* I believe I can help you... find your way to the other side.' Looking at her hand and then out through that window again, he said, 'You're worth it June.' And then pointing eagerly out into the gardens beyond, he screamed, 'SHE DID IT!' Standing in his place and looking back from June to the window and then back and forth. 'She's Flying!' Hands on his hips now, shaking his head, Dr Jason Mackie said, 'Who'd a thought?'

Chapter Thirteen

The Agent

'Kinda.'

'Kinda?' June found herself chewing at the inside of her lip.

'Yeah, kinda.'

June felt it. Marcy, her voice more schoolyard than she could have expected. It shocked, and then the shame of only now understanding that, well, she kinda shoulda known.

'Yeah.' Marcy McIntyre's words, even over the phone, which is when June usually heard them, showed a scrunched nose.

Where she sat on a perfectly grand white wicker chair looking out through the large window to the gardens of Bridges Retreat, June felt the bones within her chill. She felt those bones shake. Marcy had been her agent since she was sixteen. Just a year after her career had begun. Marcy had been there for her. She had held her hand. She had acted...

'Acted!' The word dribbling from her lips as she held the phone and tore at a toenail on the foot tucked under her.

'Yeah?' June felt her brow furrow and her nostrils flare. 'Kinda?' Shaking now. 'Yeah?' And she wasn't sure, well actually she was certain, that she had crossed that line, that little pasty line deep within her that signalled, *Ok let's be real.* June knew there was no going back. The emotion—*the sheer fucking weight of it*—scrawled, cut and burrowed a jagged line across that piece of her heart. The childlike, tender, innocent part that still remained no matter the abuse she had allowed or at least pretended not to really notice. This *thing* that had been perpetrated against her—*So many fucking times.* There was no disguising her feelings now, or that stretch of heart that she had so long sheltered behind. *Was it just denial?* June's thoughts rolled past her analytical mind as though they were offerings. Or slogans pulled on a banner? Pulled behind the plane of her sense of humour. She shook her head, got both feet under her, and knew, *knew*, that she hadn't known such fury since she was a teenager.

She looked out that window with her tongue pressed into the bottom side of her shaking mouth, tasting the sourness that pooled there. The heat in her head sickening, she said, 'You're, *telling me,* that I have to?'

'It's in your contract.' The words flat.

'Awhhh!' Again, a sound she hadn't heard herself make since she was maybe seventeen. She paced the room and was aware that the colours around her had begun to swim.

Marcy spoke with just the slightest rinse of humour, if you could call it that, coating her words, 'We were all very sad to hear of your little *accident* June. Really, we were running around just so worried.'

113

Now the squint hit her face. Like it had been thrown there. June could feel her jaw, the back of her head even, shake. Her free hand thrown up into the air, she said, 'Really?' Hating the sound of her tears in this word. 'Really!' Knowing there was no way to hide that she was upset. 'Really? You were all so worried?' But she knew there was nothing she could say here, to this woman, this person who had pretended. 'You acted! Pretended! To be like a *mother* to me!' And then, with her eyes to the ornate ceiling of this old room as she hated this feeling, this reek of weakness, June heard it... the smallest laugh she had ever heard. And how it ripped the skin of the heart that she had long believed she had left behind.

And for the moment, June was speechless.

'Well,' Marcy's voice calm, 'you surprise me June.' A breath, winding, she said, 'I thought you were a professional.' Only her nose sounding the slightest chuckle.

June's whole face... her hands... trembled.

It was all sucked out. All of that which June had believed she was—*The adult June Bonnet. And how easily it had been done,* was the thought that braced her. She knew it should have been this thought that cut what appeared to be the last thread. A thread as thin and weak as one of saliva. And it is true that a part of her—a ghost maybe, or a shell, or a cap, or an aspect of her ego—collapsed internally and folded in upon itself. This, June knew was true. She also knew that she had no time to get clear on any of this right now. What she had to do was respond to this person, this *Agent* of hers, who was demanding that she appear for a job, a contract... that she...

'I've been out of the hospital for three days,' she said.

The sound of her throat clearing, the drawing back of her scythe, Marcy said, 'Mmm. Yeah, well that's kinda on you Kiddo. You're under contract.'

Speechless, *assolutamente*.

The sound of a tapping pen on a desk, Marcy went on, 'And that contract says that if you choose not to appear, then, well, you will be liable for financial reparations.' And June could hear Marcy's lips stretch in a closed-mouthed smile.

There comes a time—or so June was considering as the ice rose into the top of her skull, and as her eyes glazed and looked out through that fantastic garden and out over and through it to the cerulean blue sky that was undusted by a single cloud and too at those small breakers that met those golden sands... when one realises that what one is looking at in a new light of a new day, is nothing but the truth. There comes a time, most often directly after this realisation, that one decides that it is better to know, no matter the length of time that this insidious thing has been hidden, that it is better to know and be done with it than to allow it to continue to be present in one's life... a moment longer.

So, June walked to the desk where her cooling coffee sat, and she slowly took a cigarette from the packet she had there. She too, picked up her cigarette lighter, and she walked to the closest of those large, beautiful, white framed windows, and with her phone dangling in her hand, she opened the window wider and sat on the sill. Placing the phone down just in front of her while hearing Marcy voice a question, June lit her cigarette, drew on it with some weight, and dabbed at the tip of her tongue and blew that smoke out. She took a breath in through her nostrils, felt that her eyelids were even, and she picked up the phone.

'Marcy? Are you still there?'

'Yes June.'

'You're a *Cunt,* Marcy. And I hope you die.' And she touched the little red phone icon before tossing it back down onto the windowsill. And then she took another draw on her cigarette, of the same brand her Daddy used to smoke.

The door to the room opened. June knew it because the air from the garden drew past her harder. And she smiled. Hearing no words from that doorway, June rest her hand that held the cigarette on her bent knee where she sat in the wide window frame and turned her face into the room.

Dr Jason Mackie stood not three feet from her, apparently naked but for a large tray which he held at hip level. His large and a little more than overstated smile lifting his whole face.

June laughed.

'Sausage?' Lifting one hand from the large tray and almost dropping it from the weight of cooked sausages piled atop it, Jason awkwardly pointed at the crispy snags.

Unwilling or unable, she didn't know which, to remove the large smile that had infected her own face, June lifted a sausage. Tears from the bag of her recent emotions pooled with this comic relief, and she spoke around her first delicious, greasy bite, 'This is kind of inappropriate.'

'Aw nah!' Jason looked down at himself, either pretending or not—who could rightly know—to only just now notice his faux par. He bent and shuffled backwards, properly shuffled, and turning to place the tray of sausages on the desk, he pointed to his skin-coloured, togs covered bum while jutting it in her direction. 'I'm wearing me togs.' His nose cinched. He walked back towards the laughing and sausage munching June as she took another draw on her

116

smoke. 'Here, give me some of that.' Taking the cigarette out of her hand and her lips, looking left and right for anyone who might catch him out, Dr Mackie took a few short drags. Blowing the smoke out, and clearly never having enough of his own theatrics, he said, 'Aw, I love it. I love a bit of a smoke.' His giggle, straight out of his own internal amusement at himself. He handed it back to the laughing June.

'Skin coloured?' she said, thinking them really *salmon* in hue.

Taking a position opposite her in the same window sill, crossing his legs so that the one leg hung and bounced, lacing his hands over his knees, looking out into the garden for all the world to see that he was caught in a reverie, he said, dreamily, 'When I was six years old,' lifting the back of his hand to cover a choke, a sob, real or pretended, 'my parents took me and my two siblings,' holding up two fingers for June, still looking out into his memory, 'for a holiday to Cairns.' He was nodding his head as he absently plucked the cigarette, again, from June's hand and drew on it and then sat there letting the smoke out as he looked at the cigarette. 'It was our first *real* holiday. You know?' His voice lifting in pitch at the last word. No way to tell if it was due to the smoke or emotion.

June's smile was beginning to hurt.

'And do you know what memory has stuck with me the most? Other than the memory of running through the palm fronds, screaming! My whole head,' raising his hands over his head to demonstrate, 'covered with green ants... biting.' His teeth now chomping. 'Terrifying!' Stopping to shudder, nodding to her and taking the now offered cigarette from her hand and smoking. 'The one memory that has stuck with me... like a symbol...?' Holding both hands—one with the

117

cigarette between two fingers—up in the shape of a roof frame. 'Sorry, I'm a bit emotional in the retelling.' He then spat out the window before coming right back to his former expression. 'The one memory that symbolised, epitomised,' nodding, 'that beautiful union between my mum and dad. At least before they divorced and tried to destroy one another.' And he laughed at this. 'Yeah. The one image,' wiping a tear that could not be seen, 'was of me mum and dad holding one another under a palm tree.' He sat, blowing out the emotion. 'My dad, tall and strong, looking down at his beautiful wife, my mum. Boy.' A sound escaping his mouth, a choked sob. 'They were so in love. Or so we all thought, eh?'

A moment passed.

Jolted from his reverie, Jason said, 'Aw. I almost forgot. *He-he*. The point was that they were both wearing skin-coloured togs. Yeah.' Pointing to the Speedos he now wore. A breath, large enough to raise and lower his whole form, he said, 'These are one pair of those actual togs.' Drawing one of the corners of his mouth, south. 'Bit creepy, eh? But I had to fight for these after he passed. Yep.' Ignoring June's laughter. 'No way was my brother and sister going to give these up without a fight.'

June's body actually bounced as she laughed, sat on that windowsill.

'It got a bit messy.' His demeanour went unchanged. Dismounting the windowsill, slowly, ungainly, a little rudely, Dr Jason Mackie walked to the desk, lifted the tray of sausages and brought them back with him. Standing before her, looking sincerely into June's wet eyes, he said, '*So come on*. As my departed dad would have said to my dear mother...' leaning in just a bit, his eyes hooded, '*take some more sausage.*'

'Oh please.'

Chapter Fourteen

Exit Stage Right

The sting of it was not nearly as rude as the feeling of the twine running through. The pinch, not nearly as awkward as the knowing that another was in control of its movement.

'And there we go.' Jason's voice was soft, his mind three layers deep. And June could not know if it was due to the focus required for the task at hand, but she was pretty sure that it was not this alone.

The *ping* of the tweezer's contact as he placed the last of the stitches into the kidney shaped tray by his side, the smell of the antiseptic, the slight hiss of his breath as she watched his shoulders relax, all played of a melody she had not before heard from this man.

Looking at him as he leant forward inspecting the site of the now mostly healed wound on her side, June rest a hand on his. Her own feelings simple, childlike, in response to the care he gave her, to the importance she was afforded. 'Thank you,' was all she said.

Like his heart was slapped of a sudden, Dr Mackie sucked in a quick breath. And although it was quick, he could not hide the fluttering of his lower lip.

He was quick to his feet. The stool he had sat on flung backwards to the ground, and the way his hand went to his chest caused alarm to ring its bell within June's own chest. She moved to get her elbows up under her. The unusual forms of worry for another, feeling like a mask upon her face. As her words were shaping in the lower arcs of her throat, she was halted by the hand he held out in front of him.

He leant back against the desk behind him with a kind of smile on his face, his head still bent, waving an arm as though he *just needed a moment* to get his breath. 'Woo!' But even this attempt was nothing more. His charade cascading down, invisible in its matter, apparent in every fibre of his movements.

'You're crying?' her words, almost too soft for even her to hear, and her legs were moving to get her off that table and onto her feet.

'No!' Too harsh. 'I'm sorry.' But the tears were running, and his eyes found hers, and whether he meant to or not, their shine expressed so much truth.

'Let me,' she said, and June could see that he was defeated. Her own heart ached, sounding like a tin drum, but still she was able to prevent herself from cooing. A strange thought. One she had never experienced though knew definitively was now called for. Still, she moved to him. Taking his hands, that he held out to her as though in defence, and holding them firmly in hers, June dipped her head and

122

looked into his eyes. Eyes still so very bright, and hard enough to show that this man had known a depth that, at the very least, bordered on an insanity. She couldn't speak then. A pain filled her own throat at what this simple vision, this slice of a moment, had shown her. And she knew at least a kind of the pain she saw in the light cast from Dr Jason Mackie's eyes. So much she hadn't known she knew. So much she got that retold her of the many things she had ignored. *Was it out of some kind of self-protection?* Her thoughts, a mirror to herself. Still, she held his hands and felt a heat on her ears as she watched him all but melt before her.

Then his mouth moved without sound. His eyes slipped his hold. *Maybe*, June wondered, for the self-same reason that her own voice, *in gratitude*, had been so small? He stared into her. His mouth moving as though for air. Her own voice vibrating from her throat in hope of finding the words for which this dear man sought.

It was when his eyes crazed that she went into him. When she took the back of his head and pressed his now wet, *so very wet*, face into her shoulder... that she felt Jason spill his guts. Without a word, Jason Mackie let it all out. And boy did she have to hold him. The force of this, the weight of it, incomparable to anything she had experienced first-hand. June leant in to him as he bawled. His hands, though gentle, *weak*, clawed at the skin of her shoulders like a thing without mind. And he smelt sweet. Holding him close, June noticed that he smelt *sweet*.

Her eyes went over her shoulder as the door opened. A waft of air, only that, as Dr Sharon Corely, her eyes having locked onto the situation, quickly, like a sprite, ducked into the room and shut the door behind her. Her hand hovering for just a split second over the lock. *Old habits*, yet she flipped it.

And as she moved swiftly, June too saw something in this woman's eyes as they locked onto hers, that spoke pages. The light in her eyes too, demonstrating the trick of the tale these two wove in order to practice their medicine. *The cost.* Without pushing her aside, in fact enfolding her also in part, Sharon got her face right up to and buried into Jason's face. And she kissed at the bones around his eyes, many times. And some time passed, in just this way.

'Bit of a trip, eh?' His usual comical candour re-apparent. His eyes fully red and puffy. And like his two companions, he roared laughing. Tripping an avalanche of the same in both June and Sharon. 'Woo!' he said, leaning into his hot tea. 'Fuck me if that didn't clean me out!' Dipping his head to one side, his eyes stretched wide to their limit. Making to take another sip of the sweet tea as his eyes rest on June, over the rim of his teacup, he said, 'Meeting you... has been like eating an emotional Vindaloo!' And he spat some tea. 'Aw I got some in my nose. Ow.'

And so, they sat that way in the small garden off to one side of his study, sipping hot tea, and letting the afternoon air breeze over them. Their faces sticky and stretched by their dried tears.

And they breathed easy together.

'Oh!' Hopping forward in his white cast iron chair and spilling a little tea before looking down at where it spilt. He placed his cup on the small round table. 'Fuck it,' he said, laughing at his own clumsiness. 'Hot,' And he ran around the table, in through the wide-open French doors and into his study.

Sharon, looking a little punch drunk from the prior emotional outpouring, lifted her shoulders. The corners of her mouth pulling down as she went in for another sip of her tea. 'Ergh?'

Jogging back out like a much younger man, holding something in his hand, Jason swung and dropped himself into his chair. And then, after a frozen moment, he dropped what he carried onto the table before June.

It looked like a calendar. Looking up, June watched Jason's eager face nodding. Confusion and some kind of excitement issuing from inside, June picked it up as Dr Mackie refolded his arms after pointing to it a second time. 'Yeah,' he said, nodding eagerly.

It cracked like a whip within her. Or... something split in the chambers of her ribcage. She couldn't be sure. But as she lifted the calendar, for that is what it was, her brow creased. The familiarity. Yet her eyes could not, maybe, well of course would not, assemble the information she was looking at. Until the words came out of her lips, 'It's an Advent Calendar?' Holding it out for Sharon to see. But Sharon only nodded like a drunk aunty.

'I know right!' Har-har-ing as he lifted his tea while looking off into another place and tilt-nodding his head as he smiled into his sip of tea.

June placed it flat on the table before her. She read her name, written at the top. She looked at all of the little square flaps, opened to show that the gifts inside had been taken out, and somehow her face creased in disappointment.

'Oh no,' Jason quickly hopped forward and dropped something else on the table, a little bag, 'I didn't eat your treats.' And he began smiling as he leant back with is teacup. 'They're all there. You can count them if you want.' This

125

time his smile told her that she was still, they all were, in the real world.

'Lucky.' She smiled, and then her heart pumped blood in such a way that it felt like a bloom.

June's eye leaked a bit. 'It's magical.' Looking up at him and seeing the intelligence of this man, open, if just for a moment, for all the world to see.

'I thought you'd like it.' And he winked, dragging a hanky from his pocket.

Sharon stood up from her chair, took two steps to her right, up to the edge of the garden, and like a proper teapot, she bent and hurled into the nasturtiums.

This act was both surprising and quite off-putting.

'Ooh I am so sorry,' Sharon said, turning her face with a little vomit hanging from her lower lip and chin, showing her honest confusion.

With tea running from his nose, Jason was up on his feet and dabbing at her with a napkin, completely unable to contain himself. He laughed so hard. Sharon too joined in, and June felt that maybe... and quite possibly for real... that she might actually be a little girl named *Alice*.

'I've got my period,' Sharon said as she resat beside June, tapping her forearm lightly as she did.

Her belly lifting her whole upper body as the laugh took its course, June said, 'Well yes. Of course.'

'I've gotta pee!' Jason said with real urgency. So he stood, undoing his pants, and blank faced, he turned and moved himself to the edge of the garden... and urinated like a horse. 'AHHH!' Like a monk. He said, 'AWWW!'

With the splashes, seriously, heard from where she sat only two metres from where her doctor took a piss, June's nose ran from the exertion of being witness to whatever this was.

'Hey Sharon!' Dr Mackie called from his still urinating stance. He stood, yanking his head, indicating that she come over to where he stood.

June watched as Sharon did. She watched as they engaged in what appeared to be a serious discussion. She watched as Sharon reached around, *and I swear to God*, though she couldn't see it in actuality, it most certainly looked... well... she shook it for him... as they continued to talk in hushed tones. And then she tucked his penis back into his pants and zipped him up... before slapping his bum like one football player to another once they had decided on their next play.

They, Dr Jason Mackie and Dr Sharon Corely, turned as one from the garden's edge and took two uncannily co-ordinated steps toward the table where June sat.

'We've got two things to tell you June Bonnet,' Jason said, breaking into a snigger before Sharon pinched his side. 'Right, argh, well. First!' And pointing to the advent calendar before him, he said, 'You're now free to go! Yayyy.'

June had to admit the last ten minutes of uncharacteristic displays, even for these two, had stolen some of the punch from this moment. 'And?' June felt her chair wobble just a teeny bit.

Coughing a very short laugh, Sharon said, 'And two!' Holding up two fingers before clamping this hand with the other before her, she cried, 'TWOOO!' Holding both hands up around her mouth as she then called to the wilds, 'WOW!'.

'Fuck me, Sharon!' Jason was laughing. 'Two. Well, I really, like I sincerely swear that it was an honest fuck up June Bug. But it appears we've served you the...' holding up his fingers in inverted commas, 'wrong tea!'

Holding her cup out from her and looking down into it, June saw for the very first time in her life... tiny little dachshunds... in the bottom of her cup. And she said, 'Aw, they can swim.'

'So,' really gripping his hands together, 'Miss June, although...' his voice began to deepen most strangely, 'you are free to go...' His teeth gritting together between wide open lips before he said, 'It may take some time for us to...' And that's when Sharon, Dr Corely, bent like a bull... and charged Dr Jason Mackie. The impact, sudden and brutal in its reality, lifting him fully off the ground and racing him headlong into that pretty summer garden... as he called, 'For us to come DOWWWWWN!'

Letting her eyes leave the impossibility of this display... as they, Dr Corely and Dr Mackie, exited to her left... June carefully placed her teacup down... on the drooping table... and said, 'Oh.'

Chapter Fifteen

The Jungle

The sweat! The sweat.

Heat like this was something that brought the belly out of a person. It boiled it down and squeezed out its juice, leaving the smell of one's true nature to paste them, evident to all.

She had been in the tropics before. It was this knowledge that had led her to believe in the possibility of it, this journey, this walk amidst the steam of nature.

Standing now, deep in the dark of this rainforest, this jungle, with the insects all about her, as they buzzed and lit and strayed at every turn, June contended that it had been an oversight. She considered that the sum, the method of calculating the realities of such a pilgrimage were, well, off.

The heat! The humidity. Even the word *humidity* made her sick with its ceaseless grime, its poring grease.

She breathed out, hoping that enough air could come in with the next breath to give her some relief. Everything now sucked from her. Or so she believed. Everything not enough, or too damn much. She wiped at her forehead, wet. Her scalp was wet. The skin at the back of her wrists, wet. *The fucking air... wet!*

She lifted her head once more to the canopy, so many metres above her. The blue of the sky, a puzzle piece only seen through the overlapping branches. Their leaves, hands touching one another, keeping everything under, in.

The strap of her backpack was wet against her skin. June was frustrated, annoyed, and resentful towards herself, and she knew why. She knew that she had done this to herself. She knew that she had allowed herself to engage in this obvious folly because of a romanticised memory of her childhood. The time she had spent in this part of the world. 'You are living in tropical paradise!' saying the words out loud. Her sounds swallowed by the incessant chatter of the forest. Her words, quoting cynically, realistically, those spoken through a television set all those years ago. Spoken to an eleven-year-old June sitting on the tiled floor of her mother's living room in Trinity Beach, in the Northern beaches of Cairns, Far North Queensland.

Kicking, well more scuffing, at the wet red clay where she sat on a log, a log that no doubt housed a thousand creepy crawling things of which at least a hundred would leave you scratching, infected, or delirious if bitten by them, June thumped down her backpack and pulled at her water bottle. Her skin prickling at the heat, the skin under her arms where the material of her singlet rubbed, stinging, and knowing there was nothing she could do in the moment to relieve this, she lifted her bottle and whined.

Yep, but she lifted her bottle to her mouth and felt the few remaining warm drops dribble into her mouth. Left feeling she'd drunk more of her own sweat than water in the effort, she said, 'Awrgh!' And she threw the bottle. Her self-pity

131

really getting into the high notes as she watched it clank and bounce onto and then off the meagre path that this *rainforest walk* afforded.

The forest sounds paused for just a wee moment, and there was no way, really, for her to prevent her upper lip from pushing up into her nostrils as they were met with the sweet stench of rotten vegetation brought to her by a slow, low, hot air.

The whir of her phone lifted her heart. She had no idea why. Trying to get her forest litter covered hands on it with the phone mostly sliding from her sweaty hands, she got it awkwardly to her tilted ear. 'Yes!' she said, like a lottery winner. Missing the first words spoken through the other end. 'Fuck.' Looking down at the screen, wiping it, feeling the dread of fear that she had disconnected. 'Argh,' she said, showing her teeth.

'June?'

'Jericho?' Hearing the desperation in her own voice. Feeling somewhat pathetic and *Princessy* in the hearing.

'Where are you?'

A sob of air, and she said, 'I'm in the fucking jungle.'

'Oh,' he said. A necessary pause. 'Look,' he said, speaking louder now like he was, and he was, from a generation that still figured that distance required some greater effort of volume, 'I've got a few papers for you to sign.'

The smile on her face, at how he was projecting, was a relief, a joy really. 'Okay?'

'To release you from your contract,' he said, severely spacing his words.

'Okay,' she said, and now she herself was speaking in like kind. Her volume ridiculous, and her words, well you can see. 'It may take me some time to get to some place I can print them out.' Laughing at herself, but still somehow unable to change course.

'I see. Well, I can action this if you give me your verbal consent.' And as if by magic, Jericho Jones, a lawyer of some considerable experience, acquired comprehension of the devices through which they communicated, and finally they began to converse like people of the age in which they lived.

'Talk soon.'

'Talk soon.' And after a few blissful moments focusing her consciousness on elsewhere, June pressed the little red phone icon and got back to her current reality.

Lifted by the call—*refreshed psychically?*—June felt a squirt of vigour. *True*, she reasoned, she was no longer even *nearly twelve* on an Outward-bound Camp with her school friends. But she was... 'Erghhh!' Hopping backwards and away... from a very large brown snake. Her hands were flapping, and to her credit she was aware of this fact and tried very hard to stop this pointless act. Though she still did hop as this very long—hard to tell exactly, but long—and thick as one of her forearms, creature, moved so smoothly that its movements belied its speed. Her heart crammed right up to her collar bones. She stood there feeling the tightness at the sides of her skull like two hands had gripped her. She was running out of space and resolutely disquieted by the huge brown snake's relaxed confidence... as it moved at her.

'Stop!' she said, with her hands held out before her, fingers spread, still hopping backwards on her toes like she'd seen those *American Footballers* do. Her internal dialogue screaming at her about the uselessness of such an image. *But really?* 'Arghhh! STOOOPPP!' she screamed, waving her arms. Her analytical mind uselessly trying to dredge up memories from that equally useless—at least in this real-life situation—movie, *Crocodile Dundee.* A movie which she knew kinda correlated with the time of her last visit to this truly *astounding natural wonderland.* And now, without any shred of decorum, June peed. She did not really know this, not exactly. It's more for your information. But she did pee.

The back of her heel caught on that, no doubt insect and fungus infected, log on which she had just been sitting as the now apparently giant—*Must be a KING BROWN... or is it a Mulga... or are they the same thing?* Came the internal cry of her shrieking Inner-Child—snake was nigh upon her.

She hit her head. Not too hard. Because the wood she hit her head against crumbled with the contact and dispersed its inhabitants, a proper legion of mites.

It was literally on her then—the snake.

Its weight, too much to be true. June's heartbeat hard and she, although frantic to remove the ceaseless mites that swarmed her head, tried so hard to be quiet. But she couldn't. She couldn't do it. Her legs went rigid under that awful weight, under that dry moving skin.

She could hear herself, with her teeth gnashing and her face shaking so fast, micro-thrashing. The insanity of the sickening tickle of those scurrying mites. The feel of rotten leaves, gelatinous, in her so tightly clenched fists. *Terror.* What else could it be? *Sadness.* Like a boot on her chest. The unspoken *rage, u*nable to penetrate June's mostly frozen form as the King Brown snake continued its truly torturous slow journey up over her splayed legs and onto her shorts.

She cried like a child with no recourse to their treatment. June cried. Her mouth opened with hardly a sound as she cried up into the sky-blue puzzle piece that was separating the canopy so high above, and she wished... she could just be better.

And the snake pressed its belly against hers. The movement slow, so deliberate. Its confidence, so clear. Its place, its position between them, unmistakeably assured. Its progress... like that of poured honey.

But it *wasn't honey*. This thought shook June's rattling mind, and she mouthed the words through her silently bawling mouth, '*Not fair. Not fair.*' Her eyes fixed shockingly wide and focused on the too large head of this serpent that moved upon her. Her tears were running over her vision like a waterfall. The light on the leaves to one side began starring, blocking parts of her sight of this snake. She made a sound. The same one that sent mothers and fathers all across the world to come running for their infants. And then she begged for her... 'Mummy.'

The snake stilled then. Or mostly. It held its place. Its head lifted. Its characteristic tongue, long and blue in the shade of light, darted, tasting the air between them. The coils of its muscled form seeming never to halt entirely. Its eyes drawing images in June's mind of a memory of Chinese checkers. Those black balls now staring, showing no sign of personality, no warmth, no empathy... just an unknowable intelligence with its intent concealed.

And again, she peed.

The whole bag of it rushing out of her and gushing down the inside of her outstretched thighs.

And June just wanted to die. Anything to be not feeling... *this*.

Her tension grew—as one most assuredly might expect it to do—as the main body of this grand creature coiled itself like a concertina so that its full weight was upon her belly and chest. It lifted its head higher. Its tongue now tasting the air inches from the tip of her nose... and that's when June really hit the wall. Never, ever, in her many games of *Statue* as a child had she gone so perfectly still. The only movement detectable was the vibration in her eardrums of her own heartbeat. And for the very first time in her life—her eyes flat and still, looking into the face of a very real and present opportunity for death—did June fully comprehend the meaning of the phrase, *as serious as a heart attack*.

Time does funny things when one is faced with moments that cause the entire nervous system to be on high alert. This June knew. She was not without her moments of high drama. Never before had she lost her entire grip on time, but she did there on that rainforest floor surrounded by the decay of this densely alive environment. The creature atop of her able to kill her with a single strike of a speed her own eyes could not measure or grasp.

Time stopped.

There can be no way to know exactly how long they remained there, these two beings of different worlds who yet now inhabited the very same. Yet we must contend that at the very least, a chilly wind most certainly must have blown through the veins of at least one of them.

She did not pass out. That much we must give her credit for. But consciousness *was* in some way delayed, stilled, creased and folded. It rang with, truly, the echoes and hummed chants of a thousand journeymen and women who chanced to stare into the face of eternity.

The snake moved before June's ribbon of time re-engaged. It pressed itself along and down over her shoulder. The dry scales of its moving body like the skin of a person of great age. An *ancient*, absently, thoughtlessly, caressing her... as though she were no more than an object in its way.

It took some time for her to realise or to come to grips with the fact that the snake was moving on. One might guess that June did not want to tempt the fate of such a conclusion if prematurely drawn. It wasn't until the great meat of the thing was completely removed from her own that she began to count to twenty. *One, one-thousand, two,* and so on. But at sixteen, June was on her feet and scrambling. And you know? She did the darnedest thing. An odd phrase, but in this case true. For June, well she lost her shit then.

She would guess later, as she ran through that forest, that she had felt somewhat overlooked. She would surmise that her next actions were likely related to her feelings that this creature did not judge her as *important enough* to consider her either an adversary or a meal. She did not consider as she ran, whacked and torn by the foliage, and even cut by the thorns of the aptly named *Wait-a-while vine,* that she was too big for the Mulga snake to devour. Nope. Did not cross her mind. Whatever the underlying and irrational emotional cause, June lifted a large stick from the ground beside her urine-soaked left shoe and ran at that snake screaming, 'FUCKER!'

In fact, she had a whole barrage of such words piled up, stacked, and ready to fly from her spit coated lips. But it appeared that this snake was not at all willing to forgive or allow such an emotional outpouring. At least when it was being directed toward it. And so naturally, the nearly eight-foot-long snake lifted its head, and a large portion of its body that bore it, and it swung with startling speed. Yes, it was not limited to its former gait. And even as June's feet, both of them, lifted off the ground—in her still functioning nervous system's response to a very real and present, and this time *possibly able to flee from*, danger—the King Brown made its move to put an end to her nonsense.

And so, as she ran through that forest just a short moment later, she spun in the air—very catlike and too impressed by this—her left hand dropped without her command, and she snatched up her backpack. She had done this without her eyes making contact with the bag, for they were busy looking over her shoulder at the snake that was already very nearly upon her.

So, with her body already leaning forward, propelled by her piss-covered feet as they ploughed into the rainforest floor... she ran for her life.

June did see it strike. A memory of *Jack be Nimble*. But her mind's ability to collate these flashes, these frames of time, would take some time. And as she ran through that jungle with no idea how long this great serpent would continue its pursuit of her, June considered three things:

One—that she had left her water bottle behind.

Two—that the heat and humidity were not the worst things about traipsing in the jungle.

And three—and this one she said out loud, 'I can run like a *Motherfucker!*'

Chapter Sixteen

Wayward

The light had cooled. The sounds had softened. And the path was somewhere else.

June's heart, beat too fast.

The bones of her face felt too small to hold her skin where it should be as she looked about her seeing nothing at all that might give her any sense of where she was.

Her skin was still wet. The sting under her arms had spread to her inner thighs, and the dimming sunlight there in the belly of the rainforest only seemed to thicken the blanket of humidity that spread too thickly upon her. She kept sucking air in through her nose, no matter that it didn't seem to get where it needed to go.

And she wanted to cry. She wanted that to make something happen. She wanted her tears to bring her the help she needed.

But June was, even as she stood there *somewhere* in that forest, clear that this would not happen.

Again, she lifted her phone, reading 14%. Her battery was shedding its charge. The only way to charge it was back at the hire car that was still sitting in a tiny car park at the entrance to the walk. A walk that the *sign* said would take her *two hours* or *twenty minutes*.

Again, she lifted her phone—no signal, none. Witnessing her right thumb tapping at the google icon, again searching, again seeing that message informing her that she had no reception, she said, 'I fucking know that!'

The screen then showing 13%.

The air was coming from her in little huffs and coughs. Her mouth tasted sour.

'Erghhh,' she said. The jungle, not missing a beat. Not a sound changed, not a squeak. She dropped her phone back into her pocket. She wiped at the sweat on her forearm, and she felt so thirsty. Thirstier than she could ever remember being. And it felt so wrong, so unjust... so true.

The light through the trees was no longer as sharp and promised only the doom that she had tried so hard to avoid accepting. It was getting late in the day, and there on the rainforest floor, June had no sense of how to decide on what she should do. Her *little self* whined at this. 'How am I supposed to know?' It whined, 'Why?' But she knew. June knew that as she looked about her, as she looked down at where she stood, that she was not only *not* on track to getting out of this little situation, but that she was not on any track at all.

And time was running out. 'How long have I been standing here?' she said, with her throat grabbing at her thirst. The sweat running down her legs proving that she was losing *more* water.

Something moved off to her right and June skittered. Knees bent and hands raised, her reactions heightened, her body's draw on her adrenaline already spent, June felt her muscles shaking.

'Who's there?' She'd made to scream it, but heard only the fear in her sounds, and the pleading.

The movement came from maybe twenty feet away. Everything so hidden this deep in the jungle. All sound amplified, exaggerated. Nothing making any sense. She decided to move. The sounds accelerating, behind her now. June moved, stepping and shoving through the foliage. The sounds of the insects like a scream now, like they had picked up on the drama unfolding beneath and beside them and had turned the volume up like an orchestra playing a film score, setting the mood.

Those noises now crashing behind her. 'Nooo!' She meant it, and she did her best to run deeper, ever deeper, into the jungle. The leaves and branches and heat, swatting at her, June's upraised arms kept pushing, pushing, pushing. Her legs shoving and bumping and scraping. Her tears shed, and she fled. Her eyes hardly able to distinguish anything but the never ending green and brown, and she pushed her way through. Now only hoping, pleading, whining, to get away from whatever was pursuing her.

And this is what June Bonnet did. Never stopping... until it grabbed her.

Tumbling out and through a dense swamp of leaves, with all noises having become one, and her heart screaming at her to *JUST KEEP MOVING,* June was gripped. And she lost her shit.

At first, she tried to escape the needles that held her arms, her hair, and then the skin of her legs. She tried. Her eyes were unable to see much of what was happening to her. Her fear, so enormous it poured out of her now as the beast that had been pursuing her finally attacked. Her chest was screaming from her exertion. Her desperation to *SURVIVE,* forcing her to turn and thrash and beat at the whole world around her... until the pain, increasing exponentially with every move, caused both of her eyes to close so very tight, and for her teeth to really bite down together hard... and for her to stop.

'STOP!'

'STOP!' she screamed, hearing her own hatred.

Hurting everywhere. Her mind running fast. Her clothes, and hair too, gripped by whatever was on her. The only weight, now held in place from every angle, was of that which pulled against her.

'WHAT?' Her only way to speak now, a scream.

'WHAT?' No idea what she was asking. The pain so rough. Every which way she moved, every micron, a tear at her skin, a pull on her clothing and hair. 'FUCK!' And the tears just leaked now, constantly, they just dribbled out of her. Breathing through her clenched teeth, her body held in place, in a hunch, feeling the attack had halted right in place, feeling no warmth of another body, no skin or fur against hers, no breathing, no snarl, no hiss or stench... June opened her eyes.

Immediately she saw the thorns, hundreds of them, thousands. Her eyes tracking, her hair pulling and tearing needles in her skin as she tried to look about her.

'I'm in a bind,' she said too loudly.

And then she laughed—threw-up in her mouth a little bit, swallowed it—and laughed. 'OW!' she cried, but it was the sweetest *ow* she had ever muttered. For June knew, now, that she had been caught not by a beast, but by a *Wait-a-while* vine.

Sure it hurt. It was nasty. And sure, June was in no way deluded that it was going to take some time to extricate herself from the serious tangle that her desperate attempts to escape had caused, but now she knew, and she said it, 'I'm alive.' Laughing with her mouth fully open, and with the delirium of the insane, June still somehow, for the first in the longest time, felt it. And she said it, 'I'm going to be alright'.

Of course, this conclusion was a result of her internal deeper inner-workings, and so had little bearing on changing her physical reality in that moment.

The *reality* was that it would take her over an hour and a half to fully remove herself from this horrible mess of inch long spikes. And therein lay the real problem. For not only was June lost, she knew this, not only was she without water or anyway to hold it, by the time she had gotten herself free of the *Wait-a-while* vines, June Bonnet was halfway into dusk.

And although she had come very close to where her bottle lay—only a few feet from where she had thrown it as she had made a full circle in her first desperate dash from the *King Brown*—June had not seen the path from which she had strayed hours earlier. But now, not having made an arc of more than sixty degrees for many hours, well, June was only meters from where she had left the path. The path that, if she had only kept following it, would have taken her out of the jungle's depths and back to her car. For she was so close

144

that if a car had passed her parked rental on the road back to Port Douglas, June would have certainly heard it.

But that didn't happen.

Not that the knowing of this would help her now.

The scream tore the skin off her fear.

The absence of light, all of it, brought the cool air to her nerves, and she whimpered. She didn't know this until she heard it in the space that followed that awful sound. And June pressed her body deeper into the crevice between the two high ridges of the fig tree roots; the place she had chosen for shelter as the last of the light winked out of her world.

It was not a human scream. Of this, June had no doubt. But as its sound—terrifying in its clarity and volume—shook through the trees about her, June was unable to dismiss that its creator must certainly be of some great size and ill-temperament.

Again, it screamed long and high and so very loud.

Was it closer? June's mind chilled. Her analytics flash-carding images of temporarily invisible aliens in the trees, hunting *Arnold*. And again, its terrible pitch scratched the drums of her ears and forced her back even further into the tree's crevice. Her fears of what nightmarish insects might inhabit her hide in the hours of darkness swept to the back of her mental closet as the creature let go another, this time longer, scream.

And June was sure it was closer.

Her back pressed to the hard wood walls of the tree roots, and her hands forced over her ears. So thirsty, and so tired.

145

'URGH!' Something crawled on her, and then she felt it move quickly up her back as she beat at herself to remove it. On her feet, June was running with her hands shoving up behind her and under her shirt. Her mouth stretched in horror. 'So many legs!' June pulled at her shirt while half tripping over the underbrush and debris as she ran into that darkest night. It was not until her shirt was off and away from her that June gave her last few shudders with her hands still rubbing over all of her skin, hair and shorts to remove anymore of whatever *could feel that way.*

'Erwuhh!' she said, just before she realised that she now stood exposed.

The blackest night had grown still. Not a cricket chirped. If such things, and she was sure they must, lived in such a jungle. Nothing. No sound. No breeze. No light. Just her own wet breathing, and then the thinnest sound leaking from her like a hole in a balloon.

June felt her knees bend.

A stick beneath her snapped!

'Arghhh-no-no-no!' And June knew then, knew it, that no matter her age, no matter the conclusions she might have drawn about herself, that under it, in that moment, she was as frail and vulnerable as any six-year-old on Earth.

'E-ARGH-ARRRRRRRRRRRRRRR!' came this monstrous sound from right above her.

Stamping her feet and clamping her hands over her ears, she stood there crying with an open mouth. And with her saliva running over, June begged to be anywhere but here, to be anyone but her.

Half-naked now, with no idea where the tree she had fled from was, and with no idea where her shirt was, bawling in real fear, June heard the forest go still once more.

Her senses piqued. Her own noises stilled. A chill ran up her skin like ice water defying gravity, and June looked up into the black night.

She paused, frozen.

A branch up there snapped!

The sound came in a rush, pushing the air around her.

A deep, croaking, huffing roar!

And June ran! Chased by the incredible sound that had to be, of this, as she ran through that jungle, she could have absolutely no doubt, coming from a monster... *Part pig, part man!*

Her ankles twisted, but she ran.

The forest tore at her naked skin, but she ran.

The horrors of what must surely await her if she was caught, hurricaned through her visual mind, but June ran and ran and ran.

The air coming up and through her hot and dry throat smelt like burnt toast to her as she fought and fell, righted herself and clawed, but she ran through that black night until her stomach ached at her to stop... and still she ran.

Her body torn, and her mind sick with the effort, desperate to escape, June ran... until she heard it. 'Water!' she laughed it. With no light. No sight. Nothing left but her need to find it. 'Water!' The image of *John Wayne* stumbling from the desert, pasted her mental walls like a poster. June stopped, listening, for that prettiest of sounds. 'Water!' unable to stop herself from saying it. Not recognising her own voice as she did. Another poster slapping up onto those same mental walls of *Doris Day* dressed as a cowgirl. And why? She did not know.

Her hands outstretched before her, slowly now, with her need increasing her caution, June walked toward the increasing tinkle of that sound.

And she could smell it...

And then the ground fell out beneath her feet.

In absolute darkness, June fell.

And time stilled, as it has want to do in moments of high drama. It almost froze, or least appeared to without any visual reference.

And June... falling... from *where* to *where?*... The result being *what?* In that moment, June felt it. And she could swear she heard it.

And so, falling, half naked... from *where* to *where*... with her hair streaming above her in the pitch black of a jungle's night... June crossed her legs, held her hands out to each side, where she connected her thumbs with her third fingers, and said, quite loudly, 'AUMMMMMMMM!'

She never even felt the impact.

Mercy.

Chapter Seventeen

Never Smile

Like a hot plate, sunlight coloured June's eyelids before they opened.

Breathing for moments, she lay still before her body began to show its pains, and the headache, dull and throbbing, beat at her to open her eyes.

She was shuddering as she tried to move.

She lifted her torso so that she sat.

It was the smell that stopped her.

The kind that tells a story before the mind can equate it. The kind of odour that speaks in tones that only the lizard brain properly comprehends. And the message was clear, *Do not move!*

Sitting on her butt with her hands planted beside her, and with her eyes looking straight out at that brown river before her, June knew she was covered head to toe in grey mud… and she knew that someone or something was watching her.

Again, images of that *Arnold classic* from the *80's* posted its reel of *the big guy* plastered in mud, much as she was now. But June knew she was no *Schwarzenegger*. And though memories of the horrors, real or imagined, from the previous night persisted, June too knew that whatever the reptile nugget of tissue in her brain was telling her, *it, this, far* outweighed the fears she had held then.

There was no movement. There was no sound. Just the smell.

Playing *Statue* again, from her lower peripheries June watched her nostrils flaring involuntarily before her left eyelid drooped from the stink; *like death wrapped in a blanket of rotten fish.* Her stomach tightened and tried to flip. The lack of food and water, leaving her feeling like the walls of her stomach were stuck together. She could only imagine that it was her headache that was preventing her from falling headlong into another desperate panic. That, or the intuitive knowing, the bottom of the gut comprehension, that she, June, was in serious and imminent danger. All sense of every other risk or peril in her life thus far, shrunk like goose skin in a frying pan, and she knew that whatever she did, she would get no second chances.

It was the push of the smell first. A hot wave of it rushed her.

Second, it was the deeply urgent flapping, and the slapping. It was this that first triggered the rapid spiral of firing nerves. Every mud-covered pore from toe to scalp, lighting in a brushfire *Mexican Wave*.

It was in a hair of a moment, as June was rising up onto her feet with her arms already in full swing with her face already set and pointed away in the direction she was moving, that she heard the grunts of the beast that would cause her to never again doubt her *small voices*.

It was real, and it was faster than anything June could have imagined or explained. Like a rifle shot, she felt it. The force of its power as it burst after her, shaking the air about her. With June's arsehole trying to lead the way, and with her knees pumping in her lower vision, she motored like she had never done before.

Funny, she would think some time later, *I knew it was a crocodile. Without even seeing it. I knew.* And she was right.

The riverbank ahead was clear. A mercy, one could imagine, but not by much. Her vision tunnelled before her. Her mud-covered tits swung free, and every foot that landed, bit into the dry riverbank. And June Bonnet thanked God... 'Aw FUCK!' It was gaining on her in bursts. Unable to stop herself from looking back every two or three steps, June was in awe of just how fast this thing moved. Oh this, and just how *HUGE* it was! Really. Astounding.

The sound of it, sending shock waves of terror over her like buckets of hot water tossed over her back. But still she ran like her life... *well it did really, didn't it.*

June didn't hear it at first. She saw the white water before she saw the aluminium craft rounding the bend in the river up ahead of her before she heard the motor really roar. All she knew was that if she didn't keep beating that ground with her sneakered feet then this day was going to be her last. She did watch. Her body was on auto pilot. Breaking all of her previous records. June watched as the boat raced straight toward the bank some twenty metres ahead of her. Her heart was leaping and the tears welling. Just like they did, regardless of her agreement, when watching *those* movies.

And June heard herself screaming something.

'YARRRRRR! YARRRRRR!' She would never know why. And without her permission, her arms were pumping the air as she kept inches ahead of the pursuing crocodile.

What happened next, June could not have believed possible if she hadn't seen it with her own eyes, and even then. *Can you imagine?* And June considered that there was no-one to tell. Which of course was old news.

As the boat hit the bank just ahead of her and continued its trajectory, June was still five metres from... but she had no way to gauge distance, and time had slipped. It had to. Too much information. Too many calculations to consider. Her feet still beating, and the crocodile still right on her tail, June had to duck as the man from that boat, running off the bow of his flat-bottomed aluminium punt, kicked off and soared—*I shit you not*—soared through the air and right past June's bugging eyes. Slowed time gave her a close-up view of his khaki shirt flapping as he flew, and a slight grin under the set eyes in his tanned face took the last of her breath... and then shit got real.

Standing there, she'd stopped running, like a city-paths runner with her hands on her hips, catching her breath, June watched this *guy* wrestle—*I know right?* —the...

'It's a crocodile,' June actually said this. With one elbow tucked into her waist, and with her hand open and extended, and her facial expression, *under the mud,* a perfect—*Like Really?*

And it took some time.

With her chest rising and falling, June watched *this guy* move like he was born to this kind of thing. Which she supposed, in that moment, he probably was. I mean *who else right?*

She made to chew a fingernail but thought better of it as *this guy* mounted what was now a clearly *at least six metre crocodile and* pulled from his belt a relatively—let's be honest—small rope and set about wrangling and roping this prehistoric terror.

June began to clap then, slowly. There was really nothing else to do.

'Really,' she said, unheard by anyone but herself. 'Oh, that's really very impressive.' As she watched this man completely dominate this monster who would most certainly have devoured her—well—about now. A hard thing to miss you when it's you who would've been its lunch.

She began to walk toward them.

'Just wait there Missy,' he said, his voice firm but not unfriendly. An ease about him. A *thing* she had not yet experienced. A... *thing*.

'Of course,' she said. 'You take your time.' Watching as he tied off a knot by the creature's side with the rope that had already been tied around the creature's massive jaws and other essential body parts. She watched as he held up a finger to her and smiled. 'Wow,' she said this as he dipped his head, took a roll of gaffer-tape from somewhere, pulled open the end with his teeth, and quickly wrapped the creature's jaws.

'Right.' Standing with one leg on either side of the croc, that smile again, and his hair falling just to his eyes, he bowed to her. He then sat down on the back of the beast and wiped his brow.

Walking to him, June said, 'Is it safe now?' Hearing something in her tone that she had only heard in movies. Not sure if she was up with that or not.

'Aw, yeah,' he said, nodding, 'he ain't going nowhere.' Concern spreading across his face, he said, 'Are you alright?'

'How did you...?' June said, circling a finger in the air. Her eyes catching a gap in his shorts. 'Are those your balls poking out of your shorts?'

Looking down at where June was pointing, he smiled and shook his head. 'I never wear em.' As though that was the matter settled.

Looking at him, her face going still for just a moment, June said, 'I can see your balls.' Registering to herself that those balls—no mistake—were hanging out of his shorts and onto the back of a crocodile that had just chased her down the bank of this very river on which she still stood.

'And I,' he said, now pointing a bloody finger at June, 'can see your tits.' That smile, never far away. He stood, saying, 'So, I guess we're even.' And then entirely without permission, *this guy*, takes two steps toward June, and lifts her fully up off the ground and starts marching toward the boat. 'Don't worry. Bazz will be by to take care of that little guy,' he said, hooking a thumb behind them at the hog-tied reptile. 'There's a whole mess of folks looking for you. So, we'd better get you sorted out, and call it in.'

Now June was not, had never been, the kind of girl to allow anyone to *cave-man* her. But she had to admit, as he held her against his chest and carried her away from certain death, *he did smell better than the crocodile.* 'What's your name?' she asked, even as he was getting her aboard.

Pushing off the bank, he got himself onboard like he was stepping through the front door. 'Danny.' The smile. 'Danny Duco,' he said, raising his eyes.

'Har.' Setting herself on a seat, catching the t-shirt he threw to her from somewhere. 'Like...'

'Yeah,' he said, speaking to her like he had known her all his life, 'my mum was a huge fan of *Grease*.' Scrunching his lips

155

as he lifted his phone and spoke loudly into it, he said, 'Yep, I've got her here now... Uh-huh, yep... Yeah, she's all good... Yep, we'll be there in about thirty minutes.' Sliding the phone back into his pocket. Turning to June as he powered up the boat and set to, he handed June a bottle of water as his eyes focused out, looking in the direction of where they were headed. He continued, 'Mum was a huge fan, but my dad, not so much.' That smile, his green eyes, dark under his brow, light over his cheek bones. 'He used to call him *Danny Fucko*.' His laughter, like a flock of gulls lifting off.

June couldn't help herself. 'You're infectious.' She knew he couldn't hear her, but she couldn't hide her smile.

'It's a Dutch name,' he went on. 'My great-grandfather emigrated here.' And he talked some more. June was sure it was to put her at ease.

...but she already was.

And as she looked at this guy, a part of her fell away. A part of her drifted out to sea. A month ago, she would have cut him away. She would have heard alarm bells. *And now maybe*, she reasoned, *it was down to what she'd just been through*, or maybe not. But whatever the reason, June was sure of one thing; she wasn't going to be running from him any time soon.

So, as Danny steered June back to civilisation, and kept his kind, strong face on the waters ahead, June let herself go for a moment.

And she considered that maybe all of this had been life's way of showing her what she really needed. And like it not, June played out the role on that big-screen in her mind, of *Oliva's Sandy*, hearing only the words of that song... *You're the one that I...*

June threw-up all down herself.

156

'Aw shit!' Danny left the controls and came to her. Taking the bottle of water from her hand and standing her up while holding her steady, dipping his head, looking into her eyes and speaking softly, he said, 'You gotta take it slow.' He took the water and poured some into his hand, and then he began to clean her up.

June was at a loss.

Smiling a smile she swore she had never seen, he said, 'You're a mess.' And then he wrapped his big arms around her, and as June pressed her face against him, he said, 'It's going to be alright.' Rocking her just a little bit. 'We'll get you as good as new.'

Chapter Eighteen

Side-Show

'Marshmallows don't always need a fire,' he said. 'They just need less corn starch.'

June rolled her smile over in bed, and her eyes held the orange light of the new day where it lay far off in the distance. The moisture from the night was already rising, burning off as the heat of a new day began to spread its hands across this open land. 'Kangaroos,' she said lazily, watching three. Her eyes were unwilling to fully wake, but June thought it looked like *a mummy, daddy, and baby* kangaroo.

'Ergh... coffee.' She was smiling, but...

Danny left the room. June sat up in the cast iron bed. Her eyes casting back to that window and the now empty paddock.

The smell.

She lifted the sheet to her nose. It was him, Danny. 'Danny Duco,' she said it, and her face stretched with the words

159

enough to cause her to wonder if she was still June Bonnet. She rubbed at her legs like she had a million times, a million mornings. The texture there was so rough that it gave her a start. Looking under the covers, confusion crossed her face, but only for a second. But it was long enough for the juices to pump, for her to have gotten a fright.

'Healing up well,' Danny said, handing her a hot cup, sitting beside her, kissing the top of her head. His hands so gentle. His care unyielding. He touched at the many places that her skin had suffered.

June sipped at her coffee, grinning, feeling. 'You're getting my juices flowing.' Not meaning to put a deep and rough German accent on it, June laughed through her nose into her coffee, covering them both.

Laughing, already standing, taking her cup with one hand and grabbing a towel from the back of a chair by the bed, Danny pressed at her with it. His smile, so easy. He dropped the towel on her head and walked from the room calling, 'You're still a mess.'

Giggling hard and squirming on the bed, June said, 'And you're still a *Crocodile Hunter!*' Her mouth forming an *O* and her eyes opening wide. And she was rewarded by the fast though surprisingly light steps that signalled Danny running back into the room. His hands already tickling at her before she had time for the first squawk to get out from her throat. 'Arp!' she cried. Her eyes rolling like a...

He was kissing at her then. His hand was reaching under the bedsheet. His fingers were already caressing where she was wet. His voice was speaking through the kisses against the skin of her neck as he said, 'I told you,' and with his kisses trailing, 'I'm a Crocodile *Preservationist.*'

160

June could feel his smile as his mouth touched her arcing body. Her hands touching as much of him as she could without breaking her *Egyptian Goddess* routine. But the truth was that she smiled more with Danny Duco than she had ever done before. 'And I like being fucked smiling,' she said into his ear as her hands stretched around his strong neck. 'Ark!' Laughing as he flipped her like she was made of pillow stuffing. 'Oh no *Mr Crocodile Hunter.* AR-P-please no, ooh wait a minute... yes, yes... aw fuck yes.'

'Well, I'm staying for a week or so,' June heard herself speaking into her telephone, looking through her *Jacky-O's.* 'Yeah, it was pretty full-on. But I've hardly got anymore scabs left.'

'Ew, I hate that word... *SCABS*,' Jason Mackie half screamed into the phone. 'Reminds me of those post war movies... I hate those.'

'So?' she asked, smiling and turning on the long jetty.

His voice, a change in it. 'Just be aware June...' A pause, a long one. 'You're... well you're moving quite fast.' The silence then, suggesting a chewing of the lip.

Taking her sunglasses from her face and squinting into the sun, she said, 'Icarus?' Not sure where that word came from. Jason Mackie laughed. 'Yes! Yes. Icarus! By God. Yes!'

Looking around for a cigarette, June said, 'But what if I never fly?' Walking to an older man leaning against the rail, smoking and looking out into the distance. June tapped him on the shoulder and mimed smoking, mouthing '*Please?*'. Sticking his smoke between his lips, still leaning, the older gentleman pulled a pack from his top pocket, flicked open

161

the lid and shook the pack, sending a single smoke higher than the rest. June smiled at this. With a grin of his own he produced a lighter, held it out to her and turned his eyes back out to sea. 'Thank you.' June puffed it and handed the lighter back to the man who took it without turning back to look at her. June wondered whether he noticed the many bruises and scratches that still covered her, faded as they were. The bruises, now mostly yellow and purple. *How could he not?* She walked back to the other side of the jetty. 'Oh, that's so good.'

Dr Mackie said, 'And what if you don't?' More lip chewing. 'June... we're not all meant to fly.'

She felt anger rise within her then. Surprised, still unable yet to contend with this, June paced, shutting out the world around her. She smoked. She paced. 'You mean my glue might not be strong enough?' she said, hearing herself, hating the juvenile indignation in her voice, feeling the blood in her face.

'It wasn't glue June,' his voice was breaking up.

'I can't hear you Jason. You're breaking up.' June stood there, holding the phone down, looking at it. Like that could do any good. Her mind running with thoughts of this still happening in this era. 'Say that again.'

But he hadn't heard her. 'It was wax June. It wasn't glue. It was wax.'

Looking at the phone, June saw that the call had disconnected. But she didn't redial.

Leaning on his shoulder, feeling the muscle there through his shirt, holding a stick of fairy floss out in her left hand,

162

tasting its sticky-sweet on her lips, her eyes on the row of little tin ducks rolling along in a line, and hearing the *clackity-clank* of the old-world mechanism blending with the other show-ground noises, close to his ear, June said, 'If you get it in one,' smiling as he sighted through the air-rifle attached by a thin chain to the side-show bench, 'you can have my arse.'

With his left eyebrow drawn high, taking his eye just off the iron sight then back again, softly Danny said, 'And if I don't?'

With a proper grin, with her hand sliding along the skin of his lower back, and with her fingers slipping under his jeans, June said, 'Then I get yours.'

'Ping!... Ping!... Ping!'

June was clapping like a teenager, feeling the light fabric of her summer dress brushing against her thighs.

'I'll take the crocodile.' Danny's smile was real as the side-show operator handed him the stuffed toy. Turning with his smile still in place, he handed the toy to June.

She ran into his arms just then, dropping her fairy-floss to the ground. She wanted to cry. She wanted to cry for reasons she felt she never had. She wanted... to hide in this man... to be *his*... for *this*... to be real. And when his hand held the back of her neck as she pressed her face into his chest, and he kissed the top of her head, silently June prayed that it could be. She begged... that this kind of reality... could be true.

No matter how hard her heart tried to tell her that she was *acting a fool,* June couldn't stop her tears. And the truth was that she didn't care anymore that she wasn't supposed to ever feel like this. She didn't care that *this* here, this *thing* that was happening to her, was the antithesis of who she *should* be!

June felt all of *that* melt away, and for a moment—there in that showground in the Far North, in the strong arms of *this guy*—June believed that if she could only feel *this* forever, then she would happily wear that *50's fucking apron...* every day of her life.

He rocked her just a little, holding her close and kissing the top of her head. Without a single damn given for what anyone else might think, Danny said, 'You're gonna be alright June Bug.'

And right or wrong, June died a little just then. And she knew, *knew it*, that a part of her... was never coming back.

They stayed like that for a time, holding one another in the middle of Sideshow Alley.

Danny nodded to an older woman who had stopped in her tracks and turned to look at them. Her eyes, those of a heart that knew what they were looking at. At his nod, she smiled a little uncertain smile. A second nod and she returned on her way, taking her husband's hand in hers and patting it as she did.

Bending, then holding her face in both of his hands and pressing his lips to hers while looking into her crying eyes, Danny slid his hands from her cheeks to his many times... and let a little water out from his own eyes. 'It's gonna be alright.' His lips not holding their form as he said those words. 'I promise.' He placed her head under his lifted chin. Sniffing hard to get some air into him, still rocking her, he said, 'I'm still getting your arse though, right?'

And the both of them laughed hard like they had not a care in the world.

'I love you.' And June knew there was no taking it back. Not two weeks with *this guy*.

His eyes did something then, they hit a thousand miles, looking right into hers, and he said, 'And oh how I love you.'

June bawled. Standing there in the middle of the way with all of the other people giving them some room—looking like they didn't want to get any on them—her pretty face dropped forward, and with her hands hanging straight by her sides and her mouth open wide... June bawled.

The world stilled then. A frame, clipped and frozen.

June, standing there out in the open with her heart torn completely in two.

Danny, only a step away with his own heart burst, as only real love can afford. His hands lifting outstretched toward this woman who had shattered his *life*, as he had purported it to be.

And how easily it had been done. Just two people—their independent selves buzzing along with their own formerly observed and decided on keen sense of self—now shattered into a million pieces... exploded right there... on the grounds of Sideshow Alley.

An older man standing by in a tented alley, not far away, holding onto a makeshift pole as his bumper-cars circled and bumped along on their makeshift floor beside him—he noticed. His snagging eye slowed itself within the illusion of time as he made to throw his spent cigarette past his round belly to the ground before him, with his right foot lifted, ready to step it out. His eye caught, and he was held there in that moment... and he too felt it. And he too knew what it was. And his heart broke a little. For not only did he know that what was happening out there on that ground just over

165

there on Sideshow Alley, was real, he knew that it could implode with just as much force... and tear one asunder. But still, with this to the air before him, and with his eyes on Danny and June, he said, 'You *go.*' Not noticing the single tear that dropped from his eye as time slipped back into its usual form... and the noise of the showground returned.

Danny's hands were nearly on June before he stopped in place as a small boy, stepping between them and holding something up in his hand, said, 'It's ok.' His little face pointed up to June. 'It's still good.' And with his free hand, he was brushing at the fairy-floss... that June had dropped only a short while before.

Chapter Nineteen

The Catch

I t was on the fucking radio!' June heard the desperation in her own voice.

'Slow down June.' But Dr Mackie's voice was not without its own urgency. 'Tortoise and the hare my dear. Tortoise and the hare.'

'I'm not a fucking tortoise!'

'You must be June,' he said, speaking steady, measured. 'Right now, you must slow yourself down.' His breathing was audible. 'You must lift your head now and look further down the road.'

She didn't speak. With her thumbnail pressed between her teeth, and her knees pushed up against the steering wheel, June sat, looking out at the flat ocean before her. The light of the late afternoon was dropping, and she felt her chest rise and fall. Her breathing was shaky. Her need was urgent, and she was gripped, braced, by a clamping pain around the bones of her eyes.

'Good.' Jason's own breath steadying. 'Now tell me.'

Wiping her nose with the back of one hand, she knew that at least she was past controlling the small tears that leaked from her eyes. Hearing the whine in her voice, the defeat, she said, 'It was all going so perfect...' And then the first sob came out. And June's head bobbed as she cried in the front seat of her rental car, with the warm sea breeze puffing in through her open window.

Jason Mackie didn't speak. He waited for her to find her next words.

'Ugh.' Dropping her feat back to the floor, June rummaged for her smokes, found them, and got one going with shaky hands. Speaking as she exhaled, leaning forward in her seat, she said, 'It had to be that bitch, Marcy. URGH!' Thumping herself back into the seat, feeling the car move, rock.

'It probably was,' he said. 'But that doesn't matter right now June. What matters is what you *do*. What matters is how you choose to respond to what has already happened.' His voice even, hopeful, he said, 'Do the dance.'

She smoked, shifting one foot back up onto the seat. Her memory offering her what she sought, she spoke softly, as though to herself, 'We were sitting in his car, eating a burger, laughing.' She took a drag, watching the thin stream of smoke wobble as it went by. 'You know? He makes me feel like I'm not me. Not the me I thought I was.' Crying now, her free hand flopping onto the other seat, she said, 'It's like I'm normal. Like I'm allowed to... laugh like that.'

'Yes June. I understand.'

Encouraged, her voice steadier now, flatter, she went on, 'It was like I was allowed to be happy. Like... I didn't have to carry all of... *that.*'

'What June?'

Sobbing a little into her hand, her voice rose in pitch, 'Me.' She shook, and her nose ran onto her upper lip. This made her angry, and she wiped it away. 'Why?' Angry, with that sense of defeat again. 'Why couldn't they just let me go... and be happy? Haven't I paid enough?'

For all that he wanted to say, Jason let the space open.

'So anyway, it came on... on the radio,' she said in a monotone, 'and they told the whole story as if I was some deranged person.' Taking a drag and lifting another cigarette out of the pack, she threw the near ended one out her window. 'Oh fuck off you silly cow,' speaking under her breath at someone looking at what she had just done. She went on, to Jason, 'You know they said I was a *Sexual Sadist?*' Scoffing as she lit the new cigarette. Blowing out smoke as she held it between her lips. Her hands busy with her gestures. She spoke around the smoke, 'Like they actually said that on the radio like it was true! And! They said I was *a violent...* something. I don't remember. I was just knocked. Sickened...'

'You did act violently June,' he said.

'Well... Yeah... Yeah, I did but *YOU* know I had a reason to. It's not like I walk around punching people in the face!'

'It's not up to me to qualify your actions June.' His tone making it clear that he didn't want to say this.

She wanted to be angry at him. But she couldn't. She folded into herself. Wanting to hang up. Wanting more not to. She needed to tell. 'But the look on his face...' She collapsed a bit with those words, with the memory of it. 'He just kinda...' But she couldn't say it.

'I want you to tell me June.'

Crying now, just crying. Sniffing, her voice broken by it, she said, 'He looked like I'd lied to him.' Her voice smaller now as she looked out at the flat ocean, she said, 'Like I'd betrayed him.' Pretending to get a grip. 'I mean, I was right there right... The guy didn't have a chance to prepare. He didn't see it coming. Hell, he tried to pretend that it was no big deal...' But she began sobbing into her hand again.

'You can't know he was pretending June.' A breath. 'Of course it would have come as a shock to hear something like that. It takes time to process.'

June tried to laugh but fell short. Breathing out long and hard, with her lips quivering, out of her control. 'But I could see it, Jason. His beautiful face flushed. Even him, with all his... strength... was embarrassed.' Crying, she said, 'I was sitting there with my mouth full of that fucking hamburger. Frozen. My eyes looking sideways at him. Seeing this man who had swept me off my fucking feet, look like he'd been played... lied to.' Again, her voice became small. 'Jason? He looked like he'd been treated... played like a fool.'

'Ah fuck it, I need a smoke. Give me a sec.' His voice trailing as he left the phone, followed by sounds of rummaging. 'Won't be a sec June. Just hold on. They're here somewhere.' His voice very light now. 'Come on you fucking things... there you are!'

A small smile at her friend, cracked through June's devastation.

Still sounding a mile away. 'Hmm-mmm, be right with you.' The sound of his chair scraping. 'Aw fuck me that's better. To be honest, I don't think I'll ever properly quit.' A small

171

chuckle. 'Right. Sorry about that. Where were we? You were saying how Danny was knocked for a six?'

June coughed a pop of laughter, and she felt her self-pity split just a little bit. 'When he said it didn't matter, I kind of died a bit.' Breathing out and shaking her head, she said, 'What else was he supposed to say?' She could hear Jason cursing on the other end of the line. 'Are you alright?' She could hear the sound of a glass placed on a table and something pouring.

'What? Yeah me? Nah, I'm good June. Just spilt some *forty-year-old*. Har. And these aren't my normal brand. I found them on the cleaner's trolley when she was clearing out one of our *guest's* rooms. She said she'd... Well, you don't need to hear all about that now do you.' A forced laugh followed. 'They're just a little bitter. So, I thought I'd have a wee nip to balance it all out. But still...'

June rubbed her eyes with her hands.

'Go on. Go on. I'm all ears.' The sound of him slurping before he said, 'Could do with some ice. But any-who, har-har.' And then another slurp sounded down the line.

June's stomach felt empty. The air felt like it didn't have enough oxygen in it. Pins and needles, small ones, were beginning in her lips and nose. She took another cigarette and lit it.

'So, what happened then June?' he said, obviously deepening his voice.

'I didn't know what to do. I don't think he did either.' Sucking smoke and breathing it right in. 'But we both knew that whatever we were in, whatever was happening, had just been knocked of its rails. We both knew that the fairy-tale...' And she couldn't say it. June Bonnet couldn't make out the words. She tried. Her mouth moved, but nothing came.

'It just melted away,' Jason said this as though he was speaking away from the phone.

'His phone rang then. He got out of the car to take the call, and when he came back, he said a call came in to the office, and he was needed. But who knows right? It was probably someone who'd just heard that this *girl* he was spending all his time with...'

'You don't know that June.'

June felt her heart braced by this support.

Jason said, 'But probably. Yeah, you're probably right.'

'Hey?'

'Well, you said it.' There was more slurping. 'What?' His voice sounding far away. Another voice, female, was talking to him. He came back on loud and clear, 'Aw fuck it. Sorry June, but I gotta go and wrangle one of the *Crazies*. One of em has *flown the coop* so to speak.' Lots of movement on his end. A chair scraping, and then he said, 'But I'll call you as soon as I get it under control. Fuckin *Loonies*! Har-har.' The sound of him gulping the last of his drink. 'Now June,' he said, serious, 'I need you to focus on what I am saying right now. Really listen June.'

'Okay?'

'URRRRRRP!' And then a cough before he said, 'Oh shit, I'm so sorry. That was rude.' Honestly sounding a little pissed. 'Don't, and I mean don't... um? Aw yeah. Don't do anything rash.'

'Really? That's the advice?'

'Yeeees,' he said this speaking way too slowly. The sound of his hand slapping on his desk appeared to break the spell he was under. 'Don't. And... aw fuck it. I gotta go June.'

Pressing the little red phone icon, June looked back out to sea with heavy eyes. In two minutes, with nothing much happening, she turned the keys in the ignition.

Chapter Twenty

Tic-Tac-Toe

There's a sense we all have. It's small, or so it appears at first.

So gentle is this sense before it's known, so slight before the use of it develops a keen recognition of it, that it goes mostly unnoticed, ignored.

It's calm, this voice, quiet and common in its delivery. In fact, it sounds much—*well let's say it plainly*—it sounds exactly like our own thoughts do, to us. So therefore, as did June Bonnet, all but a few of us assume that this small voice is our own. For this is how we hear and interpret our own cognitive thoughts. Is it not? As a voice? Its accent, tones and inflections... ours? In our language? *Yes.* And June had this precise sense in the moment she turned the key in the ignition of her car. She had the impression that it spoke to her just as one of another thousand fleeting thoughts, passing, hoping to be noticed.

But she intuited in this instance that this thought, though it appeared much like any other thought, just softer, well... that it wasn't hers.

A point here must be made. A clarity must be waded. For, *is it too much to state?* June thought as she considered this small voice that spoke from what felt like the rear of her mind, *that these are not my own thoughts?* But of course, only the person hearing that thought—in the hearing—can ever honestly know whether this thought is their own or not. A problem that centres like a drain hole in the bathtub of any person's accurate knowing of oneself. *For sure.*

But on this occasion, this voice for June was undeniably *not* created by any consciously analytic synaptic firing. For in the moment of the hearing, June Bonnet was fully immersed—drowning if we're to be honest—in the belly of her most under-developed emotions. And as such—like any person sustaining prolonged exposure to a *flash-bang*—in that moment, June was absent of any self-directed thought.

There, we said it.

'Danny's been hurt,' that's all it said, that voice, that sense.

At first June turned off the car's ignition. Still holding the key in this position, June angled her eyes skyward and a little to the left. Naturally, she was considering the validity of this *thought.* But it took only a moment for another stir, first in her gut, and then in a firing of her nervous system, to prompt her to get on board.

She started the car now without any further thought, and June accelerated in reverse. The tires of the rental, crunching on the gravel as her brakes engaged. Shifting into drive, June had the little rental car at a hundred before she knew in which direction she was headed.

Pulling into the Hospital's car park, June was out of her car and running for the front doors. Her breathing ragged, her heart rate skipping all over the show, June ran to the front desk.

'Dunny!' June said, slapping the surface of the reception counter. 'Dunny!' Her mouth too dry to form the words she meant to convey. She tried again, 'Dunny!' Her hands frantically flapping at the desktop, knocking the little bell onto the floor.

'Excuse me Miss, but can I help you?' Not at all disguising her annoyance.

'Dunny!'

'Do you need a toilet?' Speaking slowly, the receptionist was already pointing down the hall. 'If you follow the signs...'

But June was already running down the corridor.

Pushing through the next set of doors she came to, June saw a drink fountain and pressed at the little metal button on the spout. On seeing the pathetic pizzle of water that came out would require her to put her mouth fully onto the end of the thing and possibly suck, June left it too, at a run. Making her way down that hall, running all over the red, yellow and blue lines, June Bonnet was in fact so frantic that she found herself having to press with both hands against one wall on one side of that hall and then off the other opposing wall. Her analytic mind offering, *maybe this is what that song was about... Sugar Man.*

'Miss! Miss!' The man's concern was obvious.

'Dut-ter!' June tapped urgently at the man's ID tag that read *Dr Moses*. Angry at her own inability to form the simplest words, confused, alarmed, and scared for all kinds of

177

reasons, she was still in no doubt that she must find Danny.
'DUN-NEY! DUN-NEY!'
June's hands spread wide, now clawing to get past Dr Moses who was in no doubt that this person he was now struggling with in the hallway of the paediatric section of the hospital was indeed in need of psychiatric care. And he was damned if she wouldn't get it!

'So, you're a friend of Danny's?' a different doctor said, nodding his head.
'Look, I was just a bit thirsty,' she said, sipping the luke-warm tea she had been given.
'Sure, sure.' He made a note in his little book. 'The problem is, um... June Bonnet. That is your name?'
Stopping mid-sip with her mouth partially open, June said, 'Listen Fuck-Face, I know you think you've got a...' using fingers to invert the commas, '*Live-One,* but I got a message,' pausing and looking up to her right, but deciding to go with it—I mean who was gonna know?—she went on, 'that Danny had been hurt.' Showing the Doctor her forehead and the benefit of a little eye wobble for emphasis.
He was smiling now. Not a friendly one though. 'Okay June,' checking his notepad, 'the problem we have here is that there is no...' again at the notebook, 'Danny Duco at this hospital,' he said, pressing his lips together and nodding *the nod.*
She smiled one of her own then, with her tongue licking one corner of her mouth while holding the plastic cup in both hands. June lifted her right hand, and pointing at him with it

loosely, she said, 'Has anyone ever told you that you look a *lot* like Seth Rogan?'

He grinned, and then he looked out the window for just a sec. 'Hey!'

June was four steps away by the time the good doctor stood and began to wipe her tea from his face.

And she might have made it. She might have scarpered. If it wasn't for that one look back over her shoulder and the gurney being wheeled through the big flappy doors to her right by the two ambulance officers and the one other medical staff member.

The impact was really quite immense in its capacity to halt one in full *Cuckoo's Nest* flight.

'Aw, fuck me!' June croaked as she slid to the floor.

'June?' Danny lamely reached for her even as two other staff members got a hold of her. Those in charge of his escort hurried him down the hall on the blue line. 'June!' he called, with his outstretched arm still extended. 'Juuuuuuune!' The opiates administered to him on-route already in full swing.

Swatting and clawing at the two staff members trying desperately to contain her on the floor of that hospital hallway, June cried, 'DUUUUUN-NYYYYYYYY!' More out of habit now than anything.

The *Seth Rogan* lookalike approached them with a smug swagger, and he said, 'Take her away.' Pointing back down the way from which he had come. 'And don't give her anymore tea!'

'Ooh, you even sound like him.'

June lent on the door to his room.

179

'You look like shit.' That smile, so easy on his face, now sat below eyes that were not so easy to discern. Danny took his hands from behind his head where he lay on the hospital bed.

June walked to him. Her eyes running over the parts of him that were bandaged, trying to ascertain the extent of his injuries. In a haze, with her eyes still on his bandaged leg, she said, 'They told me, finally, after... well. They told me you were attacked by a crocodile?' She actually looked stunned. She was, and by more than what she had just said.

Danny didn't say anything. He took her hand. She was still not looking at his face. He said, 'Sit down June.'

She wanted to hold him. She wanted to touch his face and kiss his eyes like he had hers. She wanted... it to be yesterday. So, she sat on the chair by his bed. 'How bad is it?'

He laughed but kept his eyes off of hers. 'Well, it was real when it was happening.' Playing at his upper back teeth with his tongue before he said, 'But nothing that won't heal in a month or two.'

She looked at him now. 'You look so pale.'

'He was a big one June.' His eyes said he was serious. 'I would've been a goner if Bazz hadn't've shot him.' He smiled then, a big one. 'I think he's more cut-up about having to shoot that croc than he is about me...'. But he couldn't pull it off. He shook his head and got his tongue started on his front teeth.

'I don't...' June began.

'Stop June.'

She placed her hands between her knees with her eyes still on the leg bandaged all the way down to his toes.

'I was planning on the both of us sitting down for a talk tonight.' Taking a glass of water, he drank. 'Was hoping we could get some of all of this,' he said, pushing a hand back and forth between them, 'clear.' He was struggling to find the words.

'You mean, to find a way to tell me... that maybe we were rushing into things a bit?' She cried then. It just started coming out.

He leant across, only a small grunt to indicate that he was in any discomfort, and he took her by her hands and pulled her over to him and closed her in his arms. And Danny held her as tight as she could bare.

June hoped that his holding her like this, holding her like he could keep her together, could make everything alright. She hoped this like she was still a child who could believe this kind of thing. But she couldn't. And even still, as she collapsed in on herself against him, she knew that though he wanted to, he couldn't. And somehow, even as he kissed at the top of her head, June felt that he knew this too.

'I'm so sorry,' they both said this as one. And then again, in unison, 'No.'

Lifting her red eyed, tear stained and streaked face to his and seeing his kind leaking eyes, so strong and yet broken, looking back into hers, June saw that he knew. And she kissed him with her shaking lips, and she felt his shake just the same. Their eyes seeing one another, holding one another with the desperate knowing... that *this* could not be.

She sat herself up straight and made to straighten herself out. She began patting and flattening the bed clothes around her. 'Argh.' But she couldn't flatten out her leaking heart. June couldn't put it back together again.

'Oh, you're fucking killing me.' Danny covered his face with his big hands, and he cried like a little boy. There was no way in stopping it.

It was June's turn then, to try and hold *him* together. And they shared this awful moment, there on a hospital bed. Too broken to know how to do what they both knew they must—to say goodbye. When everything in them told them that they must not, or death must certainly fall on them in that moment... they knew they were both too... they knew this would not happen... and yet they must do this thing.

'I don't want to,' he said.

'Please?' She knew how unfair this was, but June couldn't help herself from making this useless plea.

Danny took a hard shot of air and shook his head. 'You know,' he said, his voice a merry-go-round, 'my Grandad was a hard man,' allowing a smile at his memory, 'and a drunk.' Breathing hard to control himself. 'One day he sat me down,' he said between more staggered breathing. 'It was after my Mum left.' A fact he hadn't had the time to tell June. 'He was sober that day, and he had this faraway look in his old grey eyes.' Danny took June's hands and looked into her eyes. 'He said, *Danny. You can't judge a person by what they've done. Not alone anyhow.* He said, *We're all walking a path in this life... and well, walking that path takes some fuckery to complete.*' Again, laughing at himself for the telling of this tale. 'He said, *That is, if they're brave enough to walk those extra miles.* He stopped there for a time, and I thought he'd finished. I was about eleven at the time, and to me, drunk half the time or not, my Grandad was like a God. He bent down to me then and looked me straighter in the eyes than anyone...' Danny said, choking as he lifted his eyes just briefly to hers, 'until now,' that smile peeking, 'ever had.' It took Danny a moment to get his throat working, but when he could, he went on, 'And he said, *Boy, you gotta give people the chance to walk*, then he looked past me a thousand miles. You know?

182

Like he was really seeing something or someone. And then he said, *Then you see who they are when they come back... if they come back.'*

June's heart almost tore in two. Her eyes closed so tight. She wanted to be able to say something to make this not real. When she opened them, Danny had got himself up straight and was looking right into her crying eyes.

Like the only person who had ever really seen her, he said, 'I know you think that this,' squeezing her hands in his, 'that this is because I can't or won't get past that crap we heard on the radio.' Shaking his head as he looked at her. Seeing her hope at his words, and knowing he had to go on. 'But I think you know... it's not because I'm judging you baby...' Biting at the words he desperately did not want to say. Nodding his head and seeing her grasp the meaning of his words. He got his face up to hers, their lips touching. Like he had at the showground. And stroking his hand against her cheek onto his, he said, 'And you come back to me when you're done.'

Her heart mashed. She pleaded again, 'But I feel like I need you!'

Danny took a moment then. And holding her head under his chin and stroking her hair, he said, straight, 'Then you know you can't come back until you don't.'

Chapter Twenty-One

Reflections Of...

I t was so much like it used to be, this park, this city.
It *had* been home. But now the ground under her feet
was not as firm. The trees looked like strangers. And the
birds no longer flew her air.

Standing on the new mown grass with her face angled high
to those buildings that had once fit the puzzle she had so
many times assembled, June felt her heart ache for that
which she had known—for yesterday.

'Here! Take this!' The voice of an elderly woman not fitting
the fleetness of movement, nor the speed at which she
shoved the flat square object at her, pressing it flat to June's
chest.

It was not intentional to take the thing. Even as her fingers
wrapped around the dry painted wood of the frame, June's
mouth was frogging her protest. 'Ergh, nope. Hey? Hey!'
Watching the seemingly, and she did seem, crazy old bag-
lady hurriedly side-stepping away. 'Hey? What the fuck
Lady?'

'It's yours now!' The grey mass of curly hair obscuring more than half of the wretch's cackling face as she crab-hopped away with her left arm lifted, and her fingers wiggling a farewell. 'Now, don't drop it!' she called, turning away from June with her feet still shuffling along at an ungainly trot. She moved so swiftly away that her voice already began fading, blending with the noises of pigeons and the traffic from the streets nearby. 'Seven years! Seven years! Har-har-har-har!' She cried like an urban witch, and she was gone, disappeared between some bushes and around a bend in the pathway.

'What the fuck?' June was only half-hearted in her near attempt to pursue that crazy old bugger. Sure, she felt for those who struggled... 'A fucking mirror?' Only then seeing what it was that she now held, drawing the lines between the dotty-dots of the bag-lady's words. And she almost threw the thing to the ground before her. She lifted it a few inches and all. But she didn't do it. A ghost in her mental recesses spooking at a potential curse.

Instead, June lifted the mirror a little higher, ignoring those that passed, not even bothering to imagine what they must be thinking of her. She walked off the edge of the main path. She stood there with the grass under her feet, and she looked into that mirror.

At first June saw only the sky. Its reflection painting the entire surface of the mirror in a flat cold grey. And she stared at that with her mind absent, or so it seemed.

A bird, black and large, crossed the frame, causing her to blink. Her hands angled the mirror downward so that her hair appeared to be drifting up into the bottom of the frame. And June could not grab a thought. Frozen there in the park,

June stared into that unwelcome present and felt nothing that she could clearly discern.

'And what do you see?' came the voice so deep that June felt her bowels give a tumble.

'Orp!' was all she could sound. Her head turned left and right. A slight chill on her neck informing her that the owner of that voice was behind her, directly behind her and speaking over her shoulder. And she tried to move. She made to turn on this person, but she could not, for her shoulders were pinned, held in place. And by God that pissed her off.

'Now look.' One gloved hand lifting from her left shoulder reached out and lay down over her left hand.

Frozen, with heat rising into her face, her voice unable to work, feeling a shame of an unfamiliar... but no, not so unfamiliar it appeared… and with her lower teeth sliding forward against her uppers, June felt like she might cry, '*How dare you?*' But only her mind protested. And then her analytical mind surprised her by noticing the cut of the suit jacket sleeve that covered the arm of this imposer. And you know what? June actually relaxed. *Be fucked?* June thought. But the heat subsided, and the man's smell rose to her nose. Something familiar, but out of reach.

The gloved left hand tilted hers that held the mirror, and the man's right held her firm, and he said, 'Now look.'

She could not see his face. She could not see him, for all that filled the frame of that one-foot square mirror, was June Bonnet. And without her brows moving, June was unable not to stare fully at herself.

Yes, a small part of her protested at this intrusion, this assault. But only a small part. This fact not missing June, that she was somehow more curious than afraid or offended. She felt no crawl in his touch.

And when these thoughts had run their course, June was left with nothing but her own reflection. And it looked like a picture taken of her from a time she could not remember. For who looked back at her? 'A stranger,' she answered. Her voice so soft that it hardly held the air around it.

The hand on her shoulder relaxed for a moment, and then so slightly, it pushed on her. 'What do you see?' A hardness floated in his melodious tone, an edge to his insistence.

Again, June tried to turn her head, but the eyes looking back at her from that mirror held her firm and pulled her back to face the full image in the mirror.

Unable to grasp it, that this girl in the square pane, held between her own hands, was herself. June contended to look at her as though she were the foreigner she appeared to be. First at the eyes. 'So tired,' she said, without her lips moving any more than they must. 'So sad.'

The right hand again shoving in microns. 'Look.'

And as June made to turn again at this invader—was it the light? Its angle?—those eyes in the reflection looked back, into her own. The shade of her eyes, just a quarter, were amber in that angle. Or made so in that shard of light? That quarter opening another void in the black of her too large pupils... and leading her into that image... reflected in the mirror she held. It drew her into those pupils... of the grinning girl... in that reflection.

'What do you see...?' The man's voice now excited, eager, even hungry.

Her stomach rose a little, and she fell like *Alice*... seeing her shoes turning around in the image within her own reflected inner world... of a blue and white dress... of the style she wore her hair when she was... 'Nine?'

'In you go...' said the man's voice, firm, insistent, anchoring, though drifting like a ribbon, long and real.

'I don't want to see...' June left her words far back behind her as she fell, drawn swiftly into the open holes of those pupils set in the pane of that mirrored glass. The light vacuumed and pulled behind her until it winked out, and June Bonnet was falling forward... into the rabbit hole of her own reflection.

Time slammed its door shut. The echo of its *Boom* shaking the space around her, leaving her absent of any hand-hold on the reality she had come to rely on since the years of her childhood.

Holding her hands out before her, seeing them lit by an unknown light source, June spoke, 'How can this be?' And she heard her own words bounce, echo, and tumble in the space around her. She had the very real sense that she was falling. The feeling in her gut, assuring her that she was. A breeze poured against her skin, and she said, 'Is that consciousness?' But this she only heard as she fell, dizzied by the wonder of how her words were present without her having spoken them.

Ahead of her was a small dot of light, just a dot. She felt her eyes squinting to make it out clearer, but June soon saw that it was growing in diameter at a rapid rate, and that her arms began to windmill, for she knew that she must surely hit the bottom in only seconds. And her mouth stretched wide, her eyes wider, her legs riding an unseen bicycle... and June saw that the dress flapping at her sides... was blue and white.

'ARGHHHHHHHH.' This scream, a constant companion now. Her throat was raw with it, but somehow there was no

189

end to the air in her lungs. Her scream was holding without break. The white light hole beneath her was opening so very fast... until she was passing through, and then June was landing without force of any kind. She simply, was there, in a room clearly lit and furnished with the objects of her memory.

'Where am I?' Again, the echo, but this time that sound travelled upward and into the darkness from which she had just come.

She made to fear. Really she did. And she gave it her very best. But there was nothing coming. Her fear tank, here, was empty. All June could feel was the loss.

She was left there, looking down at her *Wonderland* shoes laced around her *Wonderland* socks...

'You look like your cat's died.' The voice was familiar but *unright*, the *wrongest of right*.

Turning to that voice behind her, June screamed, well yelped really, 'Arlp!'

'Oh, stop it already,' it said. 'You act like you've just seen your ghost. Oop-har-har!'

June's eyes felt huge in her head, and she said, 'Leon?' Tiptoeing toward—well—her long dead cat... who sat before her laughing his long-dead arse off. But his laugh was much more *Mutley* than *Cheshire*.

'Oh, you should see your face,' he said, with his eyes spreading too wide. 'Oops! Wait a minute! He-he! You just did! Har-har-har-har-har-har.' He began rolling around on the black and white square tiled floor in this circular room.

Shaking her head and taking a small step back, June said, 'You're not really Leon.' And she was pouting. 'Why does my voice sound like this?'

'Har! Because you're nine. Idiot!' Laughing again with his cat face, just like that of a cat. 'And of course, I'm not really Leon. He was worm shit a decade and a half ago. Dipshit.' And then he picked his teeth with one paw's extended nail.

'This is not right,' said June, stepping back until her butt bumped the table. A table which wasn't there just a moment ago. And she considered—as seriously as one might imagine—that she had lost her very mind.

'Oh no you haven't!' Laughing, the image of her favourite pet said. 'That's what's so funny!'

'I don't want to be here anymore.'

Leon purred and then began walking, just like her pet had, towards her. Except *this* cat walked with his nails out.

Leaning back against that table, little June squinted at the sound these nails made, so loud in this little room. 'Go away,' her little voice pleaded. 'Go away!'

'Oh, but I can't, June Bug.' Coming closer, now only a half metre away. And just as he looked ready to nuzzle into her shins, Leon's shape shook, and his hair began extending in length and retracting in and out as June watched her favourite pet, her best friend pet, grow and stretch. His fur separated, exposing skin of a non-feline kind as Leon shook so violently. The bones of his face, stretching in jarring jumps.

And June, Little-June, Alice-June, almost swallowed her metaphysical tongue. 'Leee-on? Stop it! Please stop this now?'

Those eyes, once cat, now something other, shifting and growing as they held their focus on June's. Its growing and flattening mouth opening in a mewling so deep that June lost her sense of Leon. Watching him, standing now at her height, on two feet. She watched, fixed, as the patches of his

191

fur were sliding into the skin that now grew in patches of blue, both light and dark, on the top half of this creatures morphing form.

'STOP IT!' Her fingers went to her mouth, watching, unable to turn away as the creature's form popped and still shook... now taller than June... now broader... now nearly... a man.

'June Bug?'

Keeping her eyes fixed on those in the still forming face before her of this... man, she said, 'Puppa?' And she ran to him as he stood there in a moment of time, in the same blue flannel shirt that she had last seen him wear. The same year she had lost her best friend pet, Leon.

'Oh Daddy, Daddy, Daddy, I've missed you so much,' she was pleading, grasping him in her arms, over and over again. She was unable to stop herself from behaving like she was only nine. She was unable to stop herself from pushing out everything she pained. And she pressed her face into that flannel shirt... and she felt such a peace as her Daddy's big hand rest atop her head.

'It's okay June Bug,' he said, his voice so warm, so full of that sure knowing of his pure love for her. 'It's going to be alright Baby-girl. I promise.' And June felt his kiss atop her head.

June's eyes shut tighter than ever before. She needed nothing more than this that she got from her dad. But the fear arrived then, as it must do. For she knew, now not entirely separate from her adult self, that this could not last for her... not forever.

'But I need you, Daddy. Please don't go. I need you. Please Puppa?' And she held him with all of her strength... and knew the loss of her child-self. The weight of it, the never ending of it, the unreal hopelessness of it... like hot glue poured down the back of her tilted neck. 'I'm sorry Daddy,' she cried to him, her mouth moving oddly with the pain screaming throughout her bones. 'DADDY?' she cried, her voice changing as she grew in her father's arms... as *she* stretched and formed. The sounds, so awful, matching the pain that scoured every part of her knowing, and she cried, 'Daddy?'

'I'm here Baby-girl...' His voice, seeming so far away.

June was giving all she had to peek through her changing eyes. She saw him standing now, far away... 'Daddy! Daddy! I'm sorry!'

And as his image receded in clarity, as though she looked through Vaseline, as the distance between them grew, June heard his voice, so faint, say, 'I always have been, June Bug... '

In a world with no form, drifting in an ether, June felt her shoulder yank backwards... and then again! She could see her feet beneath her, no longer shod in those damned *Wonderland* shoes. With her face turning, June could see the walls of that same tunnel down which she had been drawn, all around her, falling faster as she moved so swiftly upwards... with every *Yank!*

'MISS?'

Her ears cotton wool, trying to shake her head as her arms squeezed out through that hole in the mirror's image, she cried, 'AHHHH!' June hurriedly breathed the air, even as the rest of her form, now appearing to her transparent, drew and stretched from the frame in her...

'MISS?'

Another pull on her shoulder.

And June felt time, though for an instant resumed, now slowed by ten... as her fingers loosened. The last yank,

193

snapping her back into her conscious form with a *CRACK!* So loud. A bullwhip, forcing her eyes to shut as the frame of that mirror... slipped past the second knuckle joint of her failing grip. And though her heart may have stopped for a moment, though she desperately fought to force her nerves to fire faster, June knew it was lost.

Time was slipping back into play as the mirror fell. Its reel running at normal speed as that mirror made contact with the concrete beneath her feet. The explosion of glass, too great to be justified by the force of gravity alone. The sound of it, shattering. June had only time to close her mouth and eyes to avoid the finer particles as they rose in a cloud around her.

'Are you ok Miss?' The voice elderly, feminine, familiar.

Turning to face that voice and seeing the wee older woman who had comforted her the last time she had lost her shit in this very same park, June shook her head and let this kindly lady lead her away from the debris of the fallen mirror.

They sat on a bench by the path, not ten feet from where she had just been standing.

'Oh, you poor thing,' said the elderly lady, her words like crocheted cushions, her smell like lavender and candy. She pulled a large hanky from her pocket and said, 'Now, you just hold still my dear, and I'll do my very best to get those bits of glass off you.' And she began flapping the hanky over June as though she had been doing this very thing her whole life, tutting the whole while as she did.

And so, as she sat on that park bench as the kindly lady kept flapping about her, and with her eyes fixed on the horizon, and with her voice light and filled with a pleasant melancholy, June said, 'He smelt just like always.'

'Oh, you poor dear.'

Chapter Twenty-Four

A Dozen More

She could hear her footsteps. She could hear the scrape and tap of her shoes on the wet concrete.

5am, and the sky was still heavy with the clouds that had washed the city through the night. Their shapes now beginning to appear as the first dim light of the day began to stir from its dreams, as the first glimpses of this predawn morn began to loom.

She was never one for early walks of this city's streets. She had never known a reason for such a thing. *Though*, June thought, *I have never been so entirely un-me, either.*

And so she walked those streets, dressed in tights and runners. The kind *runners* would wear. Or so June imagined. Her t-shirt was loose, and her jacket was only to protect her from the worst of more rain if it fell. And she had no idea where the cap she wore had come from. She only knew it seemed the right thing to wear.

So, she walked, learning that this city during the middle of the week was entirely vacant this time of day. The only person she had seen in the hour or so she had wandered was a man driving a small street-sweeping vehicle, and even he did not appear to be taking any notice of her. And June wondered whether any of the stories that she had read, had been written by people who had actually lived anything they wrote. For she was certain, well had been anyhow, that any inner-city street during the dark hours would certainly be filled with dangers.

Tucking her hands into her jacket pockets and strolling with a kick to her feet, June had to admit that she was more than a little disappointed, for she had seen nary a lurking fiend the whole time she had moseyed these streets. Not even a siren had blared, and everyone knew that those kicked off by the minute. In fact, when she had heard a loud clunk to her left as she passed through the centre of town, June's hair had prickled, and her faced had turned sharply to the sound. Her feet had even bounced to her toes as her knees assumed the position for a hasty escape, but all she had seen was a flashing yellow light by a roller door to the rear of a large hotel. And that door hadn't even opened. She should know because she'd waited there for a few minutes just to see. She had even pouted a small bit before her shoulder shrug set her back on her way.

No lights were shining out of shop fronts. No merry business folk were about getting an early start. There was not even a single vagrant to have to cross the street in order to avoid.

'No wonder I don't walk this early in the day.' And as she spoke these words to the empty city she had formerly thought her own, June smelt something that sunk straight into the centre of her chest and rang a big happy gong. 'Mmm,' she actually said this. And for the first time in her life, June knew what *to be led by one's nose* meant.

Her paced quickened a little, and her nose lifted to get more of that fantastic, warm, drooly smell. 'Where are you coming from?' Her toes lifting even higher with each step until June trotted—kind of like a jog. 'Ooh.' June began to swing her arms a little bit, and she bounced around the street corner.

'Oh there you are.' Literally licking her lips as her eyes landed on the red neon letters of the sign that read, 'Bakery'. And June considered just then, well she made up her mind, that *Bakery* was a part of the international language, like sex and toffee.

'I'm coming baby!' she called as she picked up her pace. For the first time, admiring those *runners* who did this so often and for so long.

By the time she arrived out front of the fully lit store, June was leaning on her thighs and looking to the sky as she caught her breath. Glancing back down the street, she was truly amazed at how close the corner was.

She was struck then, held in place with her eyes cocked. A small sound, a rhythm, finding June's ears and lifting a part of her. *A memory?* She couldn't be sure.

Standing straight, with her jaw held to one side and listening for more of that faint music, June felt her feet moving her toward the glass frontage where the light shone, and surely from where that music trickled.

Her hands on the glass looking in, June saw him working at a large bench. His dark hair netted, and his hands pounding, turning and twisting a large knot of dough. She lifted one hand to wipe away the condensation of her breath. Her

199

mind numbed by this simple sight of this man working his dough, alone in this bakery.

She didn't know how long she had been standing there. She couldn't have, for whether it be by the magic of those drums which dotted the music that vibrated the glass on which her hands pressed, or by the practiced movements of this darkly handsome man, June was out of her analytical mind. She was living in this moment in a more, um, *prehistoric zone?* Whatever it was, it was pulling on some strings. Maybe even plucking them? One thing we can be sure of is that June Bonnet's belly was entangled in that moment... by deeper yearnings. Who coulda known?

'Hey,' she said, again wiping the condensation from the glass in front of her face. 'Hey!' she called louder this time. Seeing her hands waving before her, June was then knocking before she could think better of it. 'Hey!'

The man, the solo baker, was held mid dance. The first thing he did was lift one hand, pointing his index finger to the ceiling. The next thing he did was smile.

'Oh my god.' June began wiping her palms on her jacket. 'What's wrong with me?' She began turning left and right, and really considering the option of running away as the baker bounced his way through the shop towards the front door.

'Oh hi!' she said, raising one hand as the man—younger than he had first appeared—appeared in the doorway. The small bell was sent ringing as he did. 'Hi, um, sorry to interrupt your, um, you know...' She actually went red in the face. Rarely could June not explain what she found attractive in a man, and never could she not explain what it was about one that turned her inside out... 'But this guy!' And yes, June called herself *a slut*. Chastising herself even as she did for degrading herself. But even still, she stood there with the inner thighs of her tights whooshing as they slid back and forward, trying to get a handle on this. Her own smile was spreading, and her eyes had gotten starry as she looked into this baker's huge honest smile. *I mean sure*, she thought. 'You're attractive,' this she said. 'But how?' Her head tilting sideways again. And you know what? 'Uh-har-har,' she said.

'You wanna come in?' Smiling like a boy, he stood back from the door, holding it with one hand and opening the palm of his other in a gesture of welcoming.

'So much energy.' June had no way to control what she was saying. 'And those hands,' she said, half reaching out to touch them, and hearing the guy giggle as he continued to watch her. She squinched her eyes at what she was saying but found herself still stepping in through that doorway of the *still not yet open* bakery store.

'Come, come.' He smiled. 'Welcome, welcome,' he said, leading the way through to the rear of the store.

'Well okay-y,' she said, her face going all *Wallace and Gromit*, June tip-toed, for no reason really, after the baker, winding her way through the store until she stood with a small grin and her two hands held in front of her like an audience member been brought onstage.

'Okay, okay,' he said very loudly as he dusted his hands together. His eyes focused on the flour covered bench before him. 'I am Paolo,' he said, pressing his fingers to his white t-shirt covered chest as he nodded. 'Si, si, ah your name? Please Bella?' Looking only fleetingly at her, bending, and rubbing his hands on the floured surface, laughing nervously. Or at least that's how it sounded to June.

'Uh-huh, huh.' Confused at her own response, she then said loud enough to hear her own voice crack, 'JUNE!'

201

'OKAY JUNE!' he replied in kind, and what a smile he gave her.

She lifted her hands then, half reaching. 'Oh, your eyes actually sparkle when you smile.' Withdrawing her hand before she poked him, she dropped her eyes as she stepped back, and felt them widening as they caught sight of the dense muscle of his chest.

'So okay, we make some bread, yes?' And he took one of her hands and pulled her before him, so that her back was to him. And reaching around, this Paolo took her other hand and pressed them both into the large lump of dough.

'Orp!' June was giggling before she could catch herself. 'Whoop! Har-har! Oh okay,' she said, feeling the hard muscles of his chest pressing into her back as he kneaded her hands into the dough with enough vigour to jolt her forward with each thrust. 'Uh-har!' She was really laughing now, with her lower belly pressing into the bench.

Paolo's face was close behind her ear as he said, 'Okay yes, you see?'

June wasn't exactly sure what she saw, but she sure as shit did know what she was feeling pressing into the crack of her arse from behind that white apron of his. And so, naturally, June began pressing back somewhat, extending her hands further forward with each thrust, now that she had his rhythm and everything. In fact, she'd forgotten all about the music, though it still played... somewhere to the rear of them.

'Yes, yes, very good,' he said.

She could feel his cock getting thicker, longer, harder, and the texture of the dough between her fingers, and the pure strength of his hands. The smell of the bread cooking somewhere behind them was clouding her senses, and June hardly knew that her face was turning until her tongue began protruding from between her wide-open lips, and she heard herself say, 'Awhhh.' As the next thrust pressed even harder against and kind of a little into her.

Her eyes would not shut. They appeared to be trying to, but June felt clearly that she wanted to see everything. Even as his mouth pressed against hers, her eyes were looking at the antique framed pictures on the wall.

Not sure whether she turned, or he turned her, June had her back pressed to that floured bench as Paolo devoured her mouth like one might a freshly baked panettone. 'Ew taste oh ood!' she said, and she began to slurp at his mouth. And she wondered, she did—as he got his strong hands under her arse and lifted her up onto the kneading bench—if the whole lot of him tasted like this. She would've placed a bet on it.

'Oh BELLA!' he roared, pulling his shirt off over his head and the hair net with it. He moved with such speed and strength of purpose.

Smiling like a loon, June pulled her own shirt off and helped Paolo—a little too urgently—to pull her tights down. 'AH-HAR-HAR!' she said as she felt the flour under the skin of her arse and got a glimpse of them both in the mirror mounted on the wall to the right of them.

And as he ate her pussy, June had a really tough time trying to hold onto his thick hair, and so she just resigned herself to the moment and lay back fully on that bread making bench and got her cooch devoured by the baker. 'Oh, now I get it!' she said mostly to herself as one hand went to cover her eyes and the other into her mouth to bite.

She felt two of his fingers push into her, and somehow, she could feel... 'ORHHH.' The strength of him even as he—

quite expertly—fingered her while he licked her like a kitten. And even then, she could feel his smile.

'Ahar,' he said as he picked her up from where she lay and brought her wholly to him. He began kissing her face, with his hands beneath her kneading the flesh of her bottom. Unable to stop smiling, June gripped his cock hard and jerked her hands up and down, seeing her own nipples bounce as she did. And somehow, she felt Christmassy. You know? Like when you start singing a Christmas carol in the middle of autumn... and it gets stuck in your... 'Bmm-vmmm-aufffp,' she said as she dropped her face to his cock and sucked it with more passion than her culture normally allowed or afforded. She really went to town on it. In fact, June could never remember slurping quite so much as she did on that baker's cock at just after five in the morning on that bread making bench.

She giggled some more—the open-mouthed kind with her lower lip curled up over her lower teeth—as the baker fucked her from behind and her belly slid on that floured bench back and forward as his hands held a thigh in each.

Time scattered then. I know. But it did. And June went to the *moon* in that early hour. She really did. Paolo and she danced all over that doughy table, and more than once she pulled faces that caused her to look more, well, you know. He fucked her, and she fucked him. Without a care in the world, they fucked. And though it was completely—I mean obviously—outside of the normally upheld health and safety standards—wink—of any established bakery of any standing, June had to admit that she had never been fucked with quite as much care and practiced passion as she was fucked by that bread maker that predawn morn.

And... he had the flair to offer her a tea towel to wipe herself down with, post bread bench coitus, as he did the same.

As she eased down off the bakery bench, June laughed and said, 'Oh my legs.' When they shook under her weight.

'Si, si,' he said, still smiling that big open smile. Paolo held both hands in front of him, indicating her leg's wobble. 'You okay?'

'Si, si,' she said, and they both laughed as they got their flour covered clothes back on.

When she looked at the clock, June couldn't believe that it was still only 5:23am. 'Well,' she said, inching around the corner and holding on somewhat as she did... a picture of Danny's face filled that big movie screen in her mind.

'You, okay?' Sincerely concerned, Paolo was by her side, gently holding her up. His expression pained as he said, 'I think I was maybe too hard on you?' Thrusting his hips back and forward, apparently in case she hadn't got his meaning.

His attentions were enough to give her the opportunity to disengage the image before she could let any thoughts attach and surely pull her under.

She kissed him then, sweetly. June kissed that baker like she loved him.

When they broke, and with his eyes a little misty, he said, 'Hey, wait one second.' And he bounded off into the back of the store.

June wondered whether to ask to use the bathroom, but in truth she wanted to get out of there before any people started moving around.

'Here, please.' Smiling, he handed her a parcel wrapped in white paper.

Opening the top of it, dipping her head and drawing in the sweet warm smell, June's face caught in a frown. 'Is it?' she said, one finger pointing at the parcel of buns.

'Si, si.' Leaning against the counter as if they were old friends, he shrugged and said, 'Good Friday.' Smiling, he began winging an elbow. 'A very good Friday for me anyhow hey?'

She left then, carrying her parcel of fresh hot-crossed buns.

Walking from that store with the sound of the little bell ringing as she did, June tore off a piece of sweet bun and stuck it in her mouth. She smiled in return of Paolo's infectious one and returned a wave while pointing down at the buns while rubbing a circle over her tummy before she walked out of view.

Too herself, again walking that path, still before the light had fully risen, June wondered what her mother might say if she knew what she'd just done on *this* day. And she dug into that parcel in her hands and pulled out a large chunk of a hot crossed bun and stuffed it into her mouth, feeling less about herself somehow as she did. But still, she did.

She was sitting by a small fountain in a little gardened square in the full morning sun opposite a large bronze statue of a soldier on a horse when she finished those buns. There had been thirteen of them. She smiled as she burped while looking into the water at the base of that fountain by which she sat, and she saw that her belly looked perfectly round. Believing it had to be a trick of the light on the water, without a thought, June pulled a pouting face into that reflection and rubbed her hand over her belly.

Something cracked inside June then. Like a piece of hard candy.

'Oh, you eat too much!' said a total stranger, a portly Asian man no less, pointing at her as he laughed and continued on his way. He was swallowed by the moving crowds in a blink. 'You?' Holding up her fist at what was now a lost battle, June slid off the edge of that fountain, squinting her eyes and looking into the distance above that passing crowd. She said to no-one at all, 'I think I'll have another dozen more!' And she marched off to find just that.

Chapter Twenty-Three

Aunt Joan

It was the sound of her spoon against her teacup. She felt it in her teeth. It caught the shaft of lemon light that cut through the high windows to the right of the room, causing June's eyes to drop to the lace of the tablecloth between them.

June's mind made to drift, and maybe it did.

'Are you still with us my dear?' Aunt Joan carefully placed her teacup back on the saucer before her. Her smile, one not easily explained.

'I like this place.' June tried on a smile of her own, but her lips weren't having any part of it. Her eyes were feeling tired in their sockets, like someone's thumbs rested atop them. They drifted around the tearoom at the other people who sat at their tables. People who spoke in tones suggestive of such a fine restaurant. She turned her head, leaning forward with her neck and her shoulders tilting in the same way, and June caught the eye of a dark-haired waitress looking at her in the far left of her peripheries.

'Hmm.' Aunt Joan's fingers knitted under her chin. Her blinking lashes showing eyes not stung by the years she had spent being *Aunt Joan*.

She thumped herself back in her chair. Her posture, unfamiliar in this room, seeming to draw eyes from unseen glancers. Slowly, June drew herself back upright into a *proper* position. The room around her grew like it took a sudden deep breath. June reached out and took a biscuit from the plate that sat between herself and her aunt. She lifted her chin somewhat, and she felt the dimples at the corners of her lips indent as she inspected the pink sugary icing on the top of it with the very tip of her middle finger. She placed that finger between her lips as her eyes lifted to those of that waitress as she passed their table. The contact kept and held as she walked behind Aunt Joan. She watched as this service girl took a breath through her only slightly curling smile, and she very nearly smiled herself before her eyes fell to Joan's. Watching her aunt's thin lips purse and her eyes widen somewhat.

Joan's nose did a little scrunching thing as she lifted her teacup. While sipping, she spoke over its lip, 'No lifts in *here* love.'

June coughed out little bits of the biscuit's icing across the table. Feeling her cheeks redden, she saw the waitress smile more fully as she held her small pad up to take a new order from a table of four to June's front right. She made to wipe up the fragments of icing from the tablecloth, but quickly found that she was achieving nothing but finger-painting. Her eyes tried to be hard on her aunt then as she crunched the remainder of her biscuit and wiped her hands on a cloth napkin. But maybe it was the light in Joan's eyes that prevented this charade. June was unable to do anything but smile fully as she cleared her throat and said, 'Yes, well.' And she felt good in her knowing that she loved these conversations with her aunt.

June sipped her tea and felt another elevator, one deep within her, beginning to lose its grip. Its cables beginning to slacken, threatening a fall. Maybe it was because she was *his* sister. Maybe it was this that made her feel so comfortable with her, this connection to her father.

'Don't be so hard on yourself.'

June nodded and looked out through the large framed windows to the garden outside. The table under her forearms shifting a little as her aunt readjusted herself, getting her elbows up on that fine tablecloth.

'Look at me please June,' she said, her voice a little aching, tender, strong.

She did.

'You are so very beautiful, June.' Looking down at the tabletop and then back. 'You know that.' Joan dipped her head and smiling, she said, 'And you have that light in your eyes. The same one he did.' Aunt Joan lifted her cup and put it back down a little too hard. The sound, disturbing the room but garnishing no glances. And she dropped the manners that held her expression's composure. 'But I don't think *you* know *that.*'

Looking to the garden again with her tongue pressing her right rear upper teeth, her head swung back swiftly. Her own expression pinched. 'How did he end up with *her*?' She gave a huff of air, and sitting up straighter, June said, 'I mean...? Urgh. How?'

She laughed then. Aunt Joan laughed without a care.

June watched her, unable to prevent herself from catching this outburst. And she was clear why she loved this woman, her father's sister who sat across from her at this table having tea and showing the simple uncommon strength in her ability not to care on what other's may think of her honest feelings.

The world around them now became somehow lighter, and yet somehow not.

'Oh June.' Joan's own tongue was now pressing upper teeth. Her eyes, so bright with the fire of her own intelligence. 'Really?' Her laugh was almost cruel. Her frown, and the crispness of her eyes as they looked right into June, expecting more, leant a weight. 'You know your mother wasn't always... well... so buttoned up.' And she and June both laughed hard at this. Though both felt a sadness with it. 'I remember she used to play with me.'

The clock could be heard as it ticked the next few moments.

Nodding, sipping her tea, placing her cup back down and reaching for the pot for a refill. As she did, Joan said, 'I would have thought by now June, that you knew.' An air about her, like a queen. Not only did she carry a seniority, but one that she had apparently decided to share with her much younger niece. As though they now both ran the inside line of the track.

June's lower lip pressed up, and she felt her head give a small quick shake. And she felt a little ice give, somewhere inside of her. Not a glacier, no, but some. And it was as though that very sheet of ice had hidden, no, totally obscured a thing she had not wanted to see. And yet she still couldn't make it out. And she did try. She felt that awesome frustration, anyone can feel it, but June felt it there having tea with Aunt Joan. That frustrating knowing that one was... almost able to see something. A truth, yes, that they very much needed to see.

Joan was circling her finger, slowly bobbing her head, very slowly, with her eyes wide on June's. Smiling, steady, she said, 'You can do it.'

June snatched another biscuit, and with her vision grabbing, her eyes picked up only fractured frames from around the room. That waitress again. Well, the shape of her arse just beneath where her apron tied. But it was her. June felt frustrated. 'Awrgh,' she moaned much like a womanising cad, around a really special little vanilla shortbread.

Joan looked at her while her lips pressed against her folded hands.

June felt like the room became a painting, an abstract one. 'Why can't I...?' she said, again spitting crumbs quite a ways. 'Aw fuh moi!' And immediately beginning to try again to clean this up.

'No. Really June just leave it.' Chuckling, smiling, loving her. 'You're really something,' Joan said as she reached across the table, with her bosom tilting her side-plate as she did, and she grabbed June's hand.

June halted with her mouth still open and those crumbs still dropping. At first trying to release her hand in an attempt to catch those crumbs, finally she looked into her Aunt Joan's wet eyes, and she began to cry.

And although June Bonnet had thought that she had run them dry, that her ducts had shrunken, maybe wizened, tears ran in streams down her lifted cheeks.

The waitress was there then. The one June had eyed and been eyed by. And she, plucking several tissues from the square box she held in her hand, began to dab gently, and yet with some hurry, at those rivers that ran from June's eyes. 'Oh,' was all she said... over and over.

213

Raising her own gushing eyes with her hand still linked with Joan's, and with her mouth still open and full of sweet biscuit, wet and dry, looking into the near face of this girl who sought to aid her in her emotional release, June said, 'Ow yergh oh pitty.' Spraying the girl's face with a very small handful of crumbs before sobbing harder, now only sinking deeper into her feelings of self-disgust.

And yet the waitress only tried all the harder to dry her tears. June felt the grip on her hand across the table tighten briefly. 'Oh, just leave the box!' Aunt Joan's voice cutting through the melee. Straightening, seeing the waitress had gotten the word, and after several more very quick dabs, that she had sideways quickstepped from the table. She said, *almost* under her breath, 'And get yourself a mop while you're at it.' And she lifted her tea to her mouth with her free hand, with her other still held tight, for she wasn't going to lose June just yet.

Swallowing the mess of biscuit in her mouth, her tears having seemingly ceased like a tropical rain, June sat there clearing her eyes with a bunch of blinks and a few steady breaths. Making to let go of her aunt's hand, she said, 'It's alright now Aunt Joan.'

But Joan held her fingers tight, and with a voice dry like an open field, she said, 'Oh no it is not.' And then she leant forward with her free elbow on the table, and pointing her finger straight at June, she said, 'It is absolutely not okay.' And then she released her hand before she straightened the sides of her dress, looking down at herself as she did. 'You're a fucking mess June, and I'm not too proud to say it.' Her eyes looking into June's with such love, she said, 'And I couldn't be more proud of you for the doing of it.' Her eyes began earnestly leaking that honest juice. 'My god

214

if you only knew.' She shook her head slowly from side to side. 'If you only knew how few dare to do just that.'

And then June watched the most previously unbelievable thing happen. As she sat there taking a big gulp of her tea in this fine restaurant, at this pretty table spread now with the pre-chewed crumbs of her own selection of biscuits, June watched her Aunt Joan delicately lift her fingers to her teeth... and remove a pubic hair.

She choked on a portion of that gulp of tea then. The resultant cough forcing the tea out of her face. Some came out through her nostrils, and the rest from her uncontained mouth. And from there it flew out, not in an arc, but in an ungodly spray, much like that of a cat, a large one, marking its territory. Much of it, covering Aunt Joan.

And as she sat there with her face hanging forward on her neck, and with her mouth still open, looking at her aunt who apparently was unmoved by this outburst, June heard before she felt it, the long deep burp that came out of her own, still tea dribbling, mouth.

They lost their shit then, June Bonnet and Aunt Joan. With all the world to see. They totally lost their shit.

Amidst their laughter, as those diners around them responded in their own ways, Aunt Joan paused. Lifting something from her face and looking upon it, she said, 'Oh, it's a piece of biscuit.' And they laughed some more as she wiped it on her napkin.

Now one might believe that two ladies, after such an occurrence, might, and some may suggest *appropriately*, retire from their tea party and clean themselves up. But Aunt Joan, waving away the head-shaking staff, breathed evenly. She clasped her hands together before her, and looking into June's scraped eyes, she said, 'Do you still not see June?'

Looking at her hands for a short moment and then back to June's eyes. 'That when Christian, your sweet, sweet father...' She paused, looking down again, bitten. 'When he passed away...' Looking back to June's eyes and really pressing in. 'A part, a very large part of who Jan was...' Her eyes drifting for a moment. 'The woman your father fell in love with. That woman who quite honestly brought out the very best in that dear man who loved you more than all of life itself. Yes. She did. He was a very complicated man. Of course you don't think you know this. No matter the woman you know yourself to be. But he was. And he could be crazy like a loon, loveable like a cheeky boy, and... a *man* all at once. And yet he had lived a brutality that of course you could never have known.' She stopped then and let time takes its stroll.

June watched her Aunt Joan look out through those large windows, and she saw, actually saw her drift into her memories of long ago.

When her eyes returned, they were clearer, more set. 'Now we can speak about some of those things at another time June.' Nodding her head. 'We can, and I'm sure we probably must.' Taking her hand again, with her eyes imploring June, and her voice shaking, she said, 'But surely,' frowning, quizzical, 'surely now, this far into your own life? Surely by now you must know that the picture of who we are, who we really are, *the all of it,* from then to now and what we will be... You must know that all of that cannot be truly held by the perspective that you had of him... and her... from when you were just a child.'

June felt much more of that ice inside, shed, and she felt her cheeks redden.

'No, you're not to take it that I'm saying that as though it should be lost. No. No my dear child. Absolutely not. And I am in no way saying that that picture...' Holding her hands to her own chest. Sincere, she went on, 'That *was* Christian. The best of him.' She was trying to clear her eyes. 'But surely by now you understand June that that was not, could not have been, all of who he was? Nor your mother. By God June your mum was truly someone to behold. I mean we had our differences at times, and I'm still not sure that I was altogether right in my ways when I held those opinions...' Shaking her head as she was caught in her necessary reverie. 'What I mean to say June is that surely you know that your dad chose her because she was... someone special. Absolutely unique.' Pressing her lips together, she said, 'Oh, you still don't get it do you, you poor dear.' Frowning and leaning in again, but this time with both hands. Plates and cutlery, cups and saucers spread as Aunt Joan took June's hands in hers and said, 'When he died, when your Daddy died June, a part of her, a big part of your mum June...' Not wanting it to sound like... and well deciding there was no other way, 'A part of your Mum died too. You must know this...'

A glass somewhere in the restaurant smashed on a hard floor.

'Taxi!' someone said.

Chapter Twenty-Four

Apple Sauce

They fit like new. And true, they were new. But still.
The concrete beneath her growled as she spun her
wheels. The cool air pushed between her thighs and
aerodymed around the thin fabric of her cotton undies that
held tight to the working curves of her glutes. Her white
tennis skirt, she'd thrown her racket, brushed against her
upper thighs. And under her green visor, June smiled like a
girl who had forgotten that fairy-floss was not indeed made
by fairies!

Even as she swung her arms with her elbows lifting high and
her palms making stop signs, albeit brief ones, June's eyes
behind her amber shades were alight at the pure sense of the
freedom she felt, right now, at the long-forgotten joy—and
seriously how could one forget?—at skating on a pair of
high white roller skates!

And it appeared to be contagious, at least to her, this sense
of childhood abandonment of the mundane. She was... 'On
fire!' calling this as she passed a 24hr convenience store.

'That bitch ain't on fire!' a pedestrian thought to offer their companion.

But negativity couldn't stick to her right now. Nope. June was twelve again. She was... 'Skatin!' And doing so with such aplomb and almost graceful finesse that not nearly all of the other people *sharing* this city footpath had to make drastic changes to their own course of travel in order to avoid her.

'Skatin!' she called. The rumble-growl of her red wheels click-clacking as she crossed over each line in that path. The small jiggle of that energy shaking all the way up through her, making her giggle. Her feet going awfully wide for her to keep her balance. Her stop signs becoming more like downward pats, and June knew she was probably not making any land speed records. But still... 'I'm skatin!'

'Yeah, you skatin alright,' another fellow footpath traveller confirmed, unseen.

June was picking up speed. Well, that's not true, but she believed she was picking up speed because the number of pedestrians had grown dramatically as she neared the intersection where she would need to... Yeah but that's the thing really isn't it?

'Awrp! Arp!' June said. And then she cried, 'Comin through!' And you know what? She got it then. In a flash-card of washed-out images slapping at the walls of her inner mind, June knew, remembered actually, that she didn't know how to stop... never had.

And so, as she bustled, not gently, through the small loose mass of pedestrians waiting to cross at those intersection lights, June saw more images roll through her mind. The colours like those from a magazine—*funny*—displaying her POV, and showing clearly, her only ever stopping on her skates... by crashing into stuff.

A bummer, no doubt, when one finds oneself shooting, well drifting and rolling, out into inner city traffic at ten o'clock on a Wednesday morning.

And true, June's smile did bend a little. It did. But then, you know what? June had a revelation! As a van stopped dead... 'Thank you Jesus!' came a call from one of those watching from one side of the street under a still lighted picture of a little red man, not walking. And as that van stopped dead, and another two cars, one a taxi, avoided colliding with each other, June realised, accompanied by a feeling that can only be described as a cold raw egg being cracked on her head, that... 'This is why we naturally perform stop signs...' smiling broadly again, stop signing, as she rolled across that street quite slowly, 'when we skate!'

'Something's wrong with that lady!' a child with no sense of appropriate volume levels when criticising another person, said.

'Make way!' Smiling like there certainly was something wrong with her, June called, 'Non compos mentis!' And you've probably guessed; not at all comprehending the actual meaning of these words as she called them out with a sense of true victory. Like she actually thought, in that moment, that this was something that Russell Crowe had called out to the *emperor* during *that* movie.

But still, people did scoot, and June rolled through them... much slower than she supposed.

In fact, it was not until a little while later as she turned a corner, a left so she wouldn't have to cross another street, that June became aware that more than a little of her impression of speedy travel was down to the fact that she had been travelling upwind. And the truth is that June began to feel her wide smile beginning to slide. So of course, she put more into it.

Now smiling again, back in the swing of it, though now connecting the time spaces between the click-clacking with the speed of her progress, June felt a small part of her dream, well not *her whole dream*, but still... she felt it die.

'No lady!' came a sharp happy voice popping up beside her.

'Awrp!' June's arms flailing, and her eyes only getting grabs of sight in any one direction as she fought to keep her balance. Though enough to see that a little boy was running beside her.

He said, 'You gotta lean into it!' Yelling for only reasons he knew. His arms and legs now running with exaggerated extension as he leaned into it, demonstrating.

June's open smile returned. Leaning forward and watching the wee man run up before her, June could see that in fact the little guy was right. 'Whoop!' June said, keeping her eyes locked on the little boy's form as he ran ahead of her. His black and red striped shirt bouncing. His little left hand holding a partially eaten apple out to his side. And a part of her, a real part, an entirely undeluded part of June Bonnet feared for her little helper's safety. 'Where's your Mum?' But either he didn't hear her, or he had decided that it was of no consequence. Because his pace only increased. And so too did June's.

They were nearing the end of the block, covering this distance much faster with her new technique. And June wasn't wearing her smile anymore. The skin around her hairline was beginning to prickle, and though she was still feeling somewhat exhilarated by *skatin*, she felt no urge to call it out anymore. In fact, the newfound ability to increase her speed was now only in her need to catch up to this child who ran headlong before her.

'Wait!' she called. 'Hey!' Hearing the desperation in her own voice as the boy, some thirty feet ahead of her, was closing in on the next intersection. 'HEY!'

June no longer felt like she was having fun. She no longer felt the freedom in wearing her tennis skirt while roller skating through this city she now recognised no more than she did any other anywhere. 'Wait!' Her air, she heard, signalled a kind of defeat as she stopped pumping her legs. Seeing that now there was no way that she could make it in time. Her eyes lifting, watching like a passenger as the large buses... and there were three all entering that intersection at the same time. And June realised how very loud it was. Just then in that moment, June heard the city like earbuds had been plucked from her ears. Her heart was quickening, slowing time, but only by half. And as the little boy was three headlong steps from that street, June felt herself begin to cry, and her hands lifted up to cover her mouth. Rolling on these... 'Stupid Skates!' Unable to take her eyes off... 'AUGH!' almost a squeal as she watched the little boy, not more than six or seven years old, dart to the left, avoiding the intersection. He was turning in a small circle as he hopped and waved at her. 'You little...' But smiling now, with her tears still running, June leant into it again and took that same left-hand turn crossing one leg over the other. 'MOVE IT!' Watching with some satisfaction as her words had the desired effect. Clipping a man's briefcase with her shoulder as she hooked the bend.

She was moving fast with still no knowledge of how to slow. Only now getting herself up to a more vertical position as her legs and arms adapted to her new commands, June watched the boy, still swinging the apple in one hand, laughing as he ran up two large flights of concrete stairs leading up to a large church.

Her mind calculating the odds of her making her way up those stairs, June found herself on the concrete ramp before she had consciously chosen to do so. 'Werrr!' she said, really having had no idea how this would feel. Knowing that she was already committed, June again leant into it, and she was at the top of that ramp and turning in through the main doors of the church, after the boy, before she could know why.

And, with the little scamp now running, hopping more like, backwards down the centre aisle of this very large church with his apple still in one hand, and clearly having fun and waving her on, June stopped moving. She stopped pumping anything. She just stood straight and rolled down the aisle with her features frozen and a trickle of sweat running down between her breasts. Certain that a corner of her skirt was caught up under her undies, June was fixed. Her eyes focused on the large Jesus Christ hanging from the cross directly in front of her. And she had the odd experience of floating. Well, not so odd.

She heard the gasps before the murmurs. She smelt the ladies before she saw them. And without even turning her face more than thirty degrees, June's chest caught as she recognised one of them. 'Mum?' she spoke this word flatly as she rolled down the centre isle of that church. And she saw her mother's eyes, in just a moment, as they touched on hers... and then turned away.

You know? She wanted to stop right then. June wanted to stop in the centre of that large church, in front of anyone who cared to watch, anyone who cared to judge... and just scream!

But she didn't stop. Well, she couldn't really. Not without grasping the pews, and even in her state of deeply bitten shame and rage, June still did not want to be *that* person. And so, she just rolled right on past with her heart cracking into pieces she could not have expected it would. And in that moment, nearing the image of the crucified Lord, and the organ, June felt a small child inside of her chest lay down and hope to die.

'This way!' the boy called.

And without any fuss, June angled her toes and rolled right on past the Lord with her weeping eyes held right on his, and she made her way in the direction that the small child led her.

'Excuse me!' a priest was saying as June rolled past an open doorway.

'You're excused,' she said, her voice deadpan, flat, empty. She rolled right on past and out under the sign marked *Exit*.

The boy, taking a bite from his apple as he hopped backwards, turned and swung his arm over as he did, once again begging she follow.

Her voice so small, she said, 'Where's your mother?' June skated now without thought, following the child around another corner, along a garden path and through a large iron gate.

June knew the layout of this city. That at least still remained. But she hadn't considered the geography whilst on skates. One might forgive her this oversight. But nevertheless, with momentum, and gravity too, being what it was, when June became aware of the hill... well she was already on it.

225

It's an easy thing to say in hindsight, or for those with a little more experience in such matters, what one should have done. One might suggest for instance that June simply lay herself down, or edge to her left and slow herself on the grass and take a knee at the appropriate time. But of course, any experienced person knows that in such moments, whilst engaging in such a new predicament, well one often doesn't think in such terms.

So, June was barrelling, very much so, headlong down a surprisingly steep hill, leant fully forward until her chest almost pressed to her knees. Not at all thinking, in this effort to stay on her skated feet, that she was only increasing her speed. Not at least until June felt her tears running from the corners of her eyes.

She hardly noticed the boy as he ran up the grassy rise to the left of that path. Resigned to this charade, her body gripped tightly in its attempt to preserve itself. Wobbling with the ever-increasing speed, June didn't see that the boy had dropped his apple. She didn't see that it rolled down that grassy knoll. In fact, the first she saw of it was the moment it lay directly before her left skate.

June tried to avoid it. Well, her left foot rose a bit. Just enough to gather that apple under her. For, in fear of totally losing her balance with most of her weight on her right shaking skate, June returned the balance of her weight and felt the first bite of that red apple in the wheels of her high white skate.

The effect was rapid, truly. The pull of her left leg back behind her, and the turn of her body, the juddering of her right skate, now turned sideways, and downhill on that path, her knees bending to a dancer's pose, and with her cotton undies covered arse poking out for the world to see... June watched with her eyes focused intently on that too slowly running reel as the small boy's red apple exploded, pulled into and crushed by the turn of her wheels... And June said, even as the nerves of her bare right leg signalled the imminent and awful pain she would most certainly incur... she said, 'Apple sauce!' And she laughed.

An instant, and we don't use this term loosely, after she spoke those words and heard the first crack of her own laughter, June's right sideways angled and hopping skate caught the lower end of that footpath, a lip of concrete no more than half an inch high... and June Bonnet became airborne.

She didn't know this at first. Not entirely. Time still having slowed and, well, herself not truly caring too much. It was quite a spectacle, quite a wonder to see one's own legs above oneself. And you know? June thought she felt a heart moment then. A true and real connection to those astronauts, whether real or pretend, as they moved about weightless in space or floated in a Houston swimming pool. And she considered, as the still morning's light lit on those spinning red wheels above her and her high white skates... how she didn't envy men this one thing. And that was a fact. That they would never know the real freedom of wearing a tennis skirt, and the simple pleasure of a morning's breeze against the damp cotton of one's knickers.

The impact was brutal.

As much in temperature as in the substantial whack she encountered on entry. For there was another, and now of course it appeared key, aspect of this city's geography of which June had undervalued the importance of, and for the obvious and aforementioned reasons.

The river.

Oh, sure it was a mercy of a kind. No doubt.

But?

When in Rome, one might be advised not to be wearing old-school roller skates.

The air in her locked as the cold water gripped her, and June found herself in very real danger. And she fought the near debilitating urge to draw in air. For of course there was none. And though she fought to get her face above the water line, let's be real, June had not known that she would be in this water until she was in it.

As her kicking feet fought to give her some lift, the weight of those skates was doing nothing but pulling her under.

It wasn't until she noticed that she was ladder-climbing, that June knew she was drowning.

And as the importance of things narrowed to a pinhole of focus, June was aware of nothing but... sadness. Not an exciting word. But there you have it.

Now two things occurred unbeknownst to June as she climbed her imaginary ladder in the cold waters of that city's river. The first, was that her mother was stepping into a car parked to the rear of that grand church. A car that belonged to one of those ladies who comforted her in her shame. The second, was that the priest who had called out to her as she had rolled on by his office had followed her out through that church side-exit, and on seeing the potential for what could likely occur, he had run after her down that steep hill.

If June had known these two things, she would have only been surprised by one of them.

But of course, she wasn't. For in her current predicament, June was entirely consumed with climbing that unscalable ladder. This and the haunting knowledge, a bubble of fact that had deemed itself worthy of popping up through her waning consciousness—*It takes five minutes to drown.* And even in her desperate state, June considered this piece of information, well, a little less comforting than it might first appear. For time stretched when one struggled against such a heartless foe. And June knew that she was struggling against physics. An opponent, most reluctant to change its rules.

Now surely, June would know that merely untying those weighty skates would unburden her and allow her to rise to that precious air that waited so patiently at that river's surface, only inches above her still struggling form. But I believe it prudent that we weigh in here and say simply, 'Walk a mile brothers and sisters.' And if that won't suffice, then, 'Try it.'

June saw her fingertips then, so white and still.

She saw them rising above her. That sun's light letting her know that the surface lay so close above her. And although she felt her aperture on this life retracting, she was afraid. June Bonnet feared, in that moment, one thing above all else... *That she would Never know... what it would be like... to hold...* Its grip was so strong that her mouth fished open. Her eyes locking wider... as death... for surely this was what it was... was snatching her away.

Her last thought was, *How smooth your hands are...*

The pain was like an elephant sitting on her chest.

So tight!

Her eyes snapped open in time for her to see water spouting out of her mouth before it landed back upon her face. And beyond that, the terrified face of the man she had only glimpsed as she had passed him in that church... *All those years ago.*

'Come on!' he yelled.

'UUU-UUUGH!' The air, burning as she struggled to get his weight off her enough to turn, as she fought the choking cough while desperately attempting to avoid inhaling the spittles of water that had just been expelled from her lungs.

'BREATHE!' the priest implored, taking June's face in both hands. His tears dropping to her face.

'I'm fucking trying to!' Slapping at his hands and bucking to get him off her.

Standing and calling out to the Lord, he called, 'Thank you Lord! Thank you!'

Getting her breath, on that path by the river, and seeing that her skates were still tied nice and tight, June was exhausted. Too exhausted to speak any more, and so she lay back on that muddy grass.

The priest was behind her then, lifting her shoulders and shuffling himself into a seated position so as to cradle her between his legs. Apparently considering that her protests, being so weak, were her attempts to take hold of him for comfort. And so he held her tighter and stroked at her hair.

'Oh whatever.' June lifted a single nostril and felt that it could be worse.

'Thank you, Lord, for delivering unto us this harlot!'

'Hey, wait a fucking minute!' Looking down at herself and seeing her risen tennis skirt and her white cotton undies soaked through. Her vagina was in no way, not a little bit, obscured—very little bush. 'I'm not a fucking harlot!' Her hands unable to press her skirt back down as she was rocked by this guy of God, June kinda, well, zoned out as he hushed her and stroked her hair. Thinking to herself—*If there's no wood? It's all good.*

'He-he-he,' came the familiar voice.

Regaining her focus, June saw that the little boy in the red and black striped shirt was standing before them, pointing at her vagina.

And before she could get in front of it, she said, 'At least I can't smell it.'

'Can't catch me!' He smiled as though nothing in the world at all had happened.

June was on her feet with the strength of the recently near deceased and shrugging off the attempts of the priest to contain her, *for her own good,* and getting her skates underneath her again. And pointing at the little smiling boy, she said, 'Right!' And June took off down that riverside path...   after   the   giggling   child.

Chapter Twenty-Five

Pick-up-sticks

Shaking off her umbrella, June lay it down amongst all the others outside the church doors. She looked out at the high grey sky and wondered if those drops that fell might just be a mirror to her unspilled tears.

She could feel those tears laying just under her jaw. Their sourness in contrast to the sweet smell of the rain that painted all she could see. And June felt the weight of all she had carried, all she had dragged with her, for all the years of her life.

Looking down at her flat soled shoes, in no hurry to enter these same doors she had rolled through only nine short days ago, June felt an irony, but she was unable to distinguish if that's what it truly was. Her mind's anchors were floating. She could get no purchase, no grasp.

Pulling a pack of cigarettes and a silver lighter from the jacket pocket of her black pantsuit, June moved to the far-left side of the building's concrete overhang and lit a smoke. With her right hand in her pants pocket, she scuffed one foot at the concrete floor and blew out some smoke in a narrow stream. She stood there hating the way her eyes wouldn't stop stinging, the way her lips wouldn't hold their form, and she looked out over the trees of that garden with the memory of herself rolling through that same space just days ago like a snapshot of another life, another age.

'There's no smoking here,' said the stern female voice.

Looking up at the woman responsible for this chastisement, June only nodded and turned her back, continuing to smoke. Trying to breath out more than only the smoke, June lifted her hand and wiped away a strand of hair from her brow with the tip of her ring finger, and she felt the small shake in her hand.

'Why?' June said, taking another drag. Knowing the futility of such a question, knowing that she was invulnerable to its need to be asked, she shook her head, trying to be someone much more together, someone who bore such things in their stride.

'Hey kiddo.' Behind her.

June smiled a kind of smile as her Aunt Joan stepped up beside her.

Joan uncrossed her arms and placed one hand on June's shoulder before letting it fall. 'Give me one of those.' Joan stood with her feet wide. Taking the cigarette June handed her with the lighter, this woman of a different age bent her head and lit her smoke. She breathed out the first plume around the cigarette she held between her lips and shook her head as she looked up into that raining sky.

'Did you know?' June's voice sounded small even to her.

Turning on her, her concern real, Joan said, 'No.' Her frowning eyes looking straight into June's, from under her forward tilted brow. She took June by her shoulders. 'No.

No June. I had no clue.' She stood there, pressing her lips together. 'Not until I got the call from the hospital.' Releasing June's shoulders, she turned back out to face that sky, taking a drag of her cigarette. Blowing it out with her feet again planted wide like a factory worker, she said, 'I don't think she told anyone.' She stood that way, looking down at the ground, knowing that Janice hadn't wanted to see June, even as she lay dying in that hospital bed.

'Why?' Taking the last drag from her cigarette, June pulled another from the pack. She lit it, drawing on it to give her something to do. Blowing out that smoke, her voice not holding, she said, 'Why wouldn't she see me?' But she had a clue. Of course she did.

'Don't do this to yourself June.' But her voice cracked as she said these words.

Another voice from behind them, male, said, 'The service is about to begin. And please ladies... there's no smoking on the grounds.'

'Uh-huh.' Aunt Joan turned back to her smoke, taking a big drag between two fingers before throwing it out onto the lawn. 'Come on Kid, we'd better go and get this done.' She placed her arm around June's shoulders, turning her, stopping as June dropped her smoke and pressed it out under her shoe, and they walked to the doors just as the organ music began to play.

June stopped at the doors. 'I don't want to do this.' And she meant it.

'Who does baby-doll? Who does?' And Joan, with her hand now around June's waist, walked her over the threshold.

The sound of the organ music was much louder the moment they were inside. June lifted her eyes to the high ceiling. She even took a moment to wonder how they might have considered the acoustics when they designed this place. Anything to avoid facing the crowd that were now seating themselves on the pews to either side of them.

Leaning into June and speaking softly, but with a steel in her voice, Joan said, 'You ignore them. They're only here for themselves.'

But June couldn't ignore them. Their eyes were all looking to her, looking at her as her Aunt Joan walked her down the aisle. And she felt like she was just a child again. Like she was...

'What are you looking at?' Joan's voice too, benefiting from the church's acoustics. 'Eyes front.'

June could feel her aunt shaking with her anger. And she loved her for it.

'You too Gerald.' Joan thrust her pointed hand to the front of the church. Then softer now but not much, to herself she said, 'Amazing you don't catch on fire just sitting there you old pervert.'

June felt a lift in her heart just then, and she squeezed Aunt Joan's hand tight, feeling it returned immediately. She felt her own lips curl as she watched her aunt's mouth set a small knowing smile as she led her to the front pew of her mother's funeral.

June sat, feeling no strength in her bones. The seat beneath her was hard, the room cold. The priest standing at the pulpit waiting for his moment. All about her, hushed voices. A whispered chorus of foul rumour. Some of it true.

June's eyes locked onto the casket. 'So small,' she said softly, without knowing. Her Aunt's hand again squeezing hers and placing a tissue there with her other hand. But it was Joan who wept.

The priest cleared his throat. June looked up with the eyes of a child and saw him looking at her. But her mind was full of air, and she did not know how to read his expression. She did not know how to feel. She did not know how to think. June only knew that her face was hot, and that she didn't want to be here, and that yet she must be.

The service began.

But the sounds were only that. June was unable to make out the words. The priest's voice, practiced in such things, was only a drone to June's ears. She could not bring herself to focus on anything else but that box in front of her. The one that held her mother's body.

Time rolled, the air in the room growing denser as the minutes passed by. All things heightened, lessened, narrowed and expanded without any of the usual boundaries of physics seemingly able to apply. And June felt that pressure growing from inside of her. She felt it; the small scream that grew from a corner of her inner world. She felt it bend her internal light until it became the first peep of sound, already desperate in its need to be voiced. She felt it grow and spiral like a torsion fracture breaking the glaze of her emotional walls... as though they were made of ceramic.

She did not know that she was shaking. She did not know that Aunt Joan held her as tightly as she was able. She did not know that many in that room had fixed their eyes on her. She did not know... that she was coming apart.

She did not know that she made any sound... as she felt a whole shelf of glassware, the kind one stores and treasures so that they can add it to their own home when they're grown... like a glory box lain out for display... she felt that shelf give way and all those precious gifts fall to her heart's floor... and smash to pieces.

She did not know that she was standing, or that the priest had changed his tone. She did not know that he was afraid as she stepped from her designated seat. She did not hear the squeak in his voice as he lost command of the show. She did not feel the floor beneath her feet as she moved towards that closed box that held the body of her mother who would not let her say goodbye.

She could not know whether the keening sound came from her own open lips or whether from the combined distress of some of those members of this funereal congregation. But still, June moved toward that casket. And moving as though driven by another hand, June lifted both of hers to the edge of the lid of that godawful box and felt the muscles of her arms contract as she began to push against it.

It snapped then, the rubber band that held her within her own inner world. It snapped and in rushed all the air, and the noise with it that filled this house of the promised Lord.

June's eyes squinted almost shut from the impact of it. Her right peripheries caught the movements, as well the tortured expression of that priest as he came rushing towards her. The very same man who had pulled her from the river's cold waters before she could die.

His voice was loud, high, and filled with the same righteous indignation that hounded from those others in this hallowed room who felt compelled to voice their protests at her actions.

With her head bent forward towards the still open lid of the casket in her hands, feeling that she must surely be driven into it herself from the impact of this wrath that was aimed truly at her...

'LEAVE HER BEEEE!' The voice so loud, so deep, so full of command that it closed off those other sounds in this room as though it had slammed shut a great and heavy book. A voice surely, like God himself.

Frozen in place with her left eye catching the so pale skin of her mother's cheek, slowly June turned in the direction of that awesome voice, expecting to see a man-mountain with a flowing beard of white, expecting the visage of Michelangelo's creation having stepped into this room. June's eyes drew her fully, and she saw not a mountain, but a man not taller than herself. An elderly man dressed in a black priestly uniform. His hair swept back and neat. His eyes among the oldest she had seen. His skin unable to contain an authority he carried. And he stood there some metres from where she held the lid of her mother's burial casket, and he looked at her.

She did not know that her mouth moved, trying to speak, but yet she felt her lips still as this man, this priest, moved easily toward her. No sound in the room anymore. Not a breath. Only the sound of her own heartbeat heard in her own ears.

Holding June's eyes, he walked toward her. His eyes both calm and assuring. His eyes speaking so very many words.

And June heard them all.

He was at her side as she lifted the lid fully open. And he smelt like a forest's air.

She looked at him. His eyes only a few inches away... and June felt now... that she was not alone in all of this business. She felt that she had been seen in this life, without judgement.

When he leant in toward her, June did not know that she already held the cold hand of her departed mother, but she did feel that she herself was passing from one place to another.

Softly, warmly, with honest heart, past the hair hanging by her right ear, he simply said, 'You say goodbye to your mother my child.'

With her tears now rising, June lowered her head to her mother's brow and pressed her shaking wet lips to her cool skin. With her hand squeezing the small bones of her dead mother's hand, her tears began falling from her tightly shut eyes. So much she needed to say, to give, to convey. So much she wanted to make right with this woman who had loved her, for at least those first nine years of her life. This woman who had held a promise within her. One that could now never be kept.

And as that ocean within her drew back its tide, June heard a sound bearing in from behind her. Her eyes opened, so close to her mother's hair, before June could identify the cause of that familiar sound. A small voice, she heard it echoing from somewhere near her heart. It cried, *It's the Angels coming to carry her...* But June knew it could not be... So, lifting her head and raising her face to the sound of its beating wings, June's mouth opened as that bird called its song... *t'was a currawong.*

Looking to the older man by her side, and seeing his eyes on her steady, June followed that bird's flight to the crucified Lord, to where it lit atop the left-hand side of that carven crucifix. And there it gave its call one more time.

Without any doubt, without the fear of her peers, without the crouch of her modern shame, June leant forward once again, and still holding her hand, June got her mouth close to her mother's ear and said, 'You go now Mummy. You go with him... and remember who you are.' And she kissed her mother's cheek for the very last time. She felt her most honest tears fall. June let go of her mother's hand and raised her face to follow the call of that currawong as it flew directly over her and out through the open church doors.

Sitting on a park bench by the river's side, June smoked a cigarette. Feeling the skin of her cheeks, tight with her drying tears, she breathed in the air through her nose. The rain had stopped, leaving the clouds from where it had fallen drifting fast overhead. Her eyes caught a spot of white and grey, out on the river. Watching it as it floated closer, June saw that it was a seagull sitting on the water, carried downstream. Its little face turning left and right, giving the impression that it wasn't sure how it was moving along. But going along just the same.

'Where's your skates?' said the high voice carrying in the wind.

Recognition lifted June's eyes and a small weary smile with it. She saw the little boy she had chased along this same path a little more than a week ago, and she flicked her cigarette out into the river. Sitting up straighter on the seat, June waved. 'Hey Toby,' she called, sniffing up the remnants of any tears, and using the back of her hand to wipe her eyes real quick. 'Where's your apple?'

'You crushed it.' Smiling as he walked to where she sat and hopped up beside her. 'You're not playing tennis today?' Squinting up at her, kicking his feet.

Her heart choked a little with that. Placing her hands together and leaning forward in the hope of preventing a leak. 'Nah,' she said just holding it, 'don't play in the rain.' Giving it her best go at a smile.

Turning his face out to the river, Toby said, 'It's okay to cry.'

241

And June couldn't help it. Her hand came up to try and cover it no matter that she knew it was futile. She tried to hold it in with her lower teeth on her upper lip, but when this small boy placed his hand on her back and gave her a gentle rub, June burst like a bag.

And they sat like that for a time, Toby and June. And as she fell apart, this little boy did what those who loved him did. He said, 'It's going to be alright.' But when he said, 'I promise.' Well June felt there would never be an end to her tears.

But there was an end to them. As there always is. And for a time, Toby and June talked of things that all kids talk on. Stuff that's real. Stuff you can hold in your hand.

Then letting the smile drop from his face, and looking like he was trying to work out whether it was okay to say, Toby said, 'Who died?'

June's lips formed an O, and she nodded, as much out of respect for his approach as anything. Feeling unsure of whether her lips would form the words or not and squinting with one eye while looking at his sweet face with the other, June creaked, 'My mother.' And how she wanted not to say it. How she wanted not to lay this on this young kid. But she did not know how to lie, for reasons good or bad.

Looking back out to the river, he nodded a little, chewed his lower lip a bit and then said, 'That's a tough one.'

And June nearly fell over. But she smiled so wide, so real. 'Oh, you're too much.' Her heart warmed by this wee man. She said, 'How did you know someone died?'

Nodding again, Toby said, 'I just put two and two together.'

Unable to control her face, June thought in that moment that she could learn to love a life.

'My mother died too,' he said it like... well he said it.

June felt her stomach tumble. A calamity of causes. A jumble of blames.

He turned to June then, and tapping her shoulder, he said, 'There's only one thing you gotta know.' Looking at her like she was the wee one between them.

June was gripped by his expression. Knowing that he surely must be repeating words spoken to him by those who cared for him. But still, it was a *thing*.

He chewed his cheek for a moment, and holding one finger in the air, he said, 'Ones we love can leave us June, and that can make us feel lost.' His eyes firm on hers. 'But always remember...' Moving his little face closer to hers, looking right into her eyes, he said, 'It's You you gotta love baby. It's You.'

He got up then, Toby. He got up from that park bench by the riverside, and putting his hands in his pockets, he began to walk away.

And as June watched him as he went.

Without looking back, he said, 'See yah round June Bug.'

And sitting there, June felt her heart might actually stop and die.

Chapter Twenty-Six

Cake Walk

There was hard talk. Not mere whispers in the wind. Just like the birds they pretended not to be, they squawked and danced while keeping their distance in case their intended prey was not as lame as its trail suggested. It was not that it didn't hurt. Nope. It wasn't that. It was that June knew that it couldn't really touch her, not really, unless she lay down to die.

'Oh, ease up already,' she said, batting a hand at the girl now chewing a corner of her lip after she'd brought the powder brush closer in and out as though testing the waters. But June smiled as she caught herself in the mirror in front of her, rolling her eyes. 'Just get on with it.' June lifted her chin and set that smile. There was no point in protesting too much. It was oh so familiar.

The make-up girl hurried about her task. The pressure she was under, and the consequences for this girl *to get it on and get em out* exactly to spec, June knew, far outweighed any she faced. And she relaxed her shoulders. She let go of that face she had unknowingly put on only a few minutes after walking through those outer doors.

And then she felt her stomach flip just a little bit.

Just like this city, this job now felt like it was empty, devoid of what it had contained only a few months past.

'Sorry.' June pulled her fingernail from her teeth, and instead bit down on her urge to chastise the girl for her expression. But she did poke out her tongue real quick.

Then she breathed a very big breath, and when she let it out, something slid away.

'I feel like a kid waiting for a doctor's appointment,' she said, slouching in that chair. She had long ago let go of any desire to make these make-up *artist's* job any easier. *That was*, or so she had used to contend, *part of their job*.

And under more huffs of protest from the girl who made her up, June scrunched her nose at the feeling of those thoughts. Those thoughts that now stirred in her gut. Her gut that so knew its truths. That gut that stirred its pot of toil, boil and trouble.

'Done.' The girl turned away and began prepping for the next model.

With her hands on the chair arms, June leant forward and thrust her face this way and that, looking for any *model hounds* who might seek to apprehend her if she ducked out for a quick smoke.

Then she darted.

Pushing and sliding through the morass of foul faced girls, some of them no more than children, June felt the skin of her past begin to slough.

She made it to the exit as another gut feeling flipped when she caught one girl grinning at her as she spied June slipping through the door. She held the door from closing, waiting, thinking, or trying to for just a second, about throwing all caution to the wind. And then she closed the door.

Outside, there were people, staff of one kind or another, mostly milling about, co-ordinating or being co-ordinated. None of them, from what June could tell, obviously model orientated. June stuck a cigarette between her lips, lit it and blew out the first glorious plume before her eyes rose again. The dress she wore was the very last thing on her mind. In fact, she hadn't even considered it as they dressed her. She hadn't even bothered with those predictable words that rushed from the too young designer's lips as he consulted the other staff. *Why would she?*

Rubbing her toes at the concrete and holding an elbow in the palm of her smoke free hand, June looked at the light as it cut its orange glow against those many lines of windows in the building opposite. And she felt she was somewhere else. She felt like this had all been...

'You!'

With her cigarette at her lips, June looked sideways at the *person* with the gall to speak to her like this.

The *man*, and June wasn't at all altogether proud of herself for her condescending judgements about this creature's lack of masculinity. *I mean who does that anymore?...* And yet? Anyway, as June watched this guy storming toward her, pointing under his *this is entirely unacceptable* lips, she sucked on her cigarette and showed him her best *I'm so bored right now* eyes.

She spat an imaginary tobacco strand onto the ground as he neared, and she leant against the wall and...

'Oh no you don't!' And he grabbed June's arm, pulling on it. 'That dress... ARGH!... ARGH!' he said as June's open palm made considerable and unexpectedly, for him at least, brutal

247

contact more than twice with his left jaw and eye bone. The impact bringing this *man* to his knees before a final strike took him to his arse.

Wiping the palm of her right hand against *that dress,* June smiled at the terrified expression of the floored *man* as he tried to crab-crawl back from her now pointing finger as she said, 'You don't touch people like that! Got it?' And as others came to the aid, of the aid, June smiled around her cigarette.

She smiled as she smoked the rest of her cigarette. She didn't even bother herself with the discussion that was transpiring just a few feet away from her on the loading dock. June just smoked and felt it click. That thing she knew but couldn't quite, not just yet, put her finger on. But it clicked alright. A switch. This much she got. A switch had just got flicked somewhere deep in her, just under her right ribs. She coulda heard it if it wasn't in there quite so deep. But she felt it true enough. June Bonnet felt a *switch flick.*

Blowing out the last of the smoke and holding her hand high as she flicked the butt out onto the stretch of concrete to her right side, June turned in the direction of her desired path and said to the group consoling the bloodied aid, 'Now get the fuck out of my way.' And they did. Yep. They busied the guy she popped, right out of her way. Because she meant it.

'Grrr,' she offered as she moved through them, snapping her teeth once or twice. 'Read it in tomorrow's news.'

And June walked back into the building.

Several people were rushing to the same door she was coming in through. June was thinking that they had obviously watched too many *casualty of war* scenes in their young lives, as she stepped inside, smiling at the two men who rushed by to get to their *wounded*.

'Don't you think you've hurt enough people?' Spoken through the over lip-stuck lips of a girl whom in June's opinion... was too young to have one.

But as that girl hurried past with the other *rescuers* of her ruin, June muttered, 'Oh, I think I'm just getting started.'

Standing in line, all June knew was that she was tired of this. This, and that no matter how she despised these girls who stood before and behind her in this *call-up*, she couldn't deny that they all smelt so *very* good.

And as they jostled and burned their nerves, June knew they couldn't possibly know just how alien she felt. After so many years doing just this, after so many years of having climbed this impossibly slippery rope and having reached its very top... they couldn't know just how very bored she was to be here once again.

She made to turn, to step out of line, and she felt her eyes arch, seriously, as the girl behind her placed her hands on her shoulders sharply and shoved her back into position.

'Seriously?' But she didn't turn and pop her like she did the guy outside. Nope. *You don't hit girls.* Those words, somehow, from somewhere, dragging their nails across the inner bones of her skull. And you know? No matter her indignation, no matter the disrespect even, to be treated in this way, and from some *model*, June could see neither the irony of this condescension in her scattered thoughts, nor a way out.

All June could feel was the frantic buzzing of electrons as they *Be-Bopped* throughout every fibre of her flesh and bones.

249

Her mind then flooding with images of prisoners, standing, waiting in a line for their execution.

'That's a bit dramatic,' June said under her breath and felt her facial muscles go lax like a pro as her well-honed muscle memory kicked in, and the girl before her stepped out around the wall... and down the catwalk.

'I can't feel my arms,' she said to herself. No-one else was there with an ear to hear. There was no-one who would care. So, June took her cue and began to move like a passenger. Like a passenger of a body that walked her around that same wall as the model ahead of her. A body that walked her out into the full lights, cameras and action of the high fashion world.

The response to her was enormous. Not altogether of the kind she had grown accustomed to over her long career, but still. Feeling smaller than her physical self, June wondered honestly, *How can they not know that I am in here?* As she rode inside the so-practiced forms, swells and swagger of her body... as she walked on down the line. *How can they not know how I must feel?* But these were only thoughts, only expressions in her internal world. For outwardly, June Bonnet appeared like she simply, *couldn't give a damn.*

She wanted not to walk.

She wanted to stop and point and scream.

She wanted to act out.

But for the very first time, at least as far as she could remember, June felt like a person trapped in someone else's body.

So, she did scream... inside. As she reached the end of the runway and felt her heart rip at how her body continued its programmed *strut-stop-turn and deliver*, June screamed internally like a child in the dark. She screamed like a child who had found that the monsters were most definitely real, and no-one would care to believe her.

They even clapped, these people, these... contributors.

And June screamed within herself all the way back down that long slippery path.

She screamed this way as she stepped back behind the scenes.

She screamed as those people stripped her bare and redressed her in another costume.

She screamed as they pushed and shoved at the flesh that was hers.

She screamed as she was moved back into line.

And she screamed this way, so loud inside of her, as she fought so hard to prevent her body from doing what it was making her do.

And somewhere... somewhere, either in another realm entirely, or else from a place she could not dare know... someone heard her... and somehow... they reached through... and broke the chain.

Only two steps from the end of that catwalk, June felt her grip return. *A flood of blood*, the closest words her mind could clasp to match its hot rushing gorge. And like sliding into a wetsuit, June regained... 'CONTROL!' Now of course she hadn't meant to really scream this word. We can understand. I mean, *Who in their right mind, wouldn't? Right?* Uh-huh.

But scream she did. Bellow would be a much clearer description of the sound that poured, tore, disgorged, okay spewed from June's wide-open mouth as she stopped her parade. Indeed, she stopped the entire parade. For she stood wide footed and still heeled at the end of that platform and yelled this one solitary word, 'CONTROL!'

251

The room, the entire room scratched on its record as June dragged the needle of her will across the fabric of that atmosphere. And standing there panting, her mouth maybe dribbling, well it was really, dribbling quite a deal of saliva, June saw that she had crossed a line. And just as that blood had flooded through her previously zombied form, now June felt the... 'Sparkle Dust!' And yes, she said this out loud... the... 'Sparkle Dust...' of her... 'SPIRIT!' Again yes, June felt and vocally projected, 'THE SPARKLE DUST OF MY SPIRIT... DANCING THROUGH ME!'

Someone in the very still crowd coughed. They always do. But all eyes were on her, on June, as she began to get... 'REAL!' she called, and obviously she was meaning, *with herself,* up there on that catwalk. And no, we do not mean *that* kind of real. Well, not so much.

June began to tear at the garment she had been dressed in. With her teeth set and her eyes running with honest tears, not blubbering exactly, but honestly running like a stream, June fought at her clothes like she had been plastered with the... 'UNTHINKABLE!' she screamed.

And that crowd watched June. That's all they did. In wasn't in the manual—*How to deal with such outbursts.* And further than that, there was a buzz. An unspoken, but we assure you, a most tangible b*uzz* was connecting all, really, all who were witnessing June Bonnet on this stage. And it spoke with an authority that carried. It spoke.

So, the security did not intervene. No. There were no aids rushing out to *handle* this *victim of fashion war.* Nope. No outraged designer, no friend or *peer,* coming to her aid.

Up on the end of that catwalk, alone, stood June Bonnet, clawing at, and now successfully removing the dress that she wore.

252

Yup, she was lifting it over her head. Her grunts of protest, the only sound in that large room other than the tearing of that fabric as it was stretched beyond its intent.

She threw it to the ground.

She stepped out of her... 'FUCKING URGH!'...shoes. Kicking at them because they had to... 'GO!'

And she was naked.

June stood there naked, kicking at the dress that now lay on the ground by her feet. Her hair, let's say, *disrupted,* her eyes wild, her hands just claws, with all others on that catwalk giving her plenty of space.

June stood there and looked about that room.

She looked into their faces, and into their eyes, when they could hold them. She looked at them all... like a beast.

June straightened her hair, kind of. And with her tits to the wind and her bare arse exposed for all to see, June burst forth... she took three running steps... and leapt.

June leapt from the stage.

She leapt, with all time around her slowing perspectively.

The powerful lights of that room, starring her squinting eyes. With no idea what such a physical extension can do to the muscles around one's breathing and speaking parts... June leapt... *like Jennifer in Dirty Dancing.* Or so she believed.

June leapt, screaming, 'NOVIDDY UTS ABY IN DA ORNER!' Not at all getting that it was not Jennifer's character who said this, well at least what June meant to say... nor even during that scene... at all.

She landed hard... but she landed on her feet. The crowd collectively said, 'Ooh!' As the sound of her jarring bones rang through that room. A sound akin to a plucked chicken dropped from a great height.

'I'M ARIGHT!' Still screaming without any notion of this, June began to walk... like a cowboy spent too long in the saddle.

Naked as she had ever been, June began to walk away from that catwalk.

The silence, awesome in this large space.

June took two more steps... before she heard the first clap.

Her body reanimating to a kind she found more familiar, June stopped in place. She didn't turn. No. But she stopped.

And then the room erupted... in applause.

June felt an emotion gurgle up and catch in her throat.

Turning very slowly, June looked at all those people, both left and right and even on top of that stage... holding their hands out before them, clapping. And June took two steps forward as she saw that they were sincere... *somehow*. For reasons she could not in that moment properly accept, naked June knew that these people, all of them, were honestly applauding... her.

She tried not to cry. Really. But as she looked into their eyes, and there were some serious folk in this crowd, June felt... June felt that in some way that she had never been... now, she had been... seen.

So, she bowed.

And June heard that applause explode.

And as she giggled and stood and bowed again... June felt something soft land on her back.

A shiver, a remnant of fear, only at first, crept up June's spine at this sensation.

But the applause continued.

Turning, looking to the place on the floor where it had fallen, holding the fingertips of both hands together, June saw a crumple of black cloth, and she bent to retrieve it.

'GO JUNE!' a man's voice boomed from one distant side. Whistles followed.

Holding the cloth in her hands, June opened it before her. It was a t-shirt, and gratefully she slipped it on. Its size just right to cover her bits. Now tilting her head to the man who had thrown it, June turned to the still, honestly, still applauding and smiling crowd of this show she had actually totally disrupted and probably ruined, if not just shattering its flow... she turned to them, and with a smile on her face, June ran her fingers under the single word written on the front of that black t-shirt that she now wore... *SECURITY*.

The laughter was kind, and it broke something there inside of her. Not at all feeling herself, June felt as though something cool like water had broken through a barrier within her. And it felt so good. It felt so good that no questions could follow.

So... June waved goodbye... and *they* waved to her.

Walking from that room, June was intercepted by a tall man. His suit, as well cut as his silver hair.

With her face bent in a frown, June looked at what he held in his hands.

He said, 'Excuse me Ms Bonnet?' His eyes kind, and not at all rubbed with lechery. Smiling, he went on, 'Well, I thought that you... deserve some cake.' And handing her a small plate with a large slice of chocolate cake on it, and a silver cake fork wrapped in a paper napkin, he stepped back, clapping as he did.

And with that, June Bonnet left the building.

Chapter Twenty-Seven

Ain't it Great

O h, I love these sandwiches. Did you make them yourself? Creamy. Mmm. Tuna's my fave!' Dr Jason Mackie leant his elbow on the green wooden edge of the small white rowboat. Raising his face to the full sun and pointing his free hand to June, he said, 'Come on! Put some muscle into it! Har-har.' And then he took another large bite of the sandwich.

'I ordered chicken,' she said, heaving on the oars and causing the good doctor to secure his grip.

'Oh, well that's not so good then, is it?' His mouth was opening even as he finished saying these words. He leant over the green edge, letting the chewn mix drop out and into the water. 'Oh look, they're eating it!' His fascination causing him to lean a little too far, destabilising the small boat.

'Hey!' June too had to take hold. 'Easy tiger.' Feeling the honesty of her smile, she said, 'They are tuna. Har... har.'

'Cannibals.' Dipping his finger into the lake and snatching it out, he said, 'Ooh, one nipped me!' And he placed that finger in his mouth, pulling a face. 'Maybe they think I'm a fish?'

June lifted the oars in their rings and set them inside the boat. She picked up a sandwich. Resting her arms on her knees, taking a small bite, and inspecting the remainder with one finger, she said, 'Do you think it ever gets easier?'

Looking over to the shore, something about the man fell. An edge appeared, though it was an edge with a sour note. 'What? This?' Jason continued chewing on his sandwich.

A moment passed. The air around them stilled. The pretence of an easy time on the water vanished, and with his face having slipped, Jason Mackie threw the crust of his sandwich out over the edge. His *Jason Mackie-ness* was gone. He did not turn his face to hers for a time. And that edge began to fill the small boat.

June felt it. Of course she did. She watched him begin to speak, but he stopped before any words came out. His body was shuffling, and his movements became jerky. He was building to something. What? June could not know, but she knew it must come out, and she was only hoping for a beat before he shared.

'Really?' Jason shifted, still not looking at her. First placing both elbows on the bow's edge before lifting them and bringing himself forward so that he sat there just inches in front of June. Sitting like her, with his elbows on his knees, mirroring her, he looked to his clasped hands, shaking them up and down while looking out to his right and over the surface of the lake. His lips pressed. His mouth, just a line.

And June thought she almost saw his eyes getting wet. She felt some confusion. She was unsettled by his change in demeanour. She was certain that she was looking at a great deal of emotion, for she watched as it swum beneath the

258

lenses of Dr Mackie's eyes. They almost vibrated. They shook with whatever he was fighting not to say.

He blew out a long breath. He began nodding his head a little as he turned his face back down to his hands and smiled an unfriendly smile. Lifting his face up to hers, he looked straight into June's eyes with his whites shot red and his lips pressing together harder. Looking right into her, he shook his head.

June chewed, but only a little. *Was he disappointed?* Regretting that she would feel such a thought appropriate.

'June, June, June,' he said.

She felt a little sick in her lower belly, and she placed the sandwich to one side. Watching him as he turned those now blood-shot eyes back onto her. The condescension not implied but non-verbally yelled. And she wanted to be angry about it, this treatment, but she could do nothing but look at him. And she loved him like he was... *family*? No. Maybe more than that. *But kin of a kind?* She had no doubt. And June had to figure that he was not... angry? No, she knew this. She knew this was *his* struggle right now. She knew that he didn't want to say... what he most definitely was going to say. June held it, her eyes on him, and she nodded. She gave him permission.

'Oh, I need a cigarette. Do you have any June? Of course you do.' Leaning forward, he took one from the pack she had produced, seemingly from thin air. With the smoke between his lips, Jason sat there holding the smoke to his lips as his other hand fished for a lighter.

June lit one for herself and passed the lighter to him. The boat rocked beneath them. *It was pretty out here*, she thought. But she couldn't look at that now.

Leaning across the wooden seat with one foot up, Jason smoked his cigarette. 'Oh, I do love to smoke, Juney.' He made to smile, trying on some of his old *panache*, but he was unable to hold it, even for a moment. He looked out over the water. He did not look at her. And they smoked. And they drifted.

'No current,' June said, knowing that she sat there with her eyes downcast just like a chastised child, but...

'You don't know a lot about me do you June?' Jason's eyes were still set, out there.

Drawing on the smoke, June leant to her left, dodging a line of drifting smoke that wanted to run to her eyes. She couldn't look anywhere else but at him—at him, nodding, smoking, looking elsewhere.

June didn't want to speak.

'I've been doing this a long time June.' His voice dipped, and he ashed over the edge. 'A very long time.' He took another draw. 'But you don't know what brought me to this do you? Well, how could you? Why would you?' His voice was now a drone.

June was becoming more uncomfortable. She had never seen him like this. She hadn't even considered that it was possible. And she felt naive. She felt a fear, not of Dr Mackie, but at this realisation. She felt naive in that moment, sitting on a little rowboat with her friend. And she didn't like that feeling.

She knew something was coming.

He was right back in front of her in a flash. The boat didn't sway a dot. 'Do you want to know June? Do you want to? I have to ask, you see. I must do that at least.' His eyes were almost in hers.

With her cigarette in her lips, pulling smoke, June nodded.

Nodding with her, Dr Jason Mackie said, 'I was insane June.' His eyes following hers, he said, 'I was clinically a *loon* by the age of fifteen.' Those eyes of his, searching and then resting. He went on, 'Incarcerated. And I can tell you it was no treat in those days. Of course, it still bares avoiding. But by God it was a shock to my wee red-headed system.' He flicked his cigarette. 'I was diagnosed,' nodding as a fowl expression began creasing his whole face, 'roped and stamped and shipped out to that fucking house of horrors. And let me tell you June, it was that. It was at least that.' Jason took her finished smoke from her hands and threw it overboard. He lifted two more from the pack on the wooden seat beside her, placed both in his mouth, lit them and handed one to her. And he took a time, looking out over the water again.

June's mind was empty, absent of any thought. Her fear had shifted. She only felt her heart move for this man, for what he was choosing to give—for her.

'They said I was not fit. Not fit!' Smoking. 'They forced me to take medications that they wouldn't even deem me responsible enough to know the names of.' His anger rose and flowed. It seemed to pour from him in colours. But then he calmed, so fast. His anger was only shown for a moment, like a shadow passing over his face. And his voice lower now, steady, he said, 'My family felt it was the best course of action. They didn't visit me... for five years.' Not a hint of emotion. 'They left me in there...' And now he drifted for a time.

June felt her tears roll, but she put no words to these feelings. She simply kept her eyes on him.

Looking at his hands, he said, 'Now, I did learn something June. In that place.' He nodded. 'In fact, I learned enough, it appears, to last me a lifetime. So, I guess there's no need to

261

be bitter. Yet still? Anyhow.' His eyes, his whole face, brightening. Those eyes, returning to hers. 'I wasn't crazy June. I wasn't even a little bit broken. And I guess I may not have discovered this if I hadn't been thrown into that asylum.' He played with his lip. 'There were folks in there June whose state of mind beggars description.' Taking a drag and blowing smoke. 'And some of them,' choking at the memories, 'some of them were sweet.' His eyes were showing this truth. 'Some of them were kinder to me than any single sole I have encountered before or since. Maybe ever will hey? Who knows?' Sitting taller in his seat and placing his hands on his knees. 'And I know for a fact... that some of those poor dears,' he said, his lips pressing, 'are still in such places.' He choked for a moment on this truth. 'Oh sure, they've improved somewhat. And of course, a great deal of those people can't ever really function on any safe level out here.' He gestured to the world around them. Coughing a cynical laugh, he said, 'I mean, how would we cope?'

June, with her lips closed, tongued a very small piece of food from between her teeth, and chewed.

'So any-who, I eventually convinced them that I was not actually insane... just... different. It took a bit of work that one.' He looked at her then. He really looked at her. 'Okay,' he said, rocking his head from side to side, 'it was Dr Michaels who got me out of there.' Watching her, really focusing on her reaction. He laughed, and said, 'You're the shit June. You really are.' He rubbed his knees. 'So yeah, he... this was many years ago obviously, and the good Doctor was only starting out, of course. I mean that's obvious, but anyway he said something to me one time you see. I was in the games-room... dribbling. A nasty side effect of that shit they shoved into me. And yeah, he couldn't have been more than a few years out of Uni. But he came over to where I was sitting, and he just sat there...' He gave a small smile.

June wanted to place her hand on his, to stop the rocking. The care in her eyes... at what he was giving.

'Nah, I'm alright June Bug. I'm good.' His smile, and the wave of his hand, showing otherwise. He went on, 'You know I can't really explain to you what happens to a person when they're labelled and thrown into such a situation. I can't...' puffing too fast on that cigarette, 'but I can tell you that those years seemed... felt... like an eternity.' A big breath in and out. Somewhat gathered, he said, 'You know Dr Michaels leaned on that table, reached across and took my hand. And with a smile that showed... well it showed a lot, he said, *Jason?* that's me...' Jason gave the big smile of a child as he pointed to his own chest. 'He said, *I don't think there's anything at all wrong with you.* Just like that!' And Dr Mackie coughed a sob, rubbed his knees some more and rocked back and forth on that small boat—holding his shit as best he could.

June's care creased her face. She made for him, but she stopped at his waving hands.

'Nah, I'm good June. Honestly.' But he wasn't.

So, June lifted the flask of coffee, and placing out two cups, and she poured them one.

Sipping like nothing had happened, he said, 'You know as soon as he said those words June...' Placing his cup back down. 'You know?' His hands went wide, and his fingers spread as he blew all of his air out. 'As soon as he said it,' he said with his eyes lighting wide, 'I got it! I fucking saw the whole thing unfold. I shit you not, I saw the whole damn shebang.' He was looking at her for acceptance of this fact.

263

'I saw where I was.' He left a moment of time there, as he let it go. Then so much calmer, he said, 'I sat there in that plastic chair... I can still smell the place. Funny hey? So, I looked at him when he said those words to me, and I froze. Well, I mean I was already frozen.' Jason let some saliva fall from his mouth in imitation of his former state. Laughing as he got one from June, he said, 'Yeah, I mean I just sat up in that seat, and I looked around that room... at all those unfortunate souls... and I fucking got it.'

Some time passed, and *something* passed between them.

'June, I saw the line of sanity. Funny hey? I saw it. And I know that sounds REALLY CRAZY!' he said, slamming a hand over his mouth. He watched June's eyes. Whispering now and leaning right in, he said, 'I saw it.'

June lifted another smoke. She lit it and passed it to Jason.

'It was like a painted line. A four-inch wide, yellow painted line. And it ran like a ribbon around that room.' He was in her eyes again, searching. 'And I could see who was on which side of that line June.' Jason's eyes held still in that moment They were steady, and they carried a weight. 'And I wasn't crazy June. He was right. I wasn't even a little bit insane. I mean I wasn't *sane* either. But really, who wants to be? You see June, I got a touch in that moment... har-har... it's true,' he said with a shrug. 'I did. I could see June... I could see!'

She took another smoke for herself.

Jason waited for her to light it. 'You see June,' he said, chewing his lower lip, 'ever since I could remember...' he cast his eyes around them like he was looking for listening ears, 'everything... all of it...' whispering again, with his eyes still darting, 'it all looked... wrong!' Jason pulled his face in, smiling. His hands pressed between his knees, delighted.

264

June could feel no expression on her face. In fact, she could feel nothing at all. The air about her froze. The colours fixed. All sounds whispered into a vacuum. And she sat there on that little rowboat and felt the building blocks of her inner world... rattle in their box.

'Oh, you should see your face right now.' Jason's face was delight.

A small voice... Was it her own? A memory? Saying, *This is not how it's supposed to be.* And a slice of her mind, like a thick wedge of cheesecake, slipped off its plate. Turning to her left, with her head not dipping at all, June threw up... a lot.

And as June hurled... as she watched it fly from her face... all she could hear was Jason... giggling... as he rocked the boat.

'Ooh, that's a lot!' His voice was right high. Trying to speak through his laughter, he said, 'Are you alright? Well of course you are June. Of course you are.'

It stopped as quickly as it started, and as June felt the last drips drop, she began to smile. And it was the first smile she had smiled absent of any conscious thought, in a very, very long time.

'Here drink some.' Jason placed a bottle of water in her hands with both of his. 'Gargle,' he said, demonstrating, for reasons only he could know.

Still smiling and still wiping at her mouth, June said, 'So?'

He clapped just once. 'Right you are June. So, I got it.' He gave a quick nod. 'You see, when I saw that ribbon of a line running through that room like it was a physical thing, well I got two things: One—I was not insane, and two—I was not *sane* either.' And he smiled like that was that.

June's eyebrows told the tale.

'Ew of course. Right. Well, you see I suppose it depends on the definitions we give to those words doesn't it. But,' he said, holding up a finger, 'it's pretty simple really. In order to be *sane,* by the standards of the world, you must accept... the *world,* or this order, or the system of this world... as being, well, right in and of itself.' He paused and then said, 'I know. Well, who thinks this world is right?' His eyes and brows lifting to their full extent. 'But.'

And it fell then, a small and yet so very heavy little block. No bigger than a four-dot square of Lego. It fell in June's inner existence. And she saw it. It tumbled through that metaphysical air from a very high tower. 'Aw,' June heard herself say. She felt the sound in her throat, and on her lips.

'Uh-huh,' he said. 'Crazy right?' His eyebrows again, Groucho.

'Yeah.' June felt her nose scrunch. '*They* think this is the way things are supposed to be.' And June felt her eyes searching with much of the same oddity as she had witnessed on Mackie's face. Her frown hedged her vision, and as her eyes lifted to Jason's, she said, 'They think that all of this... is..."

'I KNOW!' Almost unable to contain himself.

Now her eyes widened. 'They think this is the way it's supposed to be,' she said, her voice drifting, confounded.

Ponting, he said, 'You're confounded!' Clapping a hand over his mouth again.

'My god!' And June really had no idea who she was in that moment, speaking this way. '*They* all think this is just... set?'

Pulling the air around them with his drop in dynamic, Jason said, calm as you like, 'No, not all June. Not everyone.'

She fumbled with the cigarette pack. Her throat saying, *No,* her other stuff saying, *Damn right I am.*

Giggling again, Dr Jason Mackie said, 'You're a *Creative* June.' And then he began laughing harder than most would warrant.

June felt her head turn to cotton wool, and she swayed. Her mind made to make any kind of sense as to why she was having any kind of reaction to this information at all. Information that quite frankly, in June's opinion, meant... but did it? Somehow, and she could not deny this as her physiological reaction to this man's words attested... it did.

Again, but now not laughing one little bit, Jason Mackie said, 'You're a *Creative,* June.' He paused.

The whole world around June paused. Her intellect informing her that this was Dr Mackie's evaluation of the cause of her... *problems.* Her other faculties doing their best to assuage her of this as it produced images, hundreds of images, of shoeless people weaving, dancing in hats, beading necklaces.... and face painting.

June sat there, frowning, shaking her head.

And then Jason Mackie said, with his voice and its tone stretching, 'You will $NEVER$ fit in.'

June could only look at him. Her eyes did not want to open fully. She squinted at him. Her question? Only what it could be. 'What the fuck does that mean?' And June heard the fear, the very real fear, shaking her words as she said them.

'It means, June,' Dr Mackie said and went full Zen, 'that the main reason you have *always* felt that something was wrong... that those around you, well, that they were... kinda off. And the reason you felt that no matter how hard you tried... you never quite fit in? Well, June...' And he really appeared to be struggling to get the words out. 'June, you are living in a world that is predominantly set up for *non-creatives.*' His eyes seeking confirmation that she was following. Getting none, he continued, 'And you have spent your whole life believing that in order to be loved...' His eyes showed his sadness at the confirmation he now received from June's falling expression, and the eyes of a child that now sat in place of hers. Knowing he must continue, and quickly, he said, 'June you believed, that in order to be treated as though you had *any* value.... that you had to behave in ways that, well, quite literally....' his lips pressed, 'alienated you from... yourself.'

The air cooled, and somewhere off to June's right, a duck quacked.

And then Jason said, 'Whoops, there she goes!' And as that little boat rocked to near capsizing, he got his arms under June's pits... as she passed out in that little rowboat.

Chapter Twenty-Eight

Outta Line

Her shoes felt good on her feet.

June's shoulders moved as she swung her arms, and her hair fell just as it should. She was walking the city's streets, and the air was cool.

She was feeling *good*.

Her mind cast back to her time on the little rowboat. Just a week ago, but a lifetime. And as her feet felt the weight of her as they pressed that concrete she walked, June thought on the days since. Days spent mostly in the park. Days spent lying on the thick green grass with no thoughts to burden her. Whole days simply watching the birds at work and play. Watching those people who sat or passed, without concern. She had noticed them, just like she had the birds or the trees. Days where she too appeared to garnish as much of their attention. There were no interruptions or concerns drawn. There appeared to be no cause or need. And she knew now that they had been days separate or apart from what came before. They had been the days when she had departed from the life in which she had formally dwelt.

She had let herself go. Somewhere or sometime during that week, she had let herself go. The self, that had strangled her like a cocoon grown too tight. It had drifted from her like an aroma. It had left her like a heat. It had evaporated and taken its stain with it.

For a time, June had tried to find reason. She had tried to determine the cause of her freedom from those restraints that she had known her entire life. But she knew, as one knows those truths that require no beating pulse, that the reasons, and the map of its happening, would write themselves over time.

June *knew* now that all she was required to do was to pick her own path as she walked it. That with each step she made, *she* must be the one with whom she made agreement, and none other.

So, June walked.

'Hey sweetheart!'

June kept walking. It couldn't grate on her today. Not even a little bit. She just let her flat soles roll, her hips swing, and the ease of her smile carry her along and through the crowds around her.

Was it that they couldn't touch her? No.

Was it that she didn't care?

No.

'I'm somewhere else,' she said as she moved amongst them, walking like she threaded a line. 'But still,' she said, smiling at a man as they passed, 'I'm here.'

She walked, and her feet knew where to go.

She walked right on down the line.

June watched this world around her as she moved at her own pace. She observed, as the way before her cleared. People travelling this way and that, downstream and up. They left a path as though it were just for her.

She felt her lips curl just under her frown, unsure if what she was seeing was what it appeared to be. Still, she walked, watching as people stepped from the shops and made their own ways. Some were hurried, some not. Some were in groups or in pairs, some not. She watched them, giggling air just a little bit as they avoided her like it was nothing at all. Like the line of concrete directly before her was hers and was being left clear just for her.

And so, still walking and still keeping her pace, June let her arms swing up before her, and she clapped a single clap. Her mouth stayed open, and she looked in wonder and in a kind of awe as these people, so many people, every one of them seemingly oblivious as they left her path clear.

She stepped a little to her left... and still they made her way clear, without missing a beat. She hopped to her right, still walking. 'Har.' She clapped again. Her smile couldn't shift. Her eyes were wide. June skipped just a little. She took steps faster, and then she slowed. She held her arms out to her sides, making a face and an aeroplane noise... and still her path was made clear.

She couldn't help but stare at them, and she tried to get their attention. Really she did. But they, all of them, just carried on with their lives as though she were no cause for their particular attention, and yet...

'Wow,' she said, and she meant it. And June Bonnet wondered if this smile she carried could ever really fade.

She stuck her hands in her pockets, and she walked with greater ease than she believed she ever had before. June walked like a woman who held sway.

Now maybe she was overdoing it. Maybe she was. Maybe she was imagining things, and maybe this occurrence she was witnessing had some other explanation. I mean really, who could know?

But June felt no reason, as she walked that busy footpath in that busy city, not to *put this shit to the test*. And could you blame her?

So, leaning into the curve while heading straight for the intersection with the lights on their poles telling the tale, June held her pace. Watching as those standing at the curb, waiting for those lights to give them the *go,* parted. *Even with their backs turned?*—she thought as she moved on through them, and she walked that cleared path... out onto the street.

The intersection was busy. Of course it was. A city like this? This time of day? You bet. And this intersection, right in the heart of the city, was the kind you could cross left, right or diagonal. And June, following *her* path, had stepped out onto that street to cross it on the diagonal.

Now June took a moment to consider, as she stepped out onto that street, whether those bystanders would be vocally bound by the same *magic* that had caused them to step aside, or whether this whole effect was indeed due to some other inexplicable, or even explainable, cause.

But then June did hear them voice their concerns.

'Hey Lady!' one of them called.

Others, and there were many, voiced their objections of like kind, but June had committed herself, and so she walked her line.

273

It was immediately clear at this point, even to June, that whatever magic she had witnessed on the footpath that caused people to clear her path, well, it didn't carry to the roads. *Or maybe it's not as strong?* And she actually thought this as a taxi driver hit his brakes so hard that his car screeched very loudly and slid straight toward her.

June noticed the eyes of that driver and how very wide they got. She noticed his hands steering the wheel hard to his left in an attempt to avoid impact with her. She noticed the sounds of a car's motor revving loud and hard as a driver somewhere to her right planted their left foot on the brake. The sounds of tires kept squealing, and her feet kept moving even as the world around her slowed... even with her smile held... even as she continued to walk her path.

So slowly, in the grip of focused time, June angled her eyes to her left, looking downward as she stepped just past the yellow paint of that taxi. She felt the air of it, hot against her calf as it slid so closely by and on its way.

It was not that she wasn't aware that she had made an error of judgement. No, and it wasn't that she could agree with her chosen course of action. Not at all. It was simply that now that she was there... Well what choice did she have?

So June saw only one option—*to keep moving forward.* And so, she did just that.

Now for another, this might certainly be an occasion in which to feel an embarrassment, or even a shame at what her fellow hominids might think of what she was doing. Rational, but in that moment, in that capsule of space-time, June felt not a bit of it. Whether due to her experience as a model and the airs that can apply, or whether it was her current state of being, June was no more affected by her surrounds than if she had been walking in her Aunt Joan's Garden... when she was a child of nine.

June got the question then, as she crossed the middle of that intersection, as she held up traffic and caused such a scene. June got the meaning of that most famous Shakespearean line, and so she said it, and loud, 'To *be*! Or *not to be*! *That* is the question!' Now fair, not everyone in the vicinity was equally congratulatory about her revelation.

'You're outta line!' called a man from the crowd, oddly.

June pointed at him with her hand in the shape of a pistol, and still walking... she fired off a shot.

'Do you think the rules don't apply to you?' hollered a very large man as he hung partly out of the driver's side window of his large blue truck.

'Damn straight Big Boy!' June bellowed back with equal measure, with her smiling eyes on his.

The driver's features slipped. He shook his head with his smile growing, and he called, 'Right on!' And as he got his bulk back behind the wheel of his truck, he got to tooting its loud horn repeatedly.

A cluster of women who were somewhat more senior than June, but not nearly enough to be conducting themselves as they were, huddled like a brood on the corner to which June was headed. When on hearing their *clucking* and seeing their faces set with their self-righteous determinations to s*et her right*, June dropped her head, bent her elbows, and picking up considerable speed, she ran toward them... behaving like a chicken.

'BWARK-BWARK-BWARK!' June rushed them, laughing hard between her fowl impersonations. She laughed like a child as they ruffled and lifted to their toes, flapping about.

She felt an honest joy as they parted from her, and as they squawked in their efforts to get out of her way.

'Priceless,' she said as she made her way through them and just kept walking on her way down the path.

After ten steps or so, she said, 'Ain't it grand?' And June clapped her hands together, just the once.

When she arrived at the building, it was like she was returning to the front doors of her former school.

The time since she had been here was not so long. And yet?

She strode through the automatic doors and felt her shoes pad on the shiny floor on her way to the bank of elevators. She looked at no-one. She knew where she was going.

'Hold it!' June pressed her hand to the closing doors of the lift nearest her and slipped in. Pressing the number on the panel out of habit and turning from the double doors, June's eyes landed on the only other person in the lift, and her smile began to spread before her conscious mind gave her the facts.

'Um?' said the young lady with her eyes wider than the usual recognition of June's celebrity would normally suggest. Her fingers tracing a line as she pushed a loose strand of hair behind her right ear. Her face began reddening. 'Ah,' she said, her voice panicked. Her suit jacket brushing June as she made a dive for the *Doors Open* button. An audible sigh in time with the clack of her contact with that button.

June's smile fixed as her eyes followed this girl. 'Do I know you?' she said, turning to face both the girl and the now reopening doors.

'No, no.' The young woman's feet spread as her hands were pulling in an attempt to open those elevator doors faster. 'No I...' she squeaked, turning her pretty face over her shoulder. Her panic was clear, with her eyes stretching to their full limit as she saw June licking the knuckles of her right hand. 'Up! I've forgotten my...' And she ran out the doors. Like... ran.

'How impolite.' June stepped to the back of the lift and leant on the gold-coloured rail as she began wiping her spit off her hand.

Speaking to her reflection in the doors as they closed, June said, 'Looks like we're taking this ride alone Kid.'

'Well, he's in with a patient right now Ms Bonnet.'

Leaning on the counter, June looked over it. 'Who is it Sarah?'

Snapping the book closed, Sarah said, 'Come on June,' tilting her head at her, stern, 'if you'll take a seat, like I said, I'll call through and let him know you're here.' And she gave June her crossed arms and her lifted eyebrows.

'I'm not a child Sarah,' she said, dropping her mouth open and shaking her head. June slid her arms off the counter, and letting them fully hang, she turned and walked to the row of seats in the waiting area where she thumped herself down in a chair. 'What was that?' she called to Sarah.

'You heard me.'

She picked up a magazine and threw it back down again. 'I shouldn't need an appointment.' A little too huffy, even for her.

June decided to drop it.

And so, she waited.

She watched Sarah pick up the phone after enough time had passed to establish her *authority,* and she watched her smile a very small self-indulgent smile before she placed it back down in its cradle. And she didn't even look at June before she reseated herself in her secretary's chair.

June tongued her gums. She jiggled the foot of her crossed leg. She looked at the clock. And though she knew she had only been there for no longer than ten minutes, maybe less, well June felt something yank her chain.

Standing, with her eyes on Sarah's position, June slunk like a commando, kinda. Sliding with her back against the wall, and keeping low as she slid into the hallway, June ran on her flat shoes to that door through which she had passed so many times. And opening it, she rushed in and closed the door behind her. 'Har!' she cried, pulling a fist down, triumphant.

'June.'

Still facing the door and pressed up against it, June heard Dr Michael's voice say her name, so calm and easy. *Was he happy?* She turned with her wide-eyed smile and felt... yes, she felt love when he smiled back at her.

'Who do you think you are?' The male voice to her right was clearly indignant.

June turned to face the large man sitting in the *patient's chair,* with her eyes squinting on his doughy face. 'I,' she said taking a step forward, 'am *Not Waiting.*' Stepping over to him and extending her hand, she said, 'Who the fuck are you?'

'Um...' The man was sweating.

'June,' Dr Michaels said as he leant back in his chair and crossed his legs, 'this is Patrick, and this is *his* time.'

278

Lifting her hand robotically as Patrick extended his nervously, she clasped his hand, and said, 'Well Patrick, I am sorry but...

'Oh!' Patrick squealed, literally biting the palm of one hand and hopping in his chair. Pointing with his other hand, he said, 'You're... that girl!'

'No Patrick,' June said, 'I am *this* girl.' And she began poking herself in the chest, for clarification. She ignored his clapping and turned to Dr Michaels. 'I'm sorry Doctor but I couldn't wait any longer,' she said, her inflection demonstrating that she wasn't even a little bit sorry.

Dr Michaels' eyes smiled. 'That's alright June. I'm sure Patrick won't mind.'

'No, you go right ahead.' And Patrick settled in.

'Good luck with this one,' June thumbed in Patrick's direction, and she sat on the desk and looked at Dr Michaels. She breathed, and said, 'I came in to tell you...'

'That you're...'

'Yes...' Her eyes starred for just a moment. 'I won't be needing your services any longer.' And she was caught off guard by the bubble of emotion that stuck in her throat.

He leant forward and took June's hand.

Tilting her head, no more acts, she let him see her wet eyes, and though her lips did their little dance, June said, 'Thank you.' And she meant it.

Standing behind his desk, he reached across and drew her to him. He looked into her eyes briefly, and then he hugged her properly. He hugged her like one should hug. His voice filled with more emotion and real humanity than June had heard from him in all these years. He took her face in his big hands, and looking down into her crying eyes, he said, 'I am so proud of you June.'

279

June buried her face into his shoulder, and she wept. 'This isn't how I saw this going,' she said as she squeezed this man like the family she supposed he had become.

'Here.' Patrick was standing beside them, holding out a box of tissues while pressing a small handful against his own eyes.

'Thank you.' Dr Michaels took one and wiped at the corners of his eyes. With his mouth stretched in a smile while watching June take several tissues for herself, he said, 'Who'da thought?'

And they laughed. These three people, in this room on an upper floor of a city building, laughed together. And it felt good.

Whistling out the rest of her emotion, and using Patrick's shoulder as an anchor, June pulled herself off the desk. Turning to look at the mess they had made of it, she said, 'Sorry bout your desk Doc.'

Now wiping his nose, Dr Michaels shrugged. 'Don't worry about it.' Smiling an honest smile. 'It's mostly for show.' Their laughter again filling this otherwise serious space. Collectively, they said, 'Ahhh.'

'Well, I guess that's me.' June moved toward the doors. 'Good luck Patrick.' She slapped him on the shoulder as he moved back towards his chair. 'And I'll send you a postcard Doc.'

'Hey,' Dr Michaels called.

Turning to him, June saw him bent to an open desk drawer. She saw him smiling like a child as he pulled something from it.

June tucked in her face and then smiled. 'What is it?' And she opened her mouth as he tossed it to her. She watched as it unfolded in the air, and she caught it like a bridal bouquet.

Dr Michaels said, 'Dr Mackie and Dr Corely asked me to give you this when you came in.' His voice still inflected with an emotion, 'He said you'd earnt it.'

Still frowning over her smile, June unfolded the mustard-coloured material and saw it was a t-shirt. Smiling under a small frown as she saw that something was written on it. She held it up before her.

And time drifted and swam around that room as June felt her eyes squint a little under her frown, which creased above her small smile.

'T,R,O,J,' she said, reading the large burnt-orange letters printed on the front of it of the mustard-yellow t-shirt. Tipping her head to her left, and looking at the smaller font beneath those letters, she read, 'The Rules Of...' And she cried as her hand came to her mouth.

And she knew she was loved.

She knew she was known.

Chapter Twenty-Nine

No Need

The sand was sandy, the water was blue, and June felt that here, she could always hear the rhythm of drums deep in her heart.

Her towel was dry. The breeze was warm and... June lifted her phone.

She heard his voice, 'Hello? June?'

'Hello Dunny,' she said, giggling to herself.

'I'm sorry, I don't...

'...Oh, you weren't there yet.' Her face, flushing under the sun. Then she remembered that he had been there... but...

'Wasn't where June? Are you okay? Where are you calling from?'

Feeling a small pulse of... *Was it nerves?* June said, 'I'm sitting on a beach in Maui.' She began laughing at the raised pitch in her own voice.

'Have you had a few?' A soft and kind rumble in his voice.

I can hear you smiling, she thought.

Speaking way to loudly, she said, 'Danny, I had to call you to tell you something.'

'Okay June Bug. Go right ahead.'

June nerves were making the air around her buzz, but she couldn't waste any time on it. She swallowed, and she said, 'DANNY, I DON'T NEED YOU!' Squinting her eyes and shaking her head at herself. Wondering if he would...

Danny's voice held a deep warmth even as he raised his voice to the same level as hers, and he said, 'I WANT YOU TOO JUNE!' Laughing as he dropped his volume, Danny said, 'I want you too, June.'

The air pushed then, to fill the space between their words. The buzzing of the air around her became a hum, and June felt her mind fill with the cotton wool of a real first kiss.

And they couldn't speak for a time.

The space filled only with the sounds of their own breathing. The light around June starred, and she felt the heat of her oldest tears warm her cheeks under the tropical sun.

Danny spoke first, and softly, 'You know I could meet you there...'

June spoke softly too, 'No rush...'

The next words they spoke were in unison... their voices blending, 'We've got all the time in the world.'

'Jinx!'

The End

Printed in Great Britain
by Amazon